10/21

NEVER

SAW

YOU

COMING

ALSO BY ERIN HAHN

You'd Be Mine
More Than Maybe

NEVER SAW SAW YOU COMING

ERIN HAHN

WEDNESDAY BOOKS
NEW YORK

First published in the United States by Wednesday Books, an imprint of St. Martin's Publishing Group

NEVER SAW YOU COMING. Copyright © 2021 by Erin Hahn. All rights reserved. Printed in the United States of America. For information, address St. Martin's Publishing Group, 120 Broadway, New York, NY 10271.

www.wednesdaybooks.com

Designed by Devan Norman

Library of Congress Cataloging-in-Publication Data

Names: Hahn, Erin, author.
Title: Never saw you coming / Erin Hahn.
Description: First edition. | New York : Wednesday Books, 2021. |
Identifiers: LCCN 2021015644 | ISBN 9781250761248 (hardcover) | ISBN 9781250761255 (ebook)
Subjects: GSAFD: Love stories.
Classification: LCC PS3608.A444 N48 2021 | DDC 813/.6—dc23
LC record available at https://lccn.loc.gov/2021015644

Our books may be purchased in bulk for promotional, educational, or business use. Please contact your local bookseller or the Macmillan Corporate and Premium Sales Department at 1-800-221-7945, extension 5442, or by email at MacmillanSpecialMarkets@macmillan.com.

First Edition: 2021

10 9 8 7 6 5 4 3 2 1

This is dedicated to all the church kids.
No matter what you might've heard,
I hope you carry only this:
You deserve love, are worthy of love,
and are commissioned to love.
That's it. No caveats, conditions, or stipulations.
You. Are. Loved. Just as you are.

AUGUST

1

Meg

I was four the first time I accepted Jesus into my heart. I say *first time* because I did it at least twelve times before I turned sixteen. Better to be absolutely sure, you know? Like, what if I wasn't really feeling it the initial eleven times? Or maybe I was answering the wrong altar call? What if my heart wasn't prepared and I forgot to forgive someone who'd wronged me earlier in the day? Did those ones count? Who can be sure? We live in such conflicting times.

Better to answer at every opportunity just in case. Don't want to mess around when your eternal salvation is on the line.

All of this is to say, I'm like *super* saved. Like, if there is a punch card for gold star Christians, mine's been well earned and is ready to be cashed in. There's this billboard on the way to my nana Knudson's in the middle of nowhere, Indiana, that reads: IF YOU DIED RIGHT NOW, DO YOU KNOW WHERE YOU'D WAKE UP? And yeah. I know. I made sure of it. I'm nothing if not a planner. Hope for the best, plan for the rest. Salvation? Check. Eternity? Double-check times six.

My best friend, Vada, calls it my neurosis. That by confirming my salvation every ten months, I'm basically negating the whole thing. If I can't trust it worked the first time, who am I dealing with here? Surely, the Creator of the Universe can keep track of such things.

I told her if *she's* not going to accept Jesus, I'll have to share half of my salvations with her, so she should be grateful.

It's what I know. Salvation. It's the only certainty in my life. A week ago, that was okay with me. A week ago, I looked at my blank slate of a future and felt the giddy flip in my stomach that spoke of *Possibility* and *Discovery*. I was armed with my relentless faith and the proverbial bucketful of joy, ready to take on the world and answer the call.

Unfortunately, just like my mom and dad, last week was a *liar.*

So, it's my final night of youth group. That part was planned. It was always going to be my last time there. Only the circumstances have changed. The theater where we hold our weekly worship gatherings is dark except for the stage lights, warm and glowing around my bandmates and me. I'll miss this. Singing with them and leading kids in praise music is such an honor. It's been years since I've performed my skating programs, and this isn't the same, but it's gratifying in its own way. I'm not a professional singer, but I'm not half-bad when backed up by Jesus and my dear friend Ben's gorgeous violin.

I move to the mic, my ever-present fairy wings fluttering comfortingly around my shoulders. I chose my simple white-as-snow feather wings today. They were the first pair I ever received, years ago, from my dad. I was little then—still am, I suppose, judging by the way they fit. I was so tiny, he used to call me his sprite, and we would dance around the living room to his old My Chemical Romance albums.

My *dad*.

I shake off the memory, conjuring a beaming smile to my lips, praying the bright lights conceal the fact that it's fake.

"We have one more song tonight. I picked it special to share with you because I want you all to take care and take this to heart. And remember, Jesus and Meg Hennessey will always love you." I blow a quick kiss, spread my arms, and close my eyes, concentrating on the brush of softness at my shoulders. I press the hurt down and suck in a deep breath to soothe the ache. I'm singing "Beautiful, Beautiful" by Francesca Battistelli. It's joyful and painful at once. A girl crying out to her God, something I'm not sure I'm ready to do. It's not in me to dwell, so instead, I give the lyrics my best, impressing as much meaning and care into them as possible. In the song's final moments, I open my eyes, allowing them to adjust. I take the time to reach out with my gaze to the kids in front of me, and I will my love and prayers into them. That they might experience the consuming comfort of God's grace. May they never feel alone. May they never feel betrayed.

May they never feel like *this*.

The song ends, and the lights come on. It's over. Everything is over. I accept hugs and warm wishes for my future with my usual effervescence. (*Thank you! I love you! God Bless! PTL!*) But for once, it tires me out. Apparently, being ungenuine is exhausting. I don't bother correcting anyone on the destination of my plans, and I don't share what's in my heart. Not even with Ben. I'll miss him and his ridiculous lumberjack beard the most out of all these kids. Pretending everything is okay around him makes my insides

6 ERIN HAHN

squirm, but I'm allowing this door to close, and I'm walking away. I'm turning over a new leaf, a new life. I really hope it works out for them in there.

But I'm no longer sure it will. Not for any of us.

The clock on the wall reads seven thirty, and I'm regretting asking Vada to wait until sundown to pick me up. I was all in my feels and wanted to sneak out of my parents' two-story bungalow in Ann Arbor, Michigan, under the cloak of night. After all, I've never snuck out before—I've never disobeyed my parents, full stop—and felt I should do the thing properly. I imagined a dark house and my parents asleep in their separate beds. I would crack open my window, lifting it from its well-worn sill, and toss out a bunch of bedsheets tied end to end. I'd shimmy down to where Vada waited, her mom's car silent from being rolled in neutral down the street toward my window. I'd land with a soft thud in the dewy grass and not bother looking back as we pulled out of town, never to be heard from again, on our way somewhere explicitly *not here*.

But then my mom messed it all up with her caring.

I'm finishing my packing, holding two pairs of fairy wings in my hands and trying to decide which to bring, when she taps on my door.

"I told you," I say, petulant. "I'm running away." Because *of course* I couldn't leave without telling them first. Always the good girl. Always courteous.

"I know," she says, sitting on my bed, her hands folded over a stack of something in her lap. "I know," she repeats. "I wanted to make sure you didn't forget anything."

I straighten, tapping my chin with one finger. "I wonder what that must be like? To forget something. Something so super life-altering and important for, I don't know, nearly two decades . . ." I nail my mom with a look, daring her. Her expression narrows. She wants to say something—chastise my back talk, maybe—but she can't. She doesn't have a leg to stand on here. Instead, she swallows, her hands dancing along the object in her lap.

"Do you hate me?" she asks softly before shaking her head and refusing to meet my eyes. "Of course you do. I hate me a little bit. I have for years."

I consider this, dropping both sets of wings and flipping the lid of my suitcase over, zipping it closed. "No. I don't hate you. But"—I hold up a hand in warning—"I don't know how to feel right now. It's very jumbled." I gesture around my head. "And I don't feel like I can properly sort it out here. I was leaving next week anyway," I remind her.

Until yesterday morning, I was heading west to work at a Bible camp. I've sent my regrets via email and am trying not to feel guilty and especially irresponsible about it. I just can't imagine sitting around a fire, singing about Jesus's unerring love at a time like this. He's still who he is, but I'm . . . not sure who I am.

"Your father is moving out," she says.

I sink down beside her. "What you meant to say is he's *leaving* us," I insist. "And he's not my father, so . . ." I shrug.

That's one of the things that hasn't sunk in yet. My dad is not my dad. Not really. My real dad? Is dead. His name was Andrew McArthur, and he died at twenty years old. I can *say* it. In my head, out loud, in a text to Vada . . . but none of it *feels* real yet. It's not sticking. I don't think it's possible to reconfigure a lifetime of definites in two days. I wonder, idly, if it will take as long to undo the knowing as it took to know in the first place.

"He's been your father for nearly eighteen years."

"He's been your husband for that long, too," I say, shaking myself free of my thoughts. "If he can walk away from you, there's no reason for him to stick around for me."

"He feels terrible. He's . . ." She pauses, and I wait. She changes direction. "Declan is a good man, Meg. He's sacrificed a lot over the years, for both of us. But I need to set him free now. He deserves that much."

I don't believe that. He took off right after my mom's confession yesterday afternoon and hasn't been back. It's clear they planned to tell me together—their secret was only a secret to me, after all—but he's letting her face the fallout on her own. I don't say anything. I doubt she's fooled by my silence, but it doesn't hurt to not confirm it.

"When were you going to tell me, Mom? If the camp hadn't needed my medical records, what would you have done? Let me go my entire life believing a lie? What about you and . . . D-Dad . . ." I trip over the title. "Were you just going to carry on married to someone you don't love until you die?" My throat grows thick, choking off anything else I could say. My mom's face crumples.

"Oh, Meg." She puts down whatever is in her hand and reaches for mine. But that's all she says. No explanation or reassurances that, of course, *of course*, she was going to tell me the truth all along. That she was only waiting for the right moment. That she hadn't planned to lie for so long. I let her hands drop and stand, moving to my closet so I don't have to look at my mom's red-rimmed eyes for one more second.

She sniffs and dries her face with the backs of her hands

before standing. "I wanted you to have these." She points to the stack she was carrying. A pile of differently sized envelopes addressed in slanting cursive. "I've been collecting them over the years. One for every Christmas, including the last. They're from your great-grandmother."

"I don't have a— Oh," I say, my heart thudding painfully. "They know about me?"

"Only she does, as far as I know. Andrew's parents have been gone for decades . . . even before I met him. He has a brother, but I've only ever heard from Elizabeth. After the . . . after Andrew's funeral, and after you were born, I sent a card . . . a copy of the birth announcement. Every year, we exchange Christmas cards."

I stare at her, stunned. "You exchange Christmas cards."

She slowly nods, her brown eyes, so different from my blue ones, searching.

"Dear Andrew's family, Meg's doing great. Still clueless! Happy holidays. Love, the baby momma."

My mom winces, and I feel bad about my crassness. But I don't apologize because it's not untrue.

"And they didn't want to know me?"

My mom presses her lips together, shaking her head. "She did. She's been asking for years. Since the very first letter, even. You're all they have of Andrew, but I just couldn't . . ." She cuts off, dragging a deep breath in through her nose and out past her trembling lips. "I'm sorry, Meg. I needed to compartmentalize. Here. Read them. They're yours."

I reach for the envelope on top and trace my fingers along the fine handwriting. The name on the return address is Elizabeth McArthur. "Marquette, Michigan? Is that where you and, um, Andrew, you know . . ." I trail off, feeling awkward.

My mom pauses at the door. "No, we met at a youth group conference, actually. In Grand Rapids. His band played one of the smaller stages."

My mouth drops open, awkwardness replaced by indignation. "I was conceived at a youth group conference?"

She shrugs, and finally, it hits me how young my mom is. We're barely eighteen years apart. There's a lot more to unpack in this revelation, but first—

I whistle low. "My dad played in a Christian band."

"Just a local one. More of a church worship band, really."

"But he died in a drunk-driving accident, and he was the driver?"

"He was. I have the article somewhere in my things."

I wave her off, impatient. "My unmarried, teenage parents had sex at a youth group conference, and before you could tell my dad you were pregnant, he killed himself drunk driving?"

She frowns. "That about sums it up."

The choking feeling is returning, so I sit back down on my bed, dropping my head into my hands.

"Do you hate me *now*?" Her voice is barely a whisper.

I can't bring myself to say the words or even look at her. My head is too heavy for my body. Instead, I shake it, hot tears dripping into my lap until I hear the door close behind her.

A few hours later, I walk out the front door. My mom stands haloed in the porch light, moths circling her gleaming blue-black hair as I struggle down the steps, feeling crushed under the weight of recent revelations and my oversize suitcase. Vada pops the trunk, and I drop in my luggage, raising a hand in farewell before ducking into the car.

"I thought this was supposed to be covert," Vada mutters, reversing out of the drive.

"It was when I was running off to California. But now . . ." I trail off.

"No wings?" she asks, one red eyebrow perked. Vada and I've been best friends for almost fifteen years, and she's probably never seen me without my fairy wings. But I couldn't do it today.

"No wings," I say, facing my reflection in the darkened window. "I left them behind."

"Well," she says, tapping on the radio. "At least this makes things easier. I won't have to avoid your mom around town."

This makes me roll my eyes. "Oh, please, college girl. In a few days, you'll be off to Cali with Luke, and Ann Arbor will be nothing but a green blur in your rearview mirror."

Vada beams in a deliriously happy way that's evident even in the dark. She *glows*. Has since the night her boyfriend, Luke Greenly, announced his undying devotion to her by way of a very public, very lucrative live performance of the viral hit song he just so happened to write *about* her, which in turn saved the dive bar they both work at from extinction.

No biggie. It's not like it's messed with my expectations of romance *at all*.

Catching my smirk, she clears her throat. "So, Marquette."

"Marquette," I agree. After reading and rereading the Christmas cards from my great-grandma "Betty" over and over, I sent Vada a message, changing my destination for the third time in as many days and asking if she wouldn't mind postponing her trip to take me north. To her credit, she replied only with, "Thank God for Google Maps."

"The UP." She stretches it out like *Youuuuu Peeeeee.*

My lips twitch. "The Upper Peninsula."

"To meet your real dad's family."

"Yup."

"That's weird."

"You have no idea."

"Does his family know you're coming?"

"Nope."

"Should we call them or something?"

"And say what? 'Hey, you don't know me, but my mom boinked your dead relative eighteen years ago and surprise! It's a girl!'"

"What have I told you about using the term *boinked*? Your homeschool is showing."

I wince and swallow hard, my brain working on its usual snappy retort, but nothing comes to mind. Years of friendship has Vada pulling into a well-lit 7-Eleven parking lot and turning off her engine before facing me.

"I hear this one has those Vernors slushies you like," I say weakly.

Her dark brown eyes narrow a little, waiting me out.

"I'm fine," I insist.

"Bullshit. How could you be?"

"All right. I'm definitely not fine. I'm really . . ." I search for the term, but for the first time in my life, nothing but straight cusswords comes to mind.

Vada sighs and in a soft voice says, "Girl, if *ever* there was a moment to let it fly, now is it. It's just me and you."

A sob breaks in my throat, and Vada unlatches her seat belt, reaching for me in one smooth motion. "I'm just really, really mad," I sputter in between sobs. "Okay? I'm furious." The harsh words are strange on my lips. "My entire life has been a lie. I know—" I hiccup a breath, trying to slow the confused torrent spewing from my mouth. "I *get why* she did it. But that means I'm mad *for* her, too! What kind of *fucking horseshit* . . ." I shake my head. I can't complete *that* particular thought. Not yet. I'm mad, but I'm not blasphemous.

At least not outside my head.

"Are they really getting a divorce?"

"Supposedly, they were waiting for me to leave for college, even before the truth came out. How *gross* is that? Like, they were locked into this eighteen-year-long contract because of me. I knew they weren't blissfully happy, but this takes it to another level."

"Because they love you, Meg."

I inhale sharply, my hands trembling and my stomach sick. "I don't think that's why." I can't say the rest out loud. It's too fresh. Too raw. I'm still processing, and it all swirls round and round, the pieces floating to the surface having little to do with love.

Vada doesn't respond, giving me time. Except I'm not sure there's enough time in the world for me to face the ugly truth of what my mom has done. What was done to her. What it means for me and everything I've ever believed in.

My voice is barely a whisper when I finally say, "I don't care why they did it. I just know I have to get the fuck out of here."

"Thatta girl," Vada says, stroking my hair. "Baby steps."

This time, my sob is tinged with a little laughter. "Only

took fifteen years, but you've finally corrupted me with your heathen ways like my nana Knudson always told me you would."

Vada pulls back, her mouth wide in shock. "She did not say that. Your nana loves me!"

"She prays for you. It's not the same. She's Southern."

"Huh," Vada says, tugging the hair tie from around her wrist and looping it in her messy red hair. "Well. That explains a lot, actually." She passes me a tissue. "How about that slushy?"

I blot at my stinging face. "I *knew* that was why we came here."

"Oh, please. Give me some credit. I legitimately pulled in for a parking lot breakdown. But we *do* need to kick off the road trip right."

2

Micah

I was thirteen the first time I snuck out at night. I'd found out my dad's prison sentence meant he wouldn't be able to help me train for freshman baseball tryouts. Of course, his sentence meant he'd miss a hell of a lot more than tryouts, but *that* was the gut punch. Up to that point, my dad had always been my coach. From T-ball to coaches' pitch to Little League to majors . . . he was my batting partner, my catcher, my best friend and biggest fan.

The invite for tryouts came in the mail, and I quit on the spot. What was the point? I couldn't play without him. I didn't know how. Now I realize how stupid that was. Objectively, though, what *was* the point? I didn't know then about the heckling at school, or the dirty looks from my friends' parents, or the distrustful faces when I applied for my first summer job . . . I had no idea what was coming, but some sort of self-preservation must have kicked in because by the time shit hit the fan, I'd cut myself off.

I spent my days with my head down, wanting to crawl out of my skin, and my nights riding my bike, walking and eventually running in the dark, alone. In the light of day, I couldn't look people in the eye for fear of the disgust I'd see. At night, I could walk with my head up. My neck straight and spine tall. I worked my lungs until they felt ready to burst. All the screaming I held in at school or around my mom, I exhaled over and over until I was near collapse.

My body got stronger. Tall, powerful, and able to endure so much. Eventually, my mom figured out I was leaving. For my fourteenth birthday, she bought me a cell phone and a safety light. The following Christmas, snow cleats and cross-country skis. More recently, reflective leggings and wireless earbuds. A silent code between us. As much of a blessing and apology as she could give me.

The dirty looks are fewer since I graduated, and most people have forgotten about the things that happened when I was too young to know better, but I still prefer running at night. Old habits die hard.

Emily kept me out late tonight anyway. And by *kept me out,* I mean, she drove us, and I didn't have a choice in the matter. I'd sort of thought we were headed out for alone time, but Em's college roommate was in town, and they wanted to go to a house party on Front Street. I don't drink, don't like hip-hop, and don't frequent gross college rentals, so it wasn't my scene. I don't even know why I agreed to go. Bored, I guess. I told myself after the last time, when things went a little too far with her, I was done with it. I'm not opposed to sex, but I *am* opposed to so much as kissing a girl in the back of her car while her phone lights up with texts from guys she'd rather be with instead.

Anyway, not a great night. I'd planned to stick it out, but some guy noticed me not drinking, and when he heard my name, he said, "Wait. Allen? You aren't that pastor's kid, are you? Fuck, man . . . that was some shady shit."

I walked home, changed into my running gear, and left for the lakefront. Now I'm sprinting, my heart throbbing in time with the loud music in my ears. I go until the playlist runs out, and then I go some more. I circle around my toughest route in reverse, so I hit all the uphills tonight. My calves are burning, and my arms feel like lead when I finally allow myself to walk it off.

When I reach home again, I shake my head. My youngest sister left her bike out, and one of the twins has a light on in her car. I make my way around the yard, setting things to rights: shutting the car door and locking it, pulling the bike into the garage. There's a piece of chalk left on the porch, and I write GOOD MORNING for everyone to see on their way out the door tomorrow.

I take the stairs to my apartment, and after locking the door behind me and giving my Lab, Cash, a belly rub, I shower off the day, fall on top of my bed, and immediately fall asleep.

I wake to pounding at my front door and Cash losing his mind. With a groan, I clamber out of bed toward the source of the commotion. It's not far. My apartment above the garage is barely a studio loft, with all the emphasis on *studio*.

I pull the door open to reveal my stepdad, Brian, his hand raised to knock again.

"Hey, Cash," he says with far too much enthusiasm, acknowledging my frantic pup with a scratch behind both ears.

"You here for the dog, Bri?" I grumble, blinking against the brightness. "Because I didn't need to get out of bed for that."

"You're still in bed, Micah? It's after eight."

I don't bother responding. Instead, I walk away, leaving the door open for Brian to follow. I tug my mini fridge open and pour myself a mug of milk. They're all I have: mugs, though I don't drink coffee and don't know how to work a coffeepot. This particular one reads: LET GO AND LET GOD. It's my mom's. Everything I have is theirs. I moved into this makeshift apartment a month ago and realized pretty quickly I own *nothing*.

Brian takes a seat on my new-to-me forty-dollar thrift store couch and continues to shower affection on Cash. Leaning one hip against my table, I watch him, taking in his usual Eddie Bauer–casual appearance. If Brian owns a pair of jeans, I haven't seen them. He looks perpetually ready to teach marching band at the local high school. From the early hour and the private visit, I already know what this is about.

Or, rather, *who*.

"Your dad's parole hearing is coming up."

My fingers clench around the mug handle, and I feel it creak under pressure. I put it down on the table with a click.

"Good morning to you, too, Bri."

My mild-mannered stepdad pins me with a single brow. I imagine it's the one he uses on the clarinets when they fall out of step.

I huff out a sigh and compromise by sitting on the arm opposite him. "I haven't talked to him since the trial. It's been five years and ten months, and I'm just finally starting to say my last name in public without people giving me a wide berth." Mostly. Some families still cross the street to avoid my mom in town. How they could hold her responsible for his mistakes this many years later is beyond my comprehension. People are assholes.

"I realize this is difficult—"

"Actually, you don't. Not really."

Brian sets his jaw. "Of course. I wasn't there, during . . . but after . . ."

"No. Stop. You wouldn't be here, picking up her pieces, if you had been. So that's a stupid point to make. If he hadn't fucked up, you wouldn't be here right now."

To his credit, Brian doesn't flinch at my cussing but rather ignores it with a patient sigh born out of years of practice. He really is a good guy, and I'm being a dick. "I'm here now, though. I *am* picking up pieces, Micah. And not only hers. I've been here for all of you. I took this on because I love *all* of you."

I glare at him. I can't fault his care and love of my family since my dad went to prison. He took on a whole lot of garbage and has never made us feel like we owed him anything. That's admirable. Brian's a good guy, the best, even, except—

"You need to go see your dad. You need to forgive him."

Except for *that*. Always *that*. Over and over *that*. It's why I moved out; though clearly not far enough.

"Your mom and I were talking, and she's going to the hearing. You should go with her."

I snort humorlessly. "No, thanks."

"You can't hold on to this bitterness, Micah. It's going to eat you up inside and hold you back from enjoying the life God has planned for you."

My chest squeezes with a pang at his words, but I ignore it. "If it's all the same, no."

"Holding on to bitterness only hurts you."

"That's not true," I say. "That's religious platitudes and bullshit, and my dad was really good at those. Know what else he was good at? Cheating on his wife and stealing from his congregation, and that shit hurt everyone involved."

"Don't make your mom go alone," he pleads quietly.

"Why can't you go with her?"

"She doesn't want me there." I can tell he doesn't want to admit it. "I don't blame her," he says wryly. "It would be pretty horrific to sit next to your current husband and the father of your children while sitting across from your ex-husband and father of your other children."

"Yeah." *Horrific* is an understatement.

"Lila is strong," my stepdad says. "But no one should face that alone, and you have as much right as she does to be there. More, even, in some ways."

"Why do you say that?"

His expression is stark. "Because you're the one who's paid the most for his choices."

Somewhere between having kids five and six, my mom gave me an ultimatum: sell my drum set or find somewhere else to store it. She said she needed the space, which was true, but we both knew my endless angsty banging got on her nerves. My mom's a saint, but even she has her limits.

Brian offered to store the kit in the church basement as long as I didn't mind the worship team borrowing it from time to time.

(He offered me a chance to play with the worship team first, but we both knew *that* would be a cold day in hell.)

After this morning's news, I hit repeat on my favorite

workout. Nothing light will do. The Smashing Pumpkins' "Bullet with Butterfly Wings" is what I need. It's angry and challenging as fuck. Jimmy Chamberlin is a living legend.

One more time.

The song starts with a militaristic backbeat that slowly builds in pressure and endurance. I'm sitting on the edge of my throne, bouncing on the literal tips of my toes, ready for the moment I get to let go.

Some people scream their fury. I beat the shit out of mine.

Sweat drips in my eyes and makes my palms slick, but I squeeze my lids shut and grip my sticks even tighter. When the frantic drum solo comes up, I do my best to keep up. I'm not even close. If I were, I could be making millions. But it doesn't matter. I don't need to be. This is just for me. My shirt clings to my chest and my hair hangs in damp strands across my forehead and neck. The song ends, and I tug my earbuds out with a hearty yank, letting them drop to the cool concrete floor. I wipe my face with the bottom of my shirt, mopping up sweat and maybe tears.

When it all mixes together, it's hard to tell the difference.

Whatever it is, it's *his* fault.

"Jimmy Chamberlin, eh?"

I straighten, startled but not surprised to see James McArthur sitting on the bottom step twenty feet away. I don't ask how long he's been there. I recognized his car in the parking lot and knew he'd make his way down if he heard me.

Usually he does.

I can't bring myself to be annoyed. He's quiet and minds his own business. He's also the only adult in my life who hasn't insisted I need to forgive my dad at every turn. Like, *fuck*. I know I do. I get it. I've been force-fed the scripture since birth. I can feel the guilt and fury burning through my esophagus like acid. I know I have issues.

But I don't want to.

I sigh, reaching for a rag and scrubbing my face before standing and stretching my arms over my head and glorying at the pull in my cramped biceps. "I don't know how you could tell," I say. "No way I could keep up with the dude."

"I doubt even Jimmy could keep up with Jimmy on an off day. You did it justice, and besides, I know your routine by now."

I smirk, annoyed, but also not. Mostly because my adrenaline has been spent and I could use a nap. "More like you talked to Brian."

James doesn't deny it. He and my stepdad have been friends since they were college roommates. They're like brothers, which makes James the cool uncle I never had. I like talking to him because he doesn't have the burden of being in love with my mom. "He felt like he handled things badly."

I shrug it off, gathering up my things and heading for the stairs. James stands and joins me in the climb. "He's only looking out for my mom," I admit. "He's always been stupid for her, and this whole thing is . . . *uncomfortable.*" I grimace at the understatement. I seem to be camping out in the gray area of understatements lately.

"Brian's a big boy. He can handle uncomfortable." James gestures toward his small, air-conditioned office. One of James's seventeen jobs is part-time youth group/worship team leader at the church my mom and Brian attend. It's a small gig, so he also takes on all sorts of handyman jobs, fixing up people's houses and businesses or whatever suits him.

"I can, too," I say. I sit down in one of the guest seats.

After getting me a Gatorade from the stash he keeps under his desk, James sits next to me, forgoing his office chair.

He smiles. "I've no doubt, kid. You'd done it for years. Which is why I'm sure you could handle facing your dad at his hearing."

"But?" I ask. There's more to James's tone.

"But," he continues, "you're nineteen. In all the years I've known you, you've done right by your mom and your siblings and the church . . . out of some misguided sense of guilt or shame or restitution, I think. And I wonder if maybe for your own sake, you should *not* do that, for once."

"Who's to say I was going to?"

James smiles, but it's sad. "You only play Jimmy when you're angry, and you're only angry when you're backed in a corner, about to do something you don't want to."

"That's always."

"Seems like, doesn't it?" James agrees easily.

"I'm not ready to face him yet."

"That's fair."

"Is it, though? It's been more than five years. The last time I saw him, I was in eighth grade."

"And exactly how long are these things supposed to take?"

I grimace. "Dunno."

"Exactly. There isn't a rule book for this."

"Brian says I need to forgive him."

James nods. "Brian's right. Technically. But . . ." He leans back in his chair, crossing his ankle over his knee. "Forgiving someone before you mean it is useless. And a lie. So why force the issue? Do you think you can forgive your dad without speaking to him? Or facing your anger? Without healing your hurt?"

My lips start to twitch at James's subtle shift into Pastor Mode. I don't even think he realizes when he's doing it, but it always starts with the lean-and-leg-cross. "No."

"I'm not saying you should gloss over it and move on with your life. It won't work. Eventually, it will come up and bite you in the ass. What I'm saying is you need to heal yourself first. Then maybe you can face your dad with an open mind."

"You sound like you know a lot about this."

"Unfortunately."

"Drew?"

He doesn't answer, but his eyes dart to the photo on his desk. It's facing away from us, but I've seen it enough times to know it's of James and his older brother, Drew, taken at Summerfest in Milwaukee nearly twenty years ago.

I stand to leave, waving the unopened Gatorade at him. "I need to get to work. Thanks for this."

"Anytime."

I hesitate at the door. James is staring at the picture on his desk, lost in thought. "James," I prompt. His eyes drag to meet mine. "Thank you. Really. Are you coming by the store today?"

He brightens. "Uh, yeah. I'd better. I have to confirm a couple of online orders. Something was glitchy with the site last night, and I want to make sure they went through."

"Sure. Whatever you have to tell yourself."

James grins, whipping off his baseball hat and chucking it at me. "Get out of here, kid."

3

Meg

My first day in Marquette, I'm standing in front of Lake Superior, the coastal wind lifting and swirling around me. My magenta-striped black hair whips against my face, and I let it. Vada left an hour ago after a nice long nap in the hotel room I booked for the week. On my parents' dime. A week is all they think I'll need. I'm not so sure, but I'm happy to save my own money until I figure it out.

You might be thinking, *Wow, Meg, you really don't understand how to properly run away. First, you tell your mom you're leaving, and the next thing you know, she's footing the bill for your trip?* To which I might reply, "This is better than sleeping in Vada's car, all right?"

Anyway, I'll concede the time limit is my fault. I've been complacent and pleasant about everything they've thrown my way for my entire life. Why would that change now?

One might argue, now is exactly the time *to* change. Except I don't have any desire to talk to them and find out if my dad's moved out already or if my mom is still sad. So, here I am. *Sort of* running away.

I tuck a strand of black and pink behind my ear and fill my lungs with fresh air. The white-sand shore is filled with families and college students enjoying the sun and mild summer temps. I let my gaze fall on them from behind the safety of my sunglasses and try not to cry.

I've never felt more alone. I know my best friend just left, but it's more than that. It's all-encompassing. I mean, this is what I wanted. Before the revelations of the past few days, I wanted to take some time to be alone. To find myself and learn who I am outside of my parents and my church and even Vada . . . but I can be honest with myself and admit I barely know where to begin.

I certainly didn't plan to start like this. What a freaking mess. I thought I'd be doing a soul-search, not a self-search. I'd planned on having the benefit of knowing where I stood while I figured out what my future held . . . love- and career- and dreams-wise. A gap year to decide on a direction before starting college. But, as of two days ago, my past is as much a black hole as what lies ahead.

I mentally walk back to where my life split. I had planned to leave next week. I *was* going to road trip out with Vada and Luke . . . start in California at the Bible camp. It sounded epic to me and safe to my mom. Christian. Conservative. Modest.

Her three favorite things.

I've spent eighteen years avoiding tank tops, watching PG-13 movies, and never going on a single date. All because I was to save myself for marriage—for my future husband. I've never even kissed a boy. Forget that, I've never even held hands with a boy. I have zero idea what an orgasm feels like. Every time I've even wondered about trying to give myself one, I hear my mom's voice in my head telling me how sinful it is. Projecting, obviously. If I'd ever *actually* asked my mom about masturbation, she would've had a coronary and found me one of those metal chastity belts they used in medieval times.

When I told her I wanted to do a gap year, she about died. For weeks, I was subjected to nightly lectures about worldliness and lust and alcohol and Satanic rituals. Literal weeks. Until I found Camp Sunrise. An all-female, all-Christian dude ranch with horseback riding and a baptismal fountain on-site.

Of course, then it backfired on her. Camp Sunrise reached out looking for my entire medical history, and that was when the lies started to splinter. I'd never needed to look at my birth certificate before. I was homeschooled. I rode public transportation. I never needed to know my blood type. I feel so stupid. It was only a matter of time. Eventually, I would have seen the truth.

My lips twitch in something like derision. I'm not sure. I don't think I've ever felt derision before . . . but I've read about it plenty. My favorite romantic heroes always smirk derisively. *Dashingly.* For years, I've been hiding my smutty fan fiction collection from my mom. I'm suddenly very tempted to email her my account password. Take that. I *do* know what dry humping is.

I smile to myself. There's a stony break wall trailing out into the water about a quarter of a mile away, and I want to explore it, so I will. I climb the steps and meander along the paved surface, nodding at the families I pass, heading for the very end. I want nothing more than to sit at the very tip, the shoreline at my back, so I can feel like I'm at the end of the earth with only ceaseless rolling waves in front of me.

But when I get there, someone else is sitting in my spot.

Come the frick *on*.

I'm about to turn back when a piece of paper slaps against my shin, and I hear a voice yelp, "Fuck!"

For a second, I'm frozen as the stranger grapples with the rest of his papers in the wind.

"Can you help?" he growls, and I'm propelled by his annoyance. Which in turn annoys me.

I reluctantly swipe at the paper plastered to my shin and thrust it out to him. He looks up finally, and I shake the paper in his face, refusing to take (much) note of his darkly handsome features or stubble.

He can't be more than a year or two older than I am. How on earth does he have stubble? Vada's boyfriend Luke's cheeks are baby smooth. Granted, Ben has a spectacular beard he uses wax on daily, but he's in college.

As I get to the end of my list, it occurs to me it's possible I need more friends.

"Thank you," he says.

"You're welcome."

He turns back to his work, and I don't move. After a minute, he looks back at me. "Can I help you?"

"No," I answer automatically before shaking my head. "Actually, yes," I say, feeling emboldened. "I came down here to sit on the edge."

"I'm on the edge."

"Right. I noticed," I agree, plowing on. "But you're drawing or writing or whatever and wouldn't one of these"—I pat the large flat boulder beside me—"be a better surface?"

His black brows crease together. "I'm already here."

"Yes. I know. I just had this sort of romantic idea. Sort of a 'Keira Knightly in *Pride and Prejudice* standing on the edge of a cliff with the wind tearing at my dress' situation"—I gesture at my cutoff overalls and Birks—"minus the dress, obviously, and I drove all night to get here . . . Well, okay, my best friend drove, but that's beside the point . . . I'm like super in my feels right now after a pretty terrible day and . . ." I change direction. "Look. I'm doing this gap year thing?"

He shakes his head, chuckling low. "I'm not moving for your Instagram post."

"My . . . what? No. That's not . . ." I scoff, frustrated. "It's this thing. I'm trying to find myself. My true self. And maybe pray? I just . . . *really* need that spot. Please? I don't want to see anything but the waves of Lake Superior and . . ."

"Jesus, fine. Calm down." The kid starts gathering his stuff and shoving it into his bag.

"Oh, you don't have to completely leave. I'm not trying to kick you out."

"No, you're just trying to get me to vacate my spot so you can commune with the heavens or whatever. I get it. I don't care. I'm done anyway."

I bite my lip. "Now I feel bad."

He pauses in his packing and levels me with a look, letting out a resigned huff that softens it somehow. His eyes are brown and fringed with thick lashes and unexpected kindness. "Don't. It's a good spot. I have to get to work anyway."

"Okay. If you're sure? Thank you. I owe you one," I say, giving him a smile.

His lips lift ever so slightly, and he slides his backpack over his shoulder. "I'm Micah. Maybe I'll see you around the point."

"The point?"

"This"—he gestures to the rocks—"is called the point."

"Ah. That's . . ." *Obvious.* "I'm Meg."

"It's been interesting to meet you, Meg. Good luck with"—he waves his hand, gesturing at me—"all that."

My face heats, and it's on the tip of my tongue to defend myself, but I'm a mess, and anyway, he's not wrong.

Besides, what do I care? I've never cared what a guy thought of me, and I'm not about to start now with judgy Mr. Grumpy Pants. I want to shout something after him, like, "You should see me in my fairy wings!" but 1) I left them downstate, and 2) he's halfway down the wall, back toward solid ground.

Instead, I carefully pick my way over the boulders to the last one not submerged in the clear, probably frigid water and sit down. The rocks are gray and warm to the touch. My muscles instantly relax as I pull my knees to my chest and shut my eyes, turning my face to the sky and letting the rays soothe my nerves.

I don't know what I'm doing here, but I do know with bone-deep, 100 percent certainty this is where I'm meant to be. Right here. Not on some dude ranch in California, and definitely not at home. And I have to believe that, while every single thing that's happened over the last forty-eight hours has come as a complete shock to me, it hasn't been a surprise to God.

Which, whatever.

I don't waste any time contacting my great-grandmother. My grandparents are gone, but Elizabeth, or Betty, and my biological dad's younger brother are alive and well in Marquette. I decide to start with Betty. I love older people, and they usually love me, so hopefully this was a good idea.

In a very small way, maybe it's better Andrew *is* gone. There's none of that tense "Guess what? You're a father!" drama. But there's plenty of opportunity for rejection all the same. Which means I'm practically puking in my mouth when the door to apartment 305 at the senior center opens, and a vision in beaded scarves, bangle bracelets, and a cloud of violently purple hair smiles at me.

Like, not soft lavender fields. We're talking electric fuchsia.

And that's all it takes for me to love her.

"Meg?" she asks, and I nod, probably too enthusiastically. "Well, come on in! I love your stripes!"

"I'd give anything to achieve that shade of purple, Miss Betty," I say, testing out the name she gave me on the phone. Our call was brief. Once I gave her my name, she invited me right over. I've barely had time to plan what I am going to say or do. She has no such qualms, however, and immediately wraps me in a hug. I close my eyes, inhaling Estée Lauder and cookies. I'm trying not to overthink this, but it's easy to get caught up playing the "do we have the same attached earlobes?" game.

She closes the door behind us and gestures to a small but beautiful sitting area with a floral love seat and a Tiffany lamp. The variety of colors shouldn't work together, but they do. I sit across from Betty, and she offers me a drink. Wiping my hands down my cutoff shorts, I decline.

"Miss Betty, I need to be honest with you, I only learned about Andrew—my dad"—I swallow hard against the awkwardness of his unfamiliar name in my throat—"three days ago, and I'm pretty—"

"Good gracious, child. Three days ago?"

I nod. "So, this is very strange for me. Not this," I say, gesturing around her room. "This is lovely. I'm just not sure of the, um, etiquette . . . for a visit like this."

Betty frowns, leaning forward to peer at me through her zebra-print frames. "Three days," she repeats softly.

"Yeah. Yes," I amend, remembering my manners. I used to volunteer at the nursing home near my house in Ann Arbor. Those ladies were brutal when it came to good manners. They could generally overlook my piercings as long as I said *please* and *thank you* without prompting.

"I wondered," Betty says, seeming to come back to herself. "I've been writing for so long, and your mother would send me your photo every year. I watched you get older and more beautiful, but you never wrote. I thought maybe you didn't want anything to do with us."

My shoulders slump. "I didn't know, none of it. Not about him or how he died, about the letters, about anything." And then everything is pouring out of me at once. Growing up in a strict home, church, graduating early, my plans for a gap year and working at the Bible camp leading to the revelation that my dad wasn't my dad and my parents choosing to divorce as soon as I found out the truth.

"It's like he's been waiting for the minute he could be free of us. I don't know if they ever even loved each other. And all this time, she's been clinging to an illusion for me." My stomach churns when I consider the role my mom has been playing for *eighteen years*.

I shake my head, trying to break loose from my spiraling thoughts. "Can you tell me something about Andrew? I know almost nothing. Only that he and my mom met at a youth group conference. I don't think they were even actually together."

Betty's carefully painted lips spread into a fond smile, and I lean back into the sofa for the first time since arriving. "Andrew was handsome, charming, charismatic," she says. "Always the center of the party and ready for anything. He lived a lot of life in the twenty years he was given. As if he knew his time was short. He was always racing from one thing to the next. He'd fly into my house, front door slamming against the wall, left wide open and letting in the cold, and shout, 'Where's my best girl?'" Her voice cracks at the last part, her eyes wet. She gives me a long look. "You look very much like him. Same dark blue eyes, same easy smile. But you're very serious, too. In that way, you remind me more of James."

"Is that my uncle?"

Betty gives a sad nod. "He was barely sixteen when Andrew died. They were together, at the show and after. But James only had his learner's permit and couldn't drive. Rightly so, though he's had a difficult time forgiving himself."

"So young. That sounds horrible."

"It was awful. All-around awful. James not only lost his big brother, but his first girlfriend was in the car, too. She didn't make it. He, well . . . It was a very difficult time."

"Does James know about me?" I ask, quiet.

"Not yet."

That stings, irrational as it might be. I just arrived, after all. But it's as though I can't escape the secrets. Betty must read it in my expression and reaches out a hand, grasping mine. "I didn't want to say anything until I heard from you or your mom saying you wanted to know us. He's already lost so much."

"I understand. Maybe it's best not to . . . What if I make him sad? It's been so long. For all of you. I don't mean to dig up old memories."

Also, I'm a coward. I can fully admit to this, even if only to myself. Meeting Betty is one thing. She's elderly and has purple hair. But meeting my uncle? My dad's brother? That's a lot realer. What if he looks like Andrew What if he sounds like him? What if he doesn't want to know me?

Betty considers this but shakes her head. "No. This is a good thing. It might bring up a lot of memories, but they're not all bad. This is a second chance for all of us, including you. We're getting a little bit of our Drew back, and in turn, maybe we can give you some of the family you're missing. My son, Peter, was James and Andrew's father. He and their mother, Annabeth, died in a plane crash when the boys were very little. The boys came to live with me before James was even old enough to really remember his parents. The three of us were peas in a pod. But after Andrew was gone, it left a hole in our small family. I have a feeling you'll be the perfect fit."

I inhale sharply, then release my breath long and slow. I can do this. I can be brave. "I'd like that."

"Now. How about I show you some photos of your father?" Betty pulls out a weathered photo album from her shelf, and I'm treated to pictures of a stranger who looks a little bit familiar. It's the weirdest thing, seeing my eyes on a scrawny teenage boy's face. Andrew reminds me of the guys on the cover of my mom's old Relient K CDs. Puka shell necklaces and frosted hair tips. Baggy jeans and layered T-shirts. There's one where Andrew—my dad—has his arm slung around the shoulders of a younger boy with sandy hair—my uncle, James. Both are hamming it up for the camera. My dad is wearing a T-shirt that reads: SATAN IS A NERD. I gasp. "Oh my gosh, I have that exact T-shirt! My mom gave it to me!"

I lift my head to look at Betty. "It's in my suitcase. It's my favorite! I wear it so much, it's almost gone threadbare in places!" I try to remember back. "I used to sleep in it when I was little. I'm . . ." I trail off, a little overwhelmed. "It was *his*," I whisper. "She never told me it was his."

My eyes well up, and I swipe at the hot tears overflowing onto my cheeks. All my life, I've had something of my dad's and I never even knew. My mom never said where it came from. Only that it was an old shirt she'd found. Did he give it to her? Or did she steal it to remember him by? I shake away the thought. My mom is not a romantic. She must have found it after the fact.

Did she hide it from my da—my stepdad? Or did he, like with everything else, know all along? Somehow that thought makes it worse.

Unaware of the turmoil inside me, Betty lets out a soft chuckle, tracing the lines of her grandson's image. "He loved that shirt. Would wear it to church on Sundays and give the old conservatives fits."

"Wow. That's brave! I never wore mine to church. Maybe to youth group once or twice . . ."

Betty smiles. "Andrew had a special kind of faith. I envied it, really. God was sovereign, and rules be damned. He couldn't care less what people thought of him on Sunday mornings. It bothered some people, but Andrew sang like an angel and made worship into a real experience. No one dared ask him to step down, no matter his transgressions."

"Really?" I ask softly. "I can't imagine that."

"No? Forgive me, honey, you know my personal feelings, but has no one ever questioned your . . ." Betty gestures to the row of ear piercings lining my cartilage and the stripes in my hair.

I catch on right away and shake my head. "I wonder if that's why she allowed it? Because of how my real dad was." That seems too generous. "But no, as long as I kept my shoulders covered and didn't spend any time alone with boys, I could do what I wanted with my style. Modesty over creativity, always, but I had some freedoms, and you can be sure I made the most of them."

Betty chuckles. "And your church?"

I shrug. "Ann Arbor is pretty liberal on the surface, and our church was the same. They were okay with my fashion choices as long as I sang from a very, *very* pure heart."

My great-grandmother understands my meaning. "Ah." She looks like she wants to say more, but my phone rings, and even though I silence it immediately, the moment has passed.

We spend a few more minutes flipping through the photo album until there is a knock on the front door letting Betty know it's time to eat. She asks me if I want to join her, but it's too early for me to be hungry, so I invite her to dinner later this week instead. She and James, though I'm still nervous about meeting my long-lost uncle.

"Absolutely. Let me call James and check his availability. I'll text you later," she says.

I love her. Did I say that already? Coolest great-grandma ever.

I kiss her soft cheek, feeling like I've known her my entire life, rather than an afternoon, and drive back to my hotel where I promptly pass out on the scratchy duvet, too exhausted to check my phone and call my mom back.

Maybe tomorrow.

4

Micah

I'm exactly fourteen minutes early for work, and every second shows on the face of my boss, Dani.

"Micah!" she says, her eyes wide. "What happened?" The store is nearly empty, which isn't surprising for a quarter to four on a Monday. Even during the summer tourist season, our busyness comes in waves, timed with the kayak and canoe tours.

It's why I rarely show up on time. Usually, I pick up an iced latte next door for Dani, though, and all is forgiven.

I tuck my bike helmet under my arm. "I'm not *that* early."

"So, there's not an emergency?"

I ignore her teasing tone, heading straight for the back office. I drop my backpack in a locker, placing my helmet above it on the dusty shelf. I take my time, refilling my scratched-to-hell Nalgene from the tap. Despite the outside temp in the mid-eighties, I shiver in the air-conditioning and reach for one of the fleeces hanging beside the door. Pulling it on, I make sure the UPNorth Outfitters logo is visible and make my way to the front of the store.

"Hi, Micah," says Dani's little girl, Noel. She's swinging her legs, sitting on the counter and eating a freeze pop.

"Hey, kid," I say. As a rule, I don't care for many people. But I like Noel okay.

"What happened to your hair?" she asks, and I grimace, flattening down the sweaty fluff on top of my head. Most of the time I like her, anyway.

Dani hurries over. "I hate to cut and run, but since you're here, I need to get over to the post office before four thirty to get these online orders out."

"You know, you can have UPS pick them up," I point out for the fiftieth time.

"This is easier. You know I don't trust the internet." For someone so sensible, she's nonsensical.

"And yet, it's how you get your merch orders in the first place."

She rolls her eyes lightly, lifting a sticky Noel off the counter. "Well, that's only because James set up my website for me. Lord knows I don't manage the thing."

No, we all know who manages it. Who really manages everything around here. Well, that's not fair. Dani runs a tight ship, and the town loves her small sporting goods store. But love doesn't equal money, and James McArthur is singlehandedly responsible for keeping Dani in the black. Canoe tours and cliff jumping make us tour guides money, but it doesn't keep the lights on. The online store does that. *James* does that.

He'd do a lot more if she'd let him. Not that she can see it. Which is funny because literally everyone else can. I mean, if I can, and I'm basically useless when it comes to feelings as a whole, then it's like neon billboard in Times Square obvious.

Dani passes me the cash register keys, and I slip them

over my wrist. "Think you might have a chance to fiddle with the window display tonight? I tried to replicate your magic, but . . ." She sighs dramatically. "You're better. You have such an eye for it."

I feel the corner of my mouth twitch but quickly stifle it. "Flattery, boss?"

"Please?" she asks with a pathetic pout.

"If I have time."

She leads Noel out the front door, sending me a beaming smile over her shoulder. "You're the best, Micah!" she says. "I don't care what anyone says about you!" It's her standard farewell and meant in a completely teasing way, but it smarts. Not that she would know.

The door closes behind her with a jangle of bells, and I slump in place. A glance at my Garmin watch shows me I have at least an hour before the group of kayakers returns from their excursion, bringing my best friend, Duke, with them. In the meantime, I turn on the speakers, changing the satellite radio to a sauntering alternative station, and make my way to the front window display. Dani said she fiddled with it, but it's mostly undisturbed from last month when she asked me to feature all our water shoes.

I chew the inside of my lip, considering. It's August, so the college kids will be returning and bringing their families. I scan our NMU swag. There are other places in town to get Northern Michigan University gear, but ours is higher quality, so I pull out a few key items and place them on the counter. Then I scan our flashlights, beach towels, and day packs, choosing a few to complement the NMU colors of green and gold. I top it all off with a pair of board shorts and decide to leave some of the water shoes but toss in a pair of high-end Chaco sandals.

Cliff jumping in August is a sort of rite of passage for the NMU students, and college students have more money in August than December. It's science.

I spend a few minutes replacing the old, slightly dusty, and sun-faded display with the new one, arranging everything so it looks like you could basically pack up the window and head straight for the cliffs.

I'm finishing up when I see a flash of turquoise, and there's Duke ambling down the sidewalk, trailing eight very tired and slightly sunburned kayakers. In contrast, Duke looks as fresh as he probably did five hours ago when he pulled out. Dude is relentless. And I'm by no means out of shape. We all take turns guiding tours and have to be in top condition. It's not a hardship, honestly. What other job requires you to play outside?

But dragging heavy equipment and fishing tourists out of the water while keeping afloat requires a certain amount of stamina. I'm training to do search and rescue as a career, so this is excellent preparation, but Duke? He does this for pure fun, and it shows in every fiber of his being. He carries himself like a newborn foal, all knees and elbows strung together with rubber bands, covered in a well-worn layer of North Face and dipped in neon. Every summer for the last three, Duke's dyed his hair some varying shades of "highlighter," claiming it's so the tourists can spot him easily. I'm sure that's true, but also, it annoys his dad to no end.

I back up to allow the tour group into the store and pull out some clipboards we have sitting behind the checkout. I hand a couple off to Duke, and we disperse them through the group.

The on-the-spot surveys were another James idea. They

allow customers the opportunity to share their complaints immediately, rather than fester so they jump on Yelp to one-star us on the way home. It's not foolproof, but they can keep it anonymous, and we hand out free cone coupons for Frosty Snacks as incentive. There is nothing better after a long, hot afternoon of sweating than free ice cream.

Five minutes later, they're out the door, two pausing to glance at my display and purchase NMU merch on their way. The pair of teenage girls leaves, but after thirty seconds, one returns, slightly out of breath. She slides a small slip of paper toward Duke, who takes it with an easy grin. She waves shyly over her shoulder, and he immediately taps the number into his phone as the door closes behind her with a jangle.

I shake my head, riffling through the pile of surveys to pull the one I can only presume was hers.

"Cate with a *C*?" I ask.

"The best kind of Cate," he says.

"She in high school?"

"College. Incoming freshman."

Ah. That's lucky. Not a tourist, then.

Duke takes a swig from his Nalgene, wiping his mouth and letting out a long breath. "New display?"

"Yeah, Dani asked me to work my magic."

"And you can't turn Dani down."

"No one can."

"It would be like chastising a kitten."

"Or Noel."

Duke leans over his elbows on the counter, smudging the glass.

"You can go home," I say.

He squints one eye, scratching at his turquoise hair and letting it drop back across his forehead like a Nike swoosh. I can feel his hesitation, and my temper spikes.

"God. Please go."

He glances at the clock. "I have a few minutes. Cate with a *C* just left. Don't want to look like I'm following her."

"Stop."

He straightens with a pained look. "But last time, you said—"

I hold up a hand. "I told you it was a onetime thing. I won't do it again."

"She's your kryptonite, man."

I can't argue with that. "Maybe, but I learned my lesson. I don't need a babysitter. Go home."

He looks annoyingly reluctant, but he picks up his water, phone, and keys and is out the door without another warning. At least not a verbal one. His eyes laser-communicate "Don't even think about it" as he leaves out the back.

I grab a bottle of glass cleaner and start wiping smudges off the cases. My phone dings in my back pocket.

DUKE: Nothing good can come of it.

I roll my eyes, tapping out a middle finger emoji and silencing my phone.

Fifteen minutes later, I'm repeating the mantra as my ex, Emily, shoves the door to the shop open, her laughter tinkling and floating back over the crowd of just-out-of-college guys she took on a bachelor party tour of Black Rocks this afternoon. They follow her like puppies, their eyes tracking her long, tanned limbs and swaying ponytail as she leads them to the counter. And to me.

"Heyyyy, Micah. Can we get some of those free ice cream coupons? These guys worked their asses off for me today."

I hate when she does this. Always leaving me to be the boring rules guy.

"Sure, just a quick survey about what a great job Emily did today, and I'll go grab the coupons."

They roll their eyes but take the pens while I pretend to "look" for the stack of coupons, giving them time to actually fill out the survey.

"Oops. All out up here. Be right back."

I make my way to the back office, taking a drink of my water and checking my phone before pushing the door back into the store open and almost hitting Em.

"Sorry about that," she says. "I always feel super awkward asking for the surveys."

"I don't know why," I say, letting myself sound annoyed. "You always do a fine job."

She meets my tone with doe-eyed innocence. *Always.* "You're just so much better at asking."

"Whatever. We need to get back out there. Dani doesn't like us to leave customers unsupervised."

She grins. "Oh, Micah, such a good boy."

Yeah. That's me. I return to the desk, and the guys pass over their surveys, mostly filled out, in return for their coupons. Emily gives each and every one her winningest smile and ends up with two stalling, clearly waiting to ask her out. I feel my teeth click together. "I'll let you take care of that," I say, walking toward a display of T-shirts and pulling them out to refold. I wish I had my earbuds or had turned the radio louder after Duke left. I don't want to hear this.

"So," Emily says from behind me a few minutes later. I

turn to face her, and she's leaning against the counter. "What are you up to tonight?"

Damn it, Duke.

"Working," I say, going for bland and ignoring the stutter in the middle of my chest. *Nothing good can come of it. Nothing good can come of it. Nothing good can come of it.*

"Right. I know. But after work. Want to come pick me up?"

"I rode my bike," I say. My stomach clenches, knowing what her next words will be. What her next words *always* are.

"I'll come get you, then. We can go for a drive."

A drive. To Harlow Lake or Wetmore Landing or some other secluded spot where we can get into trouble and then she'll go back to ignoring me tomorrow.

Not today.

She walks up to me, slow and easy. "Pleeease, Micah?"

"Where's Tyler?" I ask, taking another step back.

A puzzled crease folds between her fine eyebrows. "Who?"

"That guy you were hanging with last week?"

"Oh! You mean *Taylor*. He's on vacation with his family. Some cabin on Lake Michigan. He's says it's got a—"

"Em," I interrupt. "I wasn't asking for details. I was proving a point."

"Look," she says. "Just because we didn't work out as a couple doesn't mean we can't be friends."

"Friends?" I ask, my voice strained.

"With benefits," she adds. "We were always real good at the benefits . . ."

"I'm—" The door jangles open, and I'm shocked to see the stripy-haired girl from the point. Thank God.

"Hey!" I greet with too much enthusiasm. "Um, M-Meg?"

I'm practically running to the front of the store, startling the girl. Her eyes are wide with recognition.

"Grumpy Micah?"

"Ha!" I choke out a hysterical laugh. "That's me. Welcome to UpNorth Outfitters!"

"Thank you?" she says, and her head whips around, the blunt ends of her hair flaring around her shoulders as she checks to see if there is someone else behind her.

I hold out a hand. "So good to see you."

"Okay," she says weakly. After a beat, she shakes my offered hand. Formally. Her hand is so tiny. *She* is so tiny. I hadn't noticed earlier, with her standing and me sitting, but she couldn't be more than five feet even.

"What can I help you find? I'm so glad you came," I say loudly. "Remember when you said you'd owe me one?" I whisper.

"I was being flippant," she whispers back.

"Please play along," I beg. "It will only take a minute, and I'll give you a free ice cream cone." Her lips crush together for a long second before her face smooths and she shrugs lightly as if to say, "Oh, why not?" while still holding my hand. Because I haven't let go yet. I release her immediately.

"So, what time were you thinking for tonight?"

Her eyes narrow. Mine plead with her.

"Um, well . . ." She shrugs daintily. Compulsively. We're a couple of bobbing ducks over here, and I pray Emily isn't watching closely. "I was thinking eight, but whenever you get off is good."

"Eight thirty okay? I have to check inventory."

"Of course! I can't wait?" she says, like she's checking.

"Me neither," I say, and feeling a little bold with Emily's

eyes on us, I add, "I've been thinking about it ever since I left you at the point."

Meg turns a furious red, and I almost take it back, but she tucks a magenta stripe behind her ear, revealing a row of cuffs and piercings starting at her cartilage and working down to her lobe, and I'm distracted. I've always had a thing for girls with ear piercings. Lots of them. I don't know why. Duke calls it my "pirate chick" thing, but . . .

"Awesome. Me, too. Maybe you can take me to the ice cream place you were telling me about!"

Yup. Nodding like an idiot.

Emily clears her throat behind us. "Well, I have to get going. My mom's bugging me to stop at Econo to pick up some hamburger buns."

"Okay, I'll see you, Em."

"You, too." The back door closes with a thud a few seconds later, and I release my breath.

"Is she gone?" I whisper.

Meg's dark blue eyes sparkle with mischief. "I'm not sure. She might be lurking in the dressing rooms. Better check."

I step back and run a hand through my short hair, feeling it stick up with sweat.

"I'm *so* sorry about that," I say.

"Please tell me she was an ex and not some girl asking you out?"

"Ex. Why?"

Meg's shoulders relax. "Because it takes so much courage to ask a person out, and I would feel terrible if I were part of a brush-off."

"Oh." Wow. That's . . . actually, that's super nice. "No. Nothing like that. An ex who, um, wants to be friends. But with benefits."

Meg smirks, crossing her arms over her overalls with a little clink of the fasteners. "Go on."

"She's my kryptonite," I say.

"Ah. Well, Mr. Kent, you're safe with me. No benefits here."

"Perfect," I say quickly. Meg's eyes seem to dim, and I feel the urge to backtrack, but her teasing smile returns, and I let it go.

"Actually, I did come in here for a reason," she says. "They told me next door that this is where I can get a bathing suit, even late in the season."

"Oh! Yeah." I direct her to the women's swimsuit rack. "We're running a sale on them, actually. Fifty percent off all Speedo brand."

She flicks through the smalls, barely looking. "Something wrong?"

She bites her lip. "I was hoping for a two-piece."

"Well, we don't have much in the way of bikinis, but we have some athletic tankinis, if you're into that kind of thing." I bring her around to another rack.

She looks a few over and picks one that's as many shades of pink and black as her hair and holds it to herself.

"We have dressing rooms. Want one?"

She nods shyly. I remove the keys from my elbow and unlock a room for her before returning to the counter and checking my phone.

I have five unanswered texts from Duke, the last claiming he was on his way to confirm that I was making good choices and to drive me home from work. Before I can even tap out a response, he's at the front window, staring in. I walk to the door and open it.

"She in there?" he asks, still looking.

"No. Thank God. You are the literal worst at recon. Your hair could be seen by a 747 overhead."

He ruffles his freshly showered hair and grins apologetically. "Sorry. I overreacted when you didn't respond."

"I told you I didn't need a sitter."

"You turned her away?" he asks, impressed until reason dawns. "Or she didn't ask?"

For some reason, *this* annoys me more. "*Of course* she asked. She wanted to go to Harlow Lake."

"Really."

"Yes, really. And I turned her down. I told her I wasn't doing that anymore."

"More like he pretended to have other plans with me. Hi, I'm Meg," Meg says, holding her hand out to Duke. To me, she raises the suit. "I'll take it."

"And I'm Duke. Nice to meet you, Meg." He looks at me questioningly.

"I met Meg at the point earlier, and she came in as Emily was putting on the pressure."

"So, you didn't turn her down."

"Not exactly."

"And you dragged a girl you barely know into this mess?"

"And!" Meg adds, her eyes sparkling. "He was so grumpy when I first met him! I thought I was in another dimension for a minute when he begged me to pretend to be his date."

Duke laughs. "I believe it."

"It was a deal!" I say. "You owed me one!"

"For what?" Duke asks.

"For giving up his spot at the point."

"For giving up his spot in a public space," Duke repeats dryly.

"Exactly," I say, taking the bathing suit to ring it up.

Duke follows us back to the register. "And I offered free ice cream."

"From the coupon?" he confirms. "That doesn't count. You didn't pay for that. You have to take her out properly or it's a lie."

"Oh, well—" Meg starts, no doubt seeing the glare I'm leveling at my friend.

"I just got out of one date. I wasn't trying to get another."

"Clearly," Duke mutters, and Meg snickers into her shoulder.

"That's not what I meant," I say, stabbing at the keys on the register with too much force and having to delete the wrong info and reenter everything all over again.

I read the total to Meg, who passes me cash, and I put the suit in a small paper shopping bag.

"Listen, I get off at eight thirty for real. Can I take you for ice cream? It's right down the street."

I assume she's going to say no, but she surprises me. "Sure. It's not like I know anyone else here, so you're as good as anyone." She takes the bag, pulling it over her elbow.

"It was nice to meet you, Duke. See you at eight thirty, Micah."

"Hey!" I say, stopping her as she's about to walk out. "I'm as good as anyone for what?"

"To be my first friend in town."

5

Meg

After leaving the sporting goods store, I drop off my new suit in my hotel room. I'm tempted to put it on right away, but I don't have the time or inclination to go swimming before I'm supposed to meet Micah.

Locking my room behind me, I feel my lips spread into a smile. Micah. My new friend. I know lots of people have friends. Like, kids learn how to make friends in elementary school. But the thing is, I didn't. Not really. I practically forced Vada to be my friend in the way only a four-year-old can, and later inherited Luke, Cullen, and Zack through her.

Micah is my first grown-up friend.

It was remarkably easy to make a friend, to be honest. I don't know what all the fuss is about.

I squint at the sun, still high in the sky despite it being after seven, and slide my sunglasses on. I glance up and down Third Street, trying to decide where to spend my next hour. I could get dinner. I'm definitely hungry, but a little unsure. What to eat? I can literally eat anything I want, as much or as little as I want, and no one can tell me no. I could eat specialty caramel popcorn and spicy shrimp with a Dr. Pepper. It doesn't matter if it's late in the day for caffeine and I won't sleep well. It doesn't matter if the shrimp isn't locally sourced. It *doesn't matter* if I eat while wearing my two-piece bathing suit in front of a boy.

The sheer freedom makes me giddy.

In the end, I decide on an everything bagel with cream cheese and chives at this little café on the corner, and while it's not skydiving or smoking drugs, it feels like a Big Step for me. I order a hot cocoa to go, even though it's a hundred degrees out, and take a walk on the beach. There's a large park on the shore called Lower Harbor, and I perch on a picnic table there, eating my breakfast-for-dinner and watching the sailboats on Lake Superior. A couple of college guys are throwing a Frisbee around, and while I don't ask to play, I do retrieve a rogue disk once and ask to pet their dog.

And I somehow manage to keep my purity intact. Will wonders never cease?

I sigh, leaning back on my hands, letting the breeze off the lake lift and toss my hair.

That was unfair of me, God. I don't blame my mom for having premarital sex or for having me. I don't. But even as I think it, a burst of anger flares hot. Because I *am* mad at her for projecting her life on me. I'm not saying I want to have sex before I'm married. But she clearly did and didn't die over it. Though she got pregnant and my dad *did* die, but I don't think that's related. Probably. My goodness, I might need to add therapy into my gap year plans.

I think of Vada and her Luke and feel a tiny pang in the region of my heart. Maybe I haven't met the right person, but when I do, I hope it's something like what they have. I'd give anything to have a guy look at me with half the adoration Luke has for Vada.

I tug my phone out of my pocket and unlock it to reveal a message Vada sent me earlier, after letting me know she made it home okay.

VADA: You lent me this song when I was spiraling. Now I'm passing it back to you. I love you, friend, and I'm so fucking proud of you.

VADA: YouTube Lauren Daigle "Rescue"

I dig around in my bag for my earbuds and a hair tie. After pulling my hair back, I tuck my buds in and hit Play. I'd forgotten about this song. It's weird Vada is sending this to me. Not the song part . . . that's her whole thing. It's what she *does*. But this particular song. When I sang it, all those months ago at youth group, I felt like I had it together. I sang it for her because *she* needed it. She was hurting after yet another insane brush-off from her selfish, alcoholic dad, Marcus, and this song was all I had to give her. Now, I'm the one who's a mess.

I press at the tears slipping past the edge of my dark frames and sniff. I can't help looking back at the last few days and feeling like I am all over the place. Devastated, lost, angry, bemused, amused, hopeful, rebellious, and humbled beyond reason. I'm all of those and more. I've never wanted to ask, *Why, God, why?* but for real. *Why* is this happening?

The song ends, and I straighten. I'm tempted to start it over and play it again and again until I'm completely worn down, but eff that. Not today, Satan, or however that goes.

I check the time. After eight. I blot my face, making sure my tears are clear. It's a good thing I don't wear makeup.

I jump up from the picnic table and brush off my overalls, pity party officially spent. Besides, I have an ice cream date with my new friend in fifteen minutes.

I'm walking up just as Micah is locking the front door from inside. He sees me and holds up a finger, which I take to mean he'll meet me around front. He's alone, and it's a little nerve-racking. Duke was super easygoing, and I felt like we'd get along fine with our matching hair. He would have made it less awkward. I'm not unaware we both basically bullied Micah into taking me out. Not like he didn't owe me, but Duke's teasing certainly boosted my confidence. I'm not shy, but Micah's grouchiness doesn't exactly scream, "Press my buttons."

On the other hand, something about him makes me want to poke. He's sort of cute when he grumbles. It's the eyebrows. They're so *frustrated*.

"Sorry," Micah says, jogging up from around the block. He's walking an expensive-looking, mud-splattered, and well-loved bike. "There're no alleys, so I had to go the long way."

I slip my sunglasses on top of my head and smile. "No biggie. Which way to Frosty Deliciousness?"

"Frosty Snacks," he says. "Though your name works, too." He nods, his hands full. "Follow the sidewalk up the hill. It's about a half-mile walk. Do you mind?"

"Not at all. It's perfect out. Do *you* mind? You're the one with the bike."

"My house is on the way. I figured I would drop it off."

"You live down here?" I take in the charming downtown

area. It's only a handful of blocks long, but with gorgeous views of Lake Superior and the harbor lining one side. "Lucky."

He nods again, adjusting his helmet under his arm. I take it wordlessly, holding it. "Thanks. Yeah, off one of the side streets. I mean. My, uh, parents live in the house. I live by myself above the garage."

My head falls back with a groan, as dramatic as can be. "I am so jealous. I might hate you."

The corner of his mouth lifts. "Because I live above the garage?"

"Because you live alone," I clarify. "How old are you?"

"Nineteen. To be fair, I only just moved out. It was a compromise. I go to community college, so no dorm living. It was the next-best thing."

"Whatever. It's still amazing."

"What about you?" he asks, pretending to look behind us. "You're traveling alone? How old are you?"

A little voice in my head, one that sounds exactly like my mom, whispers that I shouldn't tell a stranger how old I am *or* admit I'm alone. But she had sex with my dad when he was practically a stranger, so I push the thought away. I know where Micah works and his nosy best friend, and in a minute, I'll know where his parents live. Besides, I'm not planning to lose my virginity. We're only getting ice cream. "I just turned eighteen, and I'm alone because I left without asking. Technically. I mean, they know where I am. And the, um, girl at the front desk at the hotel, Tammy, knows me. She's expecting me," I add in case.

"Tammy Dawson?" he asks, smirking. "She's good people. Don't worry, Meg. I won't kidnap you."

"I wasn't worried. Not really. You're too type A to kidnap a hot mess like me."

"Type A?"

"Am I wrong?"

His lips twitch as he tries to look affronted. "No, you're not." He gestures to the street corner. "I'm on the right. Just a quick detour. You can stay in the driveway where all the neighbors can see you if you'll feel better."

"Okay."

Micah leads the way up a short asphalt drive that meets a cared-for navy-blue house with red brick half up its exterior and black shutters. There are flowers in window boxes and a bunch of discarded kids' bikes and skateboards in the grass. The drive is covered with stick figure chalk drawings and messages reading YOU ARE MY SUNSHINE and I ❤ MOMMY. Micah pulls his bike around to the garage door under a set of wooden stairs that must lead to his apartment. I pick up a piece of chalk and squat, tracing a couple of flowers, making a tiny garden. I hear the door slam, and Micah jogs up to me, a frantic yellow Lab in tow, as the front screen door opens. A little girl is standing on the porch with her hands on her hips.

"Where're you going?" she asks.

Micah waves her back in, slipping a leash onto the vibrating dog's collar. "None of your beeswax. Aren't you supposed to be in bed?"

"Are you getting ice cream? You said you would take me next time!"

I raise my brow. "Wow. Woooooow," I say, pretending to be offended. "You promised *both* of us ice cream? What's her name, Micah? I thought you said I was special."

His lips do that quirk thing, and he sighs, faking exasperation. "Her name is Elizabeth, and she's five."

"A younger woman, then."

He shakes his head with a grunt. "Lizzy, get to bed."

"You promised!" Even from here, I can see her lips quiver, and I immediately melt into a puddle of goo. A voice from inside calls for her, but she doesn't budge. Micah huffs, passes me the leash, and walks toward her. I follow at a distance, intrigued, pulling the dog. I'm an only child, and I've never had a pet. This entire detour is fascinating.

"Listen, Lizzy. It's too late to take you tonight. But I promise I'll check if there're any 'mistakes' and bring one home for you."

"Who are you?" she asks, looking at me and blinking huge eyes.

I love this kid. She's direct. I wave with my free hand. "I'm Meg. Nice to meet you."

"I like your hair," she says.

"And I like your style," I say. She glances down at her *Frozen* Elsa nightgown and spins once.

"I don't think it will fit you."

"Oh, man. Bummer," I say, tucking away my grin.

"Well, as fun as this is, we should get going. Lizzy, go to bed. Tell Mom . . ." He pauses, straightening. "Never mind. I'll see you tomorrow."

Lizzy goes inside, and we head out toward our original destination. I pass the dog back.

"This is Cash. He's been cooped up all day, do you mind?"

"Are you kidding?" I stop, reaching for the pup and scratching his ears. He turns his head to lick my hand, and I giggle. "Easy, Cash, not on a first date."

"So," I say after we've resumed walking. "It's new for you, too, huh?"

"Hm?" He turns to me.

"I just mean the whole living-on-your-own thing. Not having to check in."

"Oh. Yeah." He makes a face. "It's this sort of weird situation."

I think he's going to say more. He doesn't. I watch as Cash's tail wags back and forth. He is the epitome of happy, and somehow, he's made Micah 100 percent more attractive in the last five minutes. Well, that and promising his little sister ice cream. Holy bananas, this might've been a bad idea.

I clear my throat. "How so?"

"Hm?"

"How's it weird?"

"Um. Just the . . . Well. You see how young Lizzy is? So, there's me, I'm the oldest. And then Eve and Rachel who are twins. They're seventeen. Then my dad, um . . . My parents split. A few years ago, my mom married Brian, and they had, um, three more kids. Lizzy, Zeke, and Eli, who's a baby."

"Wow, that's a spread."

"Yeah. So, it's a bit crowded and chaotic and loud."

"And being type A . . ."

"Right," he agrees, relieved I'm catching on. "So, after graduation, Brian and I started getting the apartment over the garage ready for habitation. I moved in a few months ago. It's tricky. I'm there a lot, but I don't live under their roof. *Technically*. But it's an adjustment for my mom. She wants to know where I am and what I'm up to, while I say I'm a grown-ass adult and don't need a curfew. And if I were away at school, she wouldn't know."

"That's fair."

He rolls his dark eyes lightly. "You'd think."

"I found out a few days ago my dad isn't my dad," I blurt.

Micah falters. Cash pulls on the leash. Eyes wide, Micah looks at me. "What?"

"Yeah." I smile wryly. "That's exactly what I said, actually."

"So *that's* why you're here? Or *is* that why you're here?"

I shrug and motion for us to keep walking. "Kinda. I graduated early." I point to myself. "Homeschool kid. I was planning this whole gap year thing where I'd travel with my best friend out west where she's going to college. I was going to start working at this Bible camp slash dude ranch."

His brows creep farther north to his hairline. I plow on.

"Which my mom, in particular, was super into because it would keep me all"—I motion around myself wildly—"surrounded by the Holy Spirit and away from worldliness and sin, which is massively ironic because, turns out, she got knocked up at eighteen. Presumably, *not* by the Holy Spirit."

Micah's lips turn up at the corners. Sort of sardonic. Like a grizzled, dark-haired, slightly moody Nick Miller–from–*New Girl* type. I swallow hard at the thought and continue, "Anyway, apparently my real dad is dead. Died before I was born. But she—my mom, I mean—married her friend—so my stepdad? I guess?—and they never really loved each other. And he's decided he wants to cut ties and live his truth or whatever, and since I'm grown, now's the time to reveal the sham for what it is."

"Wow, that's—"

"Cold," I say. "Ice cold. My, um, dad—the living one," I clarify, "hasn't been real affectionate, for the last, oh, maybe five years? Or even, like, present, but he was my dad. Last week, I had one dad, then two, and now zero."

Micah shakes his head. "I don't even know what to say."

"I don't know why I just told you all of that. You didn't even want to take me for ice cream. You probably think I'm super weird. Full disclosure, I might be."

His mouth lifts in a real smile. "You ramble when you get worked up."

"I . . ." I falter. "Yeah. I do. Another thing I just learned about myself."

"You don't usually ramble?"

"I don't think I've ever gotten worked up before. At least not on my own account."

"Want some ice cream? It's right there." He points to a well-lit stand with a giant person-size ice cream cone on the roof.

"You sure? Maybe you're thinking you need an out after all that. I don't mind. You just met me, and I got real strange real fast." I close my eyes. "Go ahead and run. I'll give you to the count of twenty."

I feel his hand brush mine.

"Meg. Open your eyes."

I do, tremulously, and find his are piercing. I concentrate very hard on not swooning. It is way too early to be swooning. I only started finding him attractive fifteen minutes ago when I met his dog.

"First of all, you are not a reflection of your parents' bad choices." The way he says it, with 150 percent sincerity, makes me think his words are weighted with something extra. "And second," he says, smirking, "I owe two girls ice cream. What kind of monster reneges on ice cream?"

6

Micah

It's Sunday, and I'm nowhere near a church. I'm fairly certain the general consensus surrounding my beliefs is that I'm agnostic—that I'm lost—that whatever happened with my dad crushed my faith and made me into an example of what happens when pastors' kids are led astray.

Well, they're wrong.

But I won't go near a church. Or, rather, I refuse to go near the people who make up the church.

I don't hate God. He didn't do anything wrong. I don't even hate my dad most days. He's a fuckup, and I don't ever want to see him again, but I can't hate him. I tried. To be honest, I can't muster any strong emotion when it comes to him.

But I *might* hate the church.

Again, not the building. The people. Specifically, the people who comprised our old church. My dad's congregation. For all their talk of forgiveness and loving like Jesus, they sure had a fantastic time throwing my dad in jail and then shitting on his entire family. It's not like we knew what he was doing. My mom married my dad when she was two months out of high school. My sisters and I were in junior high, for fuck's sake. We were as blindsided as the rest. My mom spent an entire year barely eating, barely sleeping, barely speaking. My sisters crept into this bubble that was only the two of them and no one else. I lost everything. My dad was my best friend, pathetic as that seems now. After the scandal, it was like he was my only friend. No one wanted anything to do with us.

That was when I started climbing rocks. And rowing. And jumping off cliffs and white water rafting and backpacking off trail.

Last year, Duke and I jumped out of an airplane. That was pretty ultimate. Coincidentally, it lined up with the five-year anniversary of my dad's sentencing. It's hard to dwell when you're free-falling thousands of feet, hurtling toward the earth.

They say your life flashes before your eyes when you're seconds from dying. Mine didn't. I had no interest in seeing that bullshit play out again.

That said, it's not that I have a death wish, no matter what my mom thinks. I swear, it's nothing like that. It's sort of the opposite? It's like this intense need to have God as close as possible. To wear him like a second skin, directly over my pulse, like he could possibly contain all the messed-up pieces of me.

When there's no one else, and I'm at the end of my tether, that's where I feel God. In the waves pummeling me and the sun baking me and ground surging up around me. That's *my* fucking church.

I'm finished with my run up to the top of Sugar Loaf, and I tug a water bottle off my pack, cracking it open and pouring half of it into the flexible plastic dish I brought for Cash. He takes his fill while I gulp down the rest. I move past the wooden platform, ignoring the tourists and early-morning hikers and making my way to the rocky edge. I find us a flat, shaded surface and sit down, stretching my legs out in front of me. Cash curls up next to me, seemingly at his leisure, but if I jumped to my feet, he'd be at my heels, ready for more.

"Easy, man," I say, rubbing his scruff. "We mere mortals need to catch our breath after sprinting up a mountain."

From our perch, we have a 360-degree view, and it's probably my favorite in the world. September is still days away, but we're pretty far north, and the breeze has the slightest bite of fall to it. The fiery vines of Virginia creepers are highlighting the rest of the still-green foliage, and it's a relief. Summer is fine, but I live for winter. I have to up here. If I didn't love feet of snow and below-freezing temps, I should have moved farther away than my parents' garage.

Thinking about fall has me wondering about my new "friend" Meg. We didn't hang out long after getting ice cream last night. Only long enough for me to walk her back to the hotel. I'm undecided if that was too short or just the right amount of time. There was a whole lot of stuff to un-pack in that one session of "getting to know you."

I'll admit, I'm pretty rusty at the whole friendship thing. I met Duke post-fallout with my dad. He moved to town the following summer and is a fair-weather Unitarian, so the whole religious drama meant nothing to him.

But Meg is different. Underneath her bubbly exterior, I picked up on some serious hurt. Totally justified and seem-ingly fresh hurt, but I don't know. I'm hardly the person to talk when it comes to a healthy spiritual life. Or parental drama. Or relationship advice.

Not that she was asking for that. Advice or otherwise. She was just cute is all.

Aaaaand I'm shutting down that particular train of thought in three . . . two . . .

"All right, Cash," I say, standing. As predicted, he's quick on the uptake and scrambles to his feet. I lunge, loosening my quads as he stretches, yawning. "Show-off," I grumble.

He licks my hand with a snap in response.

"It's all downhill from here."

I'm avoiding Brian and my mom and anyone else who wants to talk about the hearing. Consequently, I'm at work even though it's Monday and I'm not on the schedule. Duke's behind the counter, taking an end-of-season inventory on sunglasses, and I'm spinning on Dani's stool, keeping an eye on things, while she's next door at the coffee shop getting brownies.

That's the perk of sharing a wall with a coffee shop. We always know when they've pulled something delicious out of the oven. And since Dani has the reflexes of a distracted five-year-old, she's the forever loser of "Nose Goes."

"How was ice cream?" Duke asks, not stopping in his movements of checking and recording.

"Huh?"

He pauses, his eyes flickering up underneath his hair, pinning me. "With Meg in the Pink Hair," he clarifies needlessly.

"Oh." I'm stalling. He knows it. "It was good."

"Good?"

"Yeah. Real good. She's nice."

"Pretty, too."

I shrug.

"Just ice cream?" he verifies.

"Just ice cream."

"Damn."

I huff. "If you hoped for more, why'd you want me to turn down Em?"

This time, he shrugs, closing the display case with a click and pulling out the key. "It's not that, exactly. I don't like Emily. She's . . ." He scrunches up one side of his face. "She uses you."

"Maybe I use her," I shoot back.

My best friend snorts, wiping away his smile. "Sorry. But no."

I don't bother arguing. "Well, Meg's not like Emily. Very much the opposite. She's a church girl." Even as I say it, I wonder if Duke can really understand the significance. It's been a few years since I attended any semblance of a youth group, but it's a whole thing. Church girls are different. There's this guilt factor associated with anything physical that's a big old flashing DON'T EVEN THINK ABOUT IT.

Meg has it written all over her. Though she seemed aware and, truthfully, sort of pissed about it. Which is very interesting. Not in the "I'd like to corrupt that" kind of way. More like in the "I'd like to explore that topic" kind of way, which is more concerning, if I'm honest. I'm spending too much time with James, I think.

I uncross my knee from my ankle. "Anyway, Meg is cool. I didn't get her number, though, and she's leaving in a few days. I don't think I'll be talking to her again."

Duke shifts to work in the next display, unlatching and moving around the merch. "Is that regret I'm detecting?"

Since it's a moot point, I decide on honesty. "Maybe a little. You know me," I say, trying to impress some significance into the words so I don't have to actually say anything significant.

Duke nods, solemn, picking up on my tone. "Fucked-up pastor's kid. Yeah. I know you."

"Right," I say shortly. "Well, I sort of got the impression that Meg could relate on some level. Which was . . . maybe cool."

"Sort of, some, maybe? Cool?" Duke asks. He drops his pen, placing both hands on the display and leveling me with a look. "That's huge, Micah. I've known you five years, and this is like the third time you've mentioned your history. Can you stop by her hotel? Do you know where she's staying?"

"I don't know, man. That's kind of weird. 'Hey, Meg, I stalked you at your hotel and am crowding on the rest of your vacation so I can dump my five years of church trauma on you, thought you might relate, wanna hang?'"

"Only if you bring Cash along. I think we might have something."

I choke on air and spin on my stool to find Meg, holding a tray of brownies and wearing a blinding grin, standing next to a bemused Dani. Holy fuck, where did she come from?

"Meg!" Duke shouts, circling the counter and enveloping the tiny girl in his giant-ass gangly limbs. He's acting like they've known each other for decades and she's been lost at sea . . . not like they met two days ago.

She holds out the brownies. "I got a job. Next door. Brownies?"

"You're kidding," I say weakly.

"Nope. They had a sign up. I walked in and interviewed

on the spot. Now I just need to figure out a place to stay and I'm good."

"You're moving here?"

A customer comes in, and Dani maneuvers around me to check in with them. Meg's smile slips for a half second. But she hitches it back up, and if I hadn't been watching so closely, I probably would've missed it. I hop down from my stool, taking the brownies and placing them on the counter before steering Meg by the elbow to the back room.

"Am I allowed back here?" she whispers.

"Are you really working next door?"

"I am?" It sounds like a question, and my stomach clenches in pity for her.

"Relax. I only meant that if you are, you can be back here. Dani is a silent partner of the coffee shop. She's technically your boss."

Meg's lips form a quiet "Oh." She looks around, her hands fidgeting with her striped T-shirt dress. I try not to notice how well-shaped her legs are. I fail. She turns to face me, skirt flaring mid-thigh. I blink. Twice.

"Dani is super nice, so that's great."

"She's the best," I agree.

"This is all happening very fast. I'm not usually this impulsive," she admits. "The opposite, actually. But I met my great-grandma the other day, right after I first met you"—she gives me a little smile before continuing—"and I love her. Is it crazy to love someone you've met only once? And soon I'm going to meet my uncle. I have an uncle!" She full on grins now, self-deprecating. "I'm rambling."

"You are."

"It must be you. You unsettle me. All I do is ramble around you."

"I'm honored."

She presses her lips together. "I know you didn't mean for me to hear whatever that was . . . but if you meant it—or even if you didn't—I would be interested in talking church trauma some time. Wow." She shakes her head. "You're right. That sounds terrible."

"Worst hangout ever."

"For real. But I can offer brownies."

I don't know why I say it. I don't know if it's her (adorable) rambling or the glimpse of her legs or her complete lack of self-awareness or that for the first time I *do* want to talk about my issues, not even for my sake, but maybe for *hers* . . .

"What are you doing tomorrow?"

"Really? Already. Um . . ."

"Not the trauma talk," I rush to clarify. "For something else."

She tucks a section of black hair behind her ear. "Oh. Okay. I have training early all week, but Maria said I'd be done before the lunchtime rush."

"I have a canoe tour at nine but should be done around one. Meet you here?"

"Sure. I'll bring sandwiches."

"Don't you want to know what I'm asking about?"

She flushes. "Right. Yes. I'm an idiot."

I bite the inside of my cheek to keep from smiling. Whatever this girl is, she's the furthest thing from an idiot. "How do you feel about jumping off cliffs?"

7

Meg

I'm about to jump off a twenty-foot cliff, and that's not even the scariest thing I have planned for today.

I'm meeting James tonight. My uncle. My dad's brother. Gah.

But for now, the cliff. Micah stands next to me, the wind tugging at his dark hair. He's bare-chested, and I'm distracted. He removed his shirt at the bottom of the cliff, leaving it in a pile with the rest of our belongings since the easiest way down is off the edge and you don't want everything to get wet.

A very pragmatic choice, is what I'm saying.

And, like, I've for sure seen guys without their shirts on before. My dad, for one. And, you know, guys on TV. But never like this. Never up close. All the way to the top of Black Rocks, I followed Micah's footsteps up the worn path, and I couldn't help tracing the ridges of his shoulder muscles with my eyes as they moved under his tanned skin. Honestly, I didn't know muscles grew like that. I am so very tempted to touch them, to see if they're as hard as they look, but that's probably one of those things that friends aren't supposed to do. And I don't want to mess up my new friendship.

I'm wondering, though, as goose bumps ripple across his pectoral muscles, if perhaps I made a mistake in choosing Micah as my Sherpa into adult friendship. I probably ought to have looked into things like "toned stomach" and "holy Jesus, are calf muscles supposed to make shapes?" prior to accepting his ice cream invite.

Too late now.

A couple of college girls stand in front of us, giggling and shrieking as they get closer to the edge. Someone in a sorority sweatshirt is recording them on her iPhone, so I'm guessing it must be some kind of pledge thing.

And here I am doing this for fun?

I shiver and Micah frowns at me. "Too cold?"

"A little. Mostly, I want to puke."

"You can swim, right?"

"You're asking me that *now*?" I choke out. To his credit, he looks sheepish at his oversight. Turns out, grumpy eyebrows spliced with ruddy cheeks is a combo I really, really like.

Look at all the things I'm learning about myself already.

I shake out my hands as the girls jump over the edge, their screams swallowed in the wind.

Oh no.

"I'm not sure this is a good idea," I say, glancing back at the path and all the people lined up behind me.

"It's a rite of passage, Meg."

"Right."

"And you're on a gap year."

"I remember," I mutter as he gently pushes me forward.

"And you wanted to feel all the feels." Closer to the edge.

"You remember I said that?"

He rolls his eyes and holds out a big hand. I try not to think as I take it. He tugs me to the side and lets the next pair go ahead of us. He dips his head close to mine and his voice is low and rumbly.

"If you're really afraid, I'll walk you back down. But only if your fear is greater than your desire to experience this."

I swallow hard. "It's just, I can't remember why I'm even doing this. This is bananas."

Micah's eyes narrow, but not in an angry way. He seems to be considering his words carefully. Finally, he says, "Would your mom let you do this?"

I quickly shake my head.

"But God created this beautiful place. He made these rocks, this sunshine, the clear waters of Lake Superior. He formed you and your sense of adventure. He even made me and my need for this rush of jumping off cliffs . . . and he introduced us." His eyes dart away from mine at that last part. I catch my bottom lip between my teeth.

"I don't know a lot about you, but I remember every bit of that first time we talked at the point. It's annoying, actually." His lips twist in a smile. "But that girl who talked a stranger into giving up his spot so she could pray and reflect and live out some *Pride and Prejudice* fantasy is definitely someone who can run off the edge of these rocks."

I inhale through my nostrils. "Okay."

"Okay?"

"Yes. I want to do it. Alone."

His smile spreads across his face, and my breath catches a little at how handsome Micah is.

"You badass," he says. "Want me to go first or second?"

I weigh the options. Either he'll be down there, in the water, waiting *for* me, or on the cliff, waiting *on* me. The image of having someone waiting for me—someone I can reach for—is too good to pass up. "First, please?"

"You got it." We're easily let back into the line. People seem more than happy to let someone else jump first.

Micah walks confidently to the edge, his bare feet picking over the sharp stones with no problem. He peeks over the top, waving at whoever is at the bottom. Once the water is clear, he turns to face me. His clever eyes quickly take me in. My arms wrapped around my middle. My trembling limbs. My pallor.

And with a smirk worthy of any romantic hero, he jumps backward off the cliff, holding my gaze until he disappears from view.

I'm not exaggerating when I say I'm pretty sure he took my heart with him.

On shaky legs, I make my way to the edge. Micah surfaces with a shake of his head, like a shaggy dog, before making his way to shore with sure strokes. Once he's there, he raises his hand.

"Now or never, Meg!"

I swallow hard, fill my lungs, and leap off into the sky.

I've got a heart to retrieve.

MEG: I think I have a crush.

VADA: . . .

VADA: . . .

VADA: . . .

VADA: I'm sorry, who is this?

MEG: Hilarious, Carsewell.

VADA: First, no fairy wings, and now a crush? You know you have the entire year to gap it up, right?

MEG: I went cliff jumping today. In a two-piece bathing suit. With a boy. Because he asked me to.

VADA: OH SHIT.

MEG: I know. RIP me.

VADA: Is it weird that I'm getting all emotional? I'm so proud of you!

MEG: Not completely. Although my mom would not be impressed.

VADA: All the more reason.

MEG: That's what Micah said!

VADA: Is Micah the name of The Boy. The Boy Who Jumps Off Cliffs?

MEG: Yes. He's the first person I met here and somehow, not on purpose, we've seen each other almost every day since?

VADA: Like serendipity or like stalking?

MEG: I couldn't possibly know for sure, but if it's stalking, I know where he lives and met his family, his dog, his best friend, and I got a job next door to where he works.

MEG: So, I think that would make me the stalker?

VADA: Definitely. But hold up. YOU GOT A JOB THERE?

MEG: Oh, right. Yeah. I did.

VADA: Meg. Does your mom know you aren't coming home?

MEG: Um . . .

VADA: Jesus H. If I wasn't in the middle of . . .

VADA: . . .

VADA: Iowa. Apparently. Luke drives so slow, we'll probably grow old and die before we make it to Cali.

VADA: Anyway! You're moving to Marquette? Because of Micah?

MEG: No. Because of my great-grandma Betty. But I need to go. I'm having dinner with my uncle and Miss Betty in forty minutes and I'm still in my suit.

VADA: MEG. WHAT. I'M IN IOWA. I MAY VERY WELL DIE HERE. YOU CAN'T JUST TELL ME YOU'RE MEETING LONG-LOST FAMILY AND FALLING IN LOVE WITH CLIFF JUMPERS AND THEN LEAVE.

MEG: Gah. I'm sorry! I promise to FaceTime you when I get back.

VADA: You better.

MEG: And I'm not in love with anyone.

MEG: It's a crush.

VADA: Sure. Tell me that again when I can see your face.

MEG: Give Luke a hug for me.

VADA: He says, YOUTUBE: Call It What You Want by Taylor Swift.

MEG: SHUT UP AND DRIVE LUKE. *kisses*

I toss my phone on the bed and flop down on my back before bouncing back up with a groan. Better get cleaned up.

I honestly haven't had enough time to formulate any expectations about my uncle, James, but if I had, he would have exceeded them within the first thirty seconds.

I spot Betty first, walking into the restaurant on the arm of a good-looking, very tall, sandy-haired man with a trimmed beard and kind eyes.

"James," I say softly.

He flashes a smile full of white teeth and answers, "Meg?"

I reach out to hug Betty first, and it feels like something I've been doing forever. James holds out a hand. "I'm a hugger," he warns. "But I'm also a stranger, so—"

I cut him off with my arms. "I'm a hugger, too," I confess. His embrace is short and sweet, and then we're sitting down at a booth.

Betty breaks the ice after the server takes our drink order. "So, what have you been up to since I saw you last?"

"I got a job," I say brightly. "And I jumped off a cliff today!"

"Black Rocks?" James asks.

"I think so, yeah? On the shore of Lake Superior? Have you been?"

Betty shakes her head, her purple hair framing her face in chin-length layers. "Not in decades. But I did go as a teen, and I remember what it was like to free-fall long enough to think, 'I'm still in the air.'"

"Unreal," I admit. "I nearly chickened out."

"I chickened out my first time. I was with your dad, actually. Wow." James laughs. "That's very weird to say." I nod like, *You're telling me.* "I was fifteen, and I got all the way up there with Drew and his friends, and I couldn't do it. Hiked back down dry. Drew teased me for months. After he died, I went back and made myself go." He shakes his head, lost in the memory. "I was stupid. Reckless. It was too early in the season, and I could have gotten hypothermia. But I didn't . . . Except this one time when I went to Dead River Falls . . . well . . ." James scratches at his beard, hesitating, and shakes his head. "Anyway. I've gone back every year on that same day ever since, because I can. You know?"

I shrug. Because while I do know, I also don't. I didn't lose Andrew. I never had him.

We order our food, and James asks me questions about school and my mom. I tell them about ice-skating, and James tells me one of his jobs is driving the Zamboni at the rink. "If you're interested in teaching, I can pass along your name. They're always looking for qualified instructors."

"That would be incredible," I say. "For so long, I couldn't bring myself to skate if I wasn't competing, but I've been missing the ice. I think I'm finally ready to go back, even if it's just teaching little ones."

"And you said you have a job already?" Betty prompts.

I sip my iced tea. "Yeah, I'm working at a coffee shop downtown? Cozy Cup? Next to UpNorth Outfitters?"

James beams. "Next to Dani's store? We know it well. Dani and I go way back."

I raise my brow at his enthusiasm, and Betty's lips quiver behind her water glass, but he doesn't seem to notice.

"Yep, that's the one. I was hired yesterday."

"Does this mean you're staying?"

"That's the plan. It's a bit of an impulse decision. My original plan was to take a gap year and travel. Well, my original, *original* plan anyway. Then I planned to work at this dude ranch until everything got flipped nose over butt, and now I'm here and I like it. I like you guys, and I've been making friends, and, I mean, I *am* learning things about myself. So, it's still a gap year. But the location is more specific. I feel at home."

"Speaking of, do you *have* a home here?"

"Not yet," I respond, undeterred. "I'm still figuring out the logistics, or rather, God is."

James hesitates, but quickly shakes it off. "I know we just met, but we're family. You're my niece. You're Drew's kid," he says like he's willing himself to believe it. "I have a pretty big place on Park Street, a few blocks from the coffee shop. An old duplex that I've been converting back to its original single-family purposes. It's a hobby of mine. And I've got more bedrooms than I know what to do with. I'd give you plenty of privacy. You'd have your own en suite bathroom, and I won't try to give you a curfew or whatever. I'm not your dad, and I'm not trying to be . . . I mean, I don't even know what that looks like, and you're an adult anyway, but . . . well. It's yours if you want it."

I blink, startled, but a warm feeling is taking over my belly. "Really? You mean it? You don't have to do that."

James seems more certain as he nods. "Absolutely positive. I'd have to rearrange some furniture . . . I'm using the space for storage right now, but I can easily shift things around. When do you need a place?"

"Um, in the next few days . . . but I can stay in the hotel room longer if—"

He shakes his head. "No need. I'll tackle the furniture first thing in the morning. I have a friend who owes me."

"Well, that's settled," Betty says. "I'm so pleased you'll

be staying with us, Meg. I've loved getting to know you after all these years."

"I'm sorry it took so long to find my way here."

"You made it. That's all that matters," Betty says kindly. "Besides, there's nothing to be sorry for. You didn't know."

James shakes his head. "I can't imagine what that must have been like. What a shock."

I shrug, uncomfortable. "Well, it was probably pretty similar to what you experienced. I only have a few days on you. My mom wasn't just keeping secrets from me. She was keeping secrets from everyone."

"Well, for my part, I need to say I'm sorry. To both of you, but especially to James." Betty's eyes take on a sheen behind her bifocals, and she reaches for James's hand, giving it a squeeze. "I was so unsure of whether or not we would ever meet Meg, but that's nothing but an excuse. I should have told you regardless. It could have made all the difference for you to know a part of Drew lived on, somewhere in the world."

James swallows hard, his Adam's apple bobbing. He clears his throat before admitting, "Maybe it would have. Or maybe it would have made it worse. I don't know. I have to trust Meg's mom in this. She did what she thought was best. It can't have been easy to be a teen mother all alone."

"Maybe if she had come clean, she wouldn't have had to be alone," I say, squirming in my seat as something that feels suspiciously like guilt crawls up my esophagus.

"Oh, but she didn't know us," Betty says, defending my mom. "She didn't really even know Drew. To be honest, I don't know how Drew would have handled things had he lived."

James straightens in his seat. "That's true. I worshipped my big brother, and I want to say he would have done the honorable thing. But he was young and selfish, too. I'm not sure what kind of dad he might've been. And I was a teenager, younger than your mom, living with my grandmother."

"So, you think this was all for the best?" I try to keep my voice casual. Curious. But I can feel my insides start to churn at the implication that my mom might have been right to lie to me.

Betty's tone is soothing. "Of course not. At most, it was the best given a difficult situation."

"Because that situation changed," I continue, ignoring Betty's placating gesture and my heart starting to race. "At first, yeah, she was a scared teen mom, but then she married her best friend. Years passed. Nearly two decades. And she still wasn't going to come clean. She was willing to hide my entire family from me for as long as she could just so the people at church wouldn't find out she'd had premarital sex. So—" I cut off, feeling awkward. "So, anyway, you shouldn't feel bad, Miss Betty. The only person who should be feeling bad here is my mother."

James and Betty exchange a loaded look, but I pretend not to notice. I'm annoyed that I've revealed so much and aware I probably sound bitter and immature. James is definitely regretting offering his home to me. Who wants an angsty teenager living under their roof? I'd been doing so well at holding all the garbage in, and all it took was one dinner to spill my guts. James clears his throat and takes a pull from his iced tea.

"So, are you a believer, Meg?" James asks, switching gears. "What I mean is, you mentioned your mom's, um . . . the church? Did you attend church growing up?"

"For sure," I say, finding my footing and answering automatically. "A little rattled as of late, but he is in control." I point to the proverbial sky.

James leans back in his seat. "Incredible. Even after all tha—well, after everything? I envy your faith."

"Aren't you a believer?" I assumed he was with his worship band job and the way he bowed his head before digging into his dinner.

James grins. "Oh, I am. But my faith is shaky and messy most days. It's also been cultivated. For years after Drew passed, though, I struggled." He pins me with his gaze. "That's part of the reason I'm not sure how I would have reacted had I known you were out there." He shakes his head. "It would have been something to hold on to, for sure. It *is* something to hold on to. Drew is here. In you. I can see it—it's incredible. In your smile and your eyes and your exuberance."

"It's like having him in front of you all over again, isn't it?" Betty says in a soft voice.

James nods.

"But?" I prod.

"But, well, as I said, I was a mess. Not much use to anyone for a long time. But maybe that can change now. What about you, Meg? Do you have questions for us? Can I tell you anything about your dad?"

I lift a shoulder, clearing a space so that the server can put my burger in front of me.

"To be honest, I'd rather hear about you guys. It's not that I don't care about my dad, but I don't miss him. I never knew about him. But the two of you? You're my family. I still have a chance to know you. And if I left, I'd miss you."

"Have you heard anything from your mom and step-dad?" James asks gently.

I shake my head. The truth is, my mom has called twice, and I responded with an *I'm safe* text. I feel terrible, and I'll need to talk to her eventually, especially since I've got a job, but I wanted to wait until I found a place to stay. I wanted to have all my ducks in a row before giving her the news.

"My dad is moving out. I don't think he's planning on checking in with me ever."

Betty frowns. "Did you fight?"

"No, never." I pick up my burger, hoping to end this line of conversation with a bite.

James raises one eyebrow. "I feel like there's more to the story, but that's okay. Just know you can talk to us."

I feel the corner of my mouth twitch around my burger. "Thank you. But I'm okay, really. Being up here, and away from it all, helps."

His eyes narrow, but he takes a bite from his panini instead of commenting.

"So, James," I say, once he's swallowed his bite. "Tell me about Dani."

"Sure. What do you want to know?"

Betty hides a smile behind her napkin, and I swirl a fry in my ketchup. "Just how long have you been in love with her?"

That night after showering, I put on Andrew's SATAN IS A NERD tee and a pair of sleep shorts. I've packed up all my stuff, and I sit cross-legged on the hotel bed contemplating my phone. James's offer to work at the rink earlier made me think of my stepdad, Declan, and how things used to be. It wasn't something my mom was into, figure skating. It was all Declan and me. He used to drive me to early-morning practices and afternoon practices and weekend competitions. We'd stay in hotels like this one and take advantage of the cable since we didn't have it at home. Declan skated as a kid but grew out of it when he hit his teens. Most girls had skate moms, but I had a skate dad. He could stitch sequins with the best of them.

I open a text and start typing.

MEG: Hey, Dad. Just checking in. There's a rink up here that's hiring. I might get a job teaching skating.

Delete.

MEG: Hi, Dad. I miss you.

Delete.

MEG: Hey, Declan. Just wondering how you're doing?

Delete.

MEG: I wish we could talk, Dad. I wish I knew what happened between us. I still love you.

I jab my finger at my phone. *Delete, delete, delete.*

I make a noise of frustration in the back of my throat. I don't have the words yet. I think about reaching out a thousand times a day, but whenever I try, nothing seems right. Instead, I click off my phone and plug it into its charger. Then I turn off the light and crawl under the covers, falling into a fitful sleep.

8

Micah

I might have to marry Meg.

Like, it's been years since my dad gave me the whole "Where do babies come from" talk, but I remember "Find a wife who bakes" being high on the Wifely Characteristics list, and these chocolate zucchini muffins are heaven in my mouth.

Also, it occurs to me now that I've been brainwashed. What the fuck kind of sex talk is that? They're lucky I didn't impregnate a girl by accident. Thank God for public school education.

(Kidding! I learned about sex from my dad's trial transcripts.)

(Yeah, I do need therapy, thanks for noticing.)

I'm sitting in the coffee shop trying not to drool on the counter as Meg pulls out another muffin tin full of gooey deliciousness. Forget Em and her guys-who-aren't-just-friends. Em who? My new kryptonite is small, dark-haired, and carrying baked goods that smell like the best thing to ever happen to anyone.

Actually, I reject the term *kryptonite*. Meg's too sweet for something so cynical. Which is probably why I can't make a move. I like her too much to fuck it up. She's . . . so nice? And cute and smart and I'm in over my head because she needs help and I feel like maybe I could be that for her.

What if all the shit with my dad happened so that I could be the friend Meg needs?

That would be . . . too much for me to consider right now.

"Where is my muffin tester? I left her around here . . . somewhere . . ." Meg says in mock confusion. She starts looking in outrageously tiny places like a coffee canister and the cookie tin. Noel's hysterical giggles ring out from the stool next to me.

"I'm right heeeeeere!"

Meg startles theatrically and peeks around the register. "Oh, there she is! Order up, Short Stack." She cuts a muffin in half and lightly blows on it before passing it to the little girl. She holds up a hand to me.

"Easy, Muscles."

"Just one more," I beg.

"I don't think this is allowed in your CrossFit diet."

My eyes narrow. "I don't do CrossFit."

A single dark brow lifts. "Powerlifting, then."

I huff out a laugh. "What?"

"Decathlons?"

"Definitely not."

She gives me an exaggerated wink. "Give me time. I'll figure it out."

"You're ridiculous," I say, feeling a little warm.

"And you're built like an archangel. What is *that* about?"

"Meg," Dani interrupts, poking her head in from the

kitchen. "I heard from a little birdie that you found a place to stay!"

Meg props a fist on her waist. "I did! Does your birdie happen to be a strapping six-foot-something bearded carpenter sort?"

Dani blushes. "Maybe."

"Well, that's a relief. I was a little concerned he was going to change his mind after I asked if he wouldn't mind me painting the bedroom something 'not taupe.'"

Dani smirks. "You'll be good for him, Meg. He can use the shake-up. I've known James a long time and consider him to be a very dear friend. I assure you he's over the moon about having a niece. It's like he's been given a new lease on life. Truly."

"Wait," I say, catching up. "*James* James?" I look at Meg, taking in her face. Her blue eyes, her nervous smile. "Holy shit, your uncle is James McArthur? That means—"

"My dad was Andrew." Meg finishes the sentence, and it sinks in and fills the space between us.

"Whoa."

"Yeah."

"Wow. Andrew. *The* Drew. Drew had a kid."

Meg flushes, and Dani motions for her to sit down. Maria is back to man the counter, and Meg circles around to sit on a stool next to me.

"Firstly, Dani, thank you for that. I feel the same. I'm looking forward to getting to know James more, and I'm so grateful to stay in his beautiful home."

"He wouldn't have it any other way. Trust me," Dani says. "I have to head back over to relieve Duke." She grabs a muffin. "Who will love you for this, by the way. I'm going to lose all my employees if you keep baking." She looks meaningfully at me.

"Hey! It's my day off!" I grumble.

"Of course, Micah. And you always come here on your days off."

I open my mouth to respond with, *What?* "So, your dad," I start instead. I try to remember what Meg told me that first night. "He met your mom at a youth conference?"

"Youth *group* conference."

I groan sympathetically. "I guess he used to play in a band?"

I shrug, but it makes sense. "Probably. James leads the worship band at church."

"He does?"

"Plays the guitar. Sings, too."

"Huh. I sing," she says. "At church. Or I did. My mom can't carry a tune to save her life. I must get it from my dad."

"I'd like to hear you sometime," I say. I don't know why.

This time, *she* shrugs. "Maybe. If I go to church."

"Maybe if I go, too."

She raises her brows at that. Touché.

"Did your mom ever tell him about you?"

Meg is shaking her head. "Nope. They met at the conference and never spoke again. By the time she knew about me and was ready to reach out, he'd died in the car accident."

"Wow," I repeat.

"Yeah. I'm the product of a youth group kid one-night stand. Bet that's not something you hear every day."

I scrunch my mouth to one side, playing with the sugar packets in front of me. "I don't know. I bet it happens about as often as any other one-night stand. But probably with a whole lot more guilt. It's my experience that church folk aren't any purer than the rest of the world; they just hide it better."

"I don't know. If you met my mom, you might change your mind."

"And if you met my dad, you might change yours," I toss back before rushing on. "But that's *whatever*. The point is, your uncle is one of my favorite people on Earth."

"James is special," she agrees. "I didn't know you had favorite people."

"I don't. Not many, anyway. Duke is okay. Noel, when she's not making fun of my helmet hair. Dani when she's not trying to convince me to take extra hours. You—" I start, and immediately swallow wrong, choking on nothing.

Meg's eyes take on a glittery quality. "Really? Me?"

"You're all right." I work at sounding casual, but I doubt I'm any good at it. "Brave enough to jump off a cliff, and you make damn good muffins."

"Worth keeping around, for sure," she quips.

"Certainly intriguing."

"I'm also good at pretending to be a girlfriend in a pinch."

"Hey! You owed me after you stole my spot."

"Sure. Little old me threatened you right out of your public space."

I change direction at her sass. "How was meeting James anyway? How's all of that been going?"

She wipes nonexistent crumbs with a clean cloth. "Awesome. Surreal. Life-changing."

"I bet."

"In all honesty, I'm not sure yet. I really like Andrew's family, and when I'm here, I can pretend that's all there is, and I *really* like that."

"Ignorance is bliss?"

She exhales forcefully. "Probably. But it's only been a few days."

"Fair enough." Not like I'm one to talk, and I've had half a decade. I glance at the clock on the wall behind Meg's head. "I should get going. I have class in thirty minutes."

"Real quick." Her navy eyes watch me. "In your opinion, is this a good idea?"

I take a second to answer, feeling oddly flattered that Meg is asking my opinion. Like I'm a trusted friend. I know this is new for both of us, but I want her to know I can be honest.

"James is solid. I've known him for ages . . . He's best friends with my stepdad, Brian, but he's also become my friend over the last few years, too. He's very cool about my issues with the church and never makes me feel like a dick for being angry. As you can probably tell, because literally everyone can, he's been in love with Dani for years. *Years.* Unrequited, but not in a slimy way. More like the 'I'll fix your leaky faucet and keep your business afloat and love you from afar' kind of way."

Meg snickers softly and leans in, and I try not to get too distracted by how mouthwatering she smells. "Can I tell you something? I don't think it's unrequited anymore. I've been watching Dani, and I get the impression that she's crushing hard on my uncle. Did you see her face when I mentioned his handsome, bearded self?"

I sit back. "Actually. I did. You think?"

"I do. One hundred percent. So . . . *you* don't think I'm making an unsafe or impulsive choice by moving in with a grown man who is practically a stranger?"

"Well, when you put it like that, it does sound a little

shady. But no. I don't. He's not a stranger; he's your dad's brother. And maybe you never met your dad, but I promise I would never suggest you move in with the guy if I didn't trust him with my life. I'd let my younger sisters move in with him, if that helps."

Meg unleashes her smile full force, and I rise to my feet and pull my jacket off the back of my chair before I decide to do something embarrassing like forge her a promise ring out of staples and tack nails.

"See you tomorrow?" she asks.

"Tomorrow. If you happen to have any muffins left . . ."

"I'll put one aside for the wrestler?"

I sling my backpack over my shoulders. "Nice try."

She nods. "Right. Of course. I'll be saving the last one for the personal trainer."

"You're ridiculous."

"And you are blushing. Get out of here, Micah." Meg circles back around the counter right as a second customer walks in.

And I leave before I can be talked into staying all afternoon.

I'm on a run with Cash when everything goes to hell later that night. I've just managed my way to the top of the massively steep hill on Ridge Street, and my phone rings, interrupting my playlist. I tap my screen, assuming it's my mom wondering if I'll be eating with them, when I see a number I don't recognize. I'm out of breath, so I let it go, but it starts up again almost immediately. By the third time through, I answer.

"This is Micah."

"Hi, Micah, this is Dawn Blakely with the *Detroit Free Press*. Do you have a few minutes to answer some questions?"

My gut ices over as heat floods my face. What the hell?

"How did you get this number?"

"Google. Micah, your father's parole hearing will be in a few weeks. How do you feel about his chances of getting out of prison?"

I let the loop of Cash's leash slide up my arm so that my hand is free to rake through my damp hair. "No comment," I say through clenched teeth.

"Will you be attending your father's hearing, Micah?"

"No comment."

"It's rumored that several of your father's accusers plan to make an appearance. Are you planning to confront the women in his defense?"

"What?" I'm stopped short. "No! I was a kid when this happened. Why would I confront anyone?"

"At the last trial, you said you believed your father."

"I was thirteen. He's my dad. *Of course* I wanted to believe him."

"Do you think the families deserve restitution for what was stolen from them by your father?"

"Of course, but—"

"According to the trial transcripts from five years ago, your mother planned to file bankruptcy."

My head is spinning. "Sh-she did." I swallow. "We lost everything. Just like those families. I wish they could be paid back, but we don't have the money. He had it. He never gave it to us."

"You don't think they should get restitution, then."

"I don't think anything," I say. "Listen, I'm not sure where you got this number, but—"

"Google," she repeats.

"Fine, whatever." My hand waves wildly in the air in front of me, and Cash hops around my feet, impatient, tangling me in his leash. "I'm pretty sure I'm not allowed to talk to you about legal things, and since I was barely thirteen when this all went down, I'm not a very credible source. So, no, I don't plan to be at the hearing, and I don't plan to defend my father, and I'm not responsible for the harm done to those families. Please leave us alone."

I hang up with a stab of my finger and release a slow, shaky breath. My phone lights up instantly with messages from my mom and Brian. There's another text from my sister Rachel telling me to come home ASAP and three emails from news sites in my in-box.

What the hell happened?

I sprint home, which Cash takes as some sort of challenge. My mom is watching from the screen door when we run up, and before she can panic, I wave her off.

"I'll be right down. Let me shower first, okay?"

I don't give her a choice, taking the stairs to my place three at a time. I fill up Cash's water dish and drink a full glass from the tap before turning the shower to hot and jumping in. After thirty seconds, where I perform the fastest hair rinse and body scrub-down in the history of mankind, I'm dressed and throwing open the front door of my parents' house.

"The *Detroit Free Press* called, and"—I refresh my phone—"I now have five emails from various outlets looking to talk about the hearing. What happened?"

"The victims have hired a lawyer. They plan to sue for damages."

"Sue who? He's in jail."

"And they want to keep him there, but if they can't, this is the next-best solution in their minds," Brian says quietly. My younger siblings have gone to bed, but Rachel and Evie are sitting at the dining room table, ignoring the steaming cups of tea my mom has placed before them.

She motions to a third for me, and I jerk my head in a silent response like, *Really, Mom?*

"Fine by me," I say. "He can rot."

"You don't believe that. He's your father."

"He's not," I say, obstinate.

Brian clears his throat. "Micah, there's more. The video is making the rounds on the news again."

I stop in my tracks. The room tilts, and my stomach lurches.

"So far only a few local stations, but—"

My breath strangles in my throat. "Jesus."

"We called the station right away," my mom says. "Telling them to cease and desist playing the clip. Brian contacted his lawyer, too. You were a minor, so they can't legally show it on the news. Unfortunately, that does little to stop people from using it on the internet. The source is private, and it's nearly impossible to track them all down."

I sink onto the couch, burying my head in my hands with a groan. "When will this end?"

"I'm so sorry, Micah."

"I was thirteen," I say. "I had no idea what was happening. He lied to me over and over, and I believed him because he was my dad!" I'm pulling at the ends of my hair and shaking my head. "Why can't they leave me alone?"

"They want to make an example out of your father. This has nothing to do with you," my mom insists.

"That's all well and good, Mom, but regardless, I'm once

again the poster child for religious hypocrisy. Did you know I asked a girl to homecoming freshman year, and her mom made her tell me no because I might grow up to be a sex predator? She actually said that to me. Just like that. Kids would hide their wallets in PE when I was around. I've finally started getting past it all, and it's happening again."

"You don't even look the same," my mom says. "You won't be recognized."

"Too late," Evie says, holding up her phone. "'Notorious Pastor's Kid All Grown Up,'" she reads. "Some clickbait site. Looks like pics from one of your kayak tours." Rachel grabs it from her to check it out.

"At least you look good. Everyone is commenting about how hot you are." She makes a face. "Never mind. Don't read the comments. Assholes," she grumbles, typing rapidly on the screen.

"Doesn't matter. Nothing I haven't already heard. I should have taken Brian's last name when you offered."

My mom shakes her head. "You shouldn't have to change yourself because of what he did," she says softly.

"Too late," I mutter. I'm pulling out my phone, clearing my screen of texts and looking for Duke's name. "I have to get out of here."

"Where are you going?"

"Somewhere else," I say.

I go back up to my apartment, lapping the small space while cussing out my bad luck. Eventually, I pull out my phone and open the search engine. It doesn't take long to find what I'm looking for. Right there, with only a few short taps, is my thirteen-year-old self, earnest and recklessly loyal to a man who didn't come close to deserving it.

My smooth face is lit with the camera's glare, and I'm

wearing my Easter Sunday suit and tie. A reporter, someone whose name I've long forgotten, jabs a mic in my direction. All of this is totally illegal, by the way. I was underage, and my mom swears she never gave permission to film me. I wonder idly if the reporter was fired afterward.

I can mouth the questions as she fires them off, though it's been ages since I've watched this clip. The last time I saw it, I threw my laptop at the wall and cracked the screen. Thankfully, it was a hand-me-down. Now, my heart beats a steady thrum in my veins. I'm in complete control even though I know what is coming next. This is the part that went viral. The lines that condemned me to be the poster child for the modern hypocrisy of the church.

Her: "Do you believe your dad is innocent, Micah?"

Me, loud and clear and full of pride: "My dad didn't do anything wrong. He's a pastor. His job is to help these people, and they turned on him like the Sanhedrin turned on Jesus. They are crucifying my dad just the same."

There's more, but that's the worst of it. And the picture it represented was taken out of context and refitted and made into memes. The delusional ramblings of an eighth grader. Used as the butt of a joke. *I* was the joke.

My dad should have been the joke. He was the one who lied and stole and cheated. He was the one who broke the trust and faith of so many people. He was the one who led women into his office and used his position of power over them. He didn't rape anyone, according to the evidence, but he certainly wielded his influence inappropriately. Marriages broke up over him. So many lives were altered and ruined, and I know, logically, why people ostracized my family.

I get how it all looked.

But fuck, it hurt all the same.

I swipe the screen away, vowing to never look again, before pulling up my text messages.

MICAH: Meet me at Marquette Mountain in twenty?

DUKE: That bad, eh?

MICAH: You have no idea. You in?

DUKE: Absolutely.

SEPTEMBER

9

Meg

My uncle James's house is so cute, I might never leave. The man is mega-talented at reno. I've seen some of the other houses on this hilly street, and let's just say they're a lot prettier at night. I'm definitely getting a deal compared to the college students living on either side of us.

Plus, I don't have to pay rent. I'm not sure how I feel about that part. James's argument is that Andrew would never charge me rent, so he won't either. I wanted to argue that neither of us really know what my biological father would have done, but I suppose it stands to reason that the twenty-year-old version of Andrew wouldn't approve of his potential future offspring paying rent to his little brother.

I'll just keep bringing him home leftover baked goods instead. The man can update a midcentury craftsman with the skill of an HGTV star, but he burns spaghetti noodles. It's been a few days, and the beginning was pretty uncomfortable. Like when James admitted that he only bought Hot Pockets and cereal and usually ate out, and I admitted that

I've never watched an R-rated movie, not even the funny ones . . .

But my uncle roommate and I seem to be getting into a sort of routine. James left me money on the counter this morning to buy groceries. And I laughed so hard watching the highly inappropriate *Super Troopers* that I almost busted a rib. I can't stop making meow jokes every chance I get, mostly because he always laughs. It's a win-win.

To stave off awkwardness, my bedroom is on the other side of the house from his. He installed a lock for me, and I have my own outside entrance that dead bolts. Not that I don't trust him, but this is all very new, and honestly, I don't think either of us are really sure what this relationship is supposed to look like. Landlord and renter? Parent and child? Uncle and grown niece? A mashup of all three? Presumably, because I have my own door, I can come and go as I please. But because he's my flesh and blood, I feel this nagging need to explain where I'm going at all times. Thankfully, yesterday morning at work, Dani brought me a small dry-erase board with magnets.

"It goes on the fridge," she explained. "My roommates and I used one in college. We used it to write grocery lists or leave messages about broken things or where we were headed . . . it's not a requirement, but it helps with being considerate."

The woman is a godsend. I'm guessing my dear first-time uncle must have hit her up for advice. Regardless, the board is perfect. Just the right amount of accountability. Plus, I'm learning that James is a nerd who likes to tell church-dad jokes in his spare time, which is very sweet. And nerdy. Did I mention the nerdy?

This morning: *How do you make holy water? YOU BOIL THE HELL OUT OF IT.*

At lunchtime, I dropped off some essentials and saw: *Why couldn't Jonah trust the ocean? BECAUSE HE KNEW THERE WAS SOMETHING FISHY ABOUT IT.*

I answered back with: *Who was the smallest person in the Bible? KNEE-HIGH MIAH.* Which I had to google because, again, this is a level of nerdy that even I, a lifelong Sunday school participant, cannot compete with.

So when I hear the rumble of the garage door this evening, I make quick work of what is left of my grilled cheese and dash down the long hallway back to my side of the house. Before I get too far, I hear his low chuckle as he reads my joke, and I smile. This is going to work out just fine.

I'm staring into space the following night, humming and daydreaming, as the last bit of the evening's rays stream through the picturesque bay windows of the Cozy Café, painting everything in a pretty, nostalgic shade of amber. This town is so freaking cute. Ann Arbor is cute, to be sure, but this is a whole other level because it's also quaint and small enough that people still bother to smile at strangers.

Like every single person who has walked past today. More often than not, they've also stopped in, Maria's baking the bread crumbs to their wandering appetites. Maria wasn't kidding when she hired me. She barely makes it out of the back until the after-work crowd is finally headed home, and once she does, she's covered head to toe in cocoa powder and ground espresso beans. I would be more than happy to help her bake, but someone has to manage the wily sorts.

And that someone is me. I've never had a real job before. I've babysat neighbors and taught Sunday school, but I've never had a paycheck. Well, technically, I still haven't, but I've been assured it's coming. I like working. I like manning this counter and teasing smiles out of grumpy old men and giving out free samples to little kids.

I like having something to do. A purpose. It's not my life's ambition, sure, but it's mine.

The chime over the window rings out, and my eyeballs are assaulted by turquoise hair and lurid plaid.

"Gah, Duke, you should warn a girl before unleashing all of that." I automatically turn to pour him a steaming Americano, his usual. Which I only know because in the handful of days I've worked here, he's come in twice each shift, presumably on his way in and out next door, and ordered the exact same thing. He pulls up a seat at the counter and lifts the glass display dish, snatching a giant snickerdoodle. I stab the button on the register with a smirk and pass him his finished drink.

"*Wicked*?" he asks, nodding to the speakers tucked away at the corner of the room.

"*J'adore* Kristen Chenoweth," I say with a wistful tilt of my head.

He nods, taking a sip. "You remind me of her."

I raise a brow. "I'll take that as a compliment."

"It is. You're both tiny and sassy."

I beam, more than happy to be either of those things, though I never expected to hear them from Duke and his punk-rock hair aesthetic. "You surprise me."

He takes a chunk out of the cookie with his teeth. "I have an older sister who's a theater nerd. She played Elphaba in a big-deal community production and made me practice lines with her. We must have watched the *Behind the Scenes Wicked* special a thousand times."

"Lucky! I had to watch it alone. No siblings, and although my best friend, Vada, is probably *the* biggest music geek in the world, she only tolerates Broadway musicals on a purely professional level."

"You're from downstate, right? Have you seen anything live in Detroit?"

"Oh gosh, a few. I got to see *Hamilton* last fall."

His gasp is one of pure delight. "You did not!"

I glance at the clock. We're minutes from closing, so I grab a cookie for myself, taking a nibble. Holy cow, it's buttery and delicious. "I did. It wasn't as good as the original cast, obviously, but it was still the best thing I've ever seen."

Duke groans. "I'm so jealous. I tried to convince Micah to make a trip down with me, but he's saving up for school."

I shake my head. "That darn responsible kid."

"Right?"

"*Anastasia* is coming in December," I say.

He nods. "Oh, I know. To Michigan Theater."

"Want company? I'm not nearly as fiscally responsible as Micah."

"Seriously?"

"I mean, we'd have to get tickets, but absolutely. I would love to have a theater buddy."

"I'm in. Maybe Micah would even go this time with the proper motivation." The way he eyes me makes me think I'm that motivation, but I choose to ignore it.

"Whatever, either way, you and I are going. The haters can get their own tickets."

He laughs and tosses the rest of his cookie in his mouth, brushing the crumbs away and standing. "I should get back," he says between chews. "Dani will need help closing up."

"Skedaddle, then. I have mopping to do."

He saunters off, all long legs and pointy elbows, and I can't help the smile spreading across my face.

I'm riding the high of cementing *another* friendship when I get back that night and decide it's past time to call my mom. She's expecting me home any day, and seeing as how I unpacked my suitcase into the dresser in my shiny new bedroom, that's definitely not happening.

For being the easiest decision of my life, I've had a heck of a time building up the confidence to tell my mom about it.

I scroll to her number on my phone and take several deep breaths. I perch on the edge of my bed before changing my mind and standing. I kick off my worn Converse and let my toes sink appreciatively into the lush carpet. My feet hurt from standing for so many hours in a row. It's been never since I've had to do that. Is it weird that I'm happy about tired feet?

I pace, doing my breaths again, and deciding this won't help calm me, I step outside. I shut the door behind me and walk out onto to the soft lawn James mowed this morning. The grass is cool and damp and moonlit, and I pull my old worn cardigan over my shoulders, wrapping it closed at the waist. James has a small bench between two trees that overlooks a weedy garden. I make my way to it but don't sit and, before I can second-guess, hit Call.

Micah picks up on the first ring.

"Meg?" His voice is a deep grumble in my ear, and I find myself rubbing the goose bumps prickling on my arms.

"I have to call my mom, and I'm freaking out."

"Okay. About what?"

"About staying."

"What?"

I exhale. "And getting a job and moving in with my uncle."

"Meg," he says, and I can picture him shaking his head in exasperation.

"I know."

"Meg," he repeats.

"Yes?"

"You haven't told your mom any of it? She thinks you're coming home still?"

"Tomorrow. On a bus. Which, obviously, I don't have a ticket for."

"Tomorrow," he repeats flatly.

"I think. Ish."

"Ish."

"Why do you just keep repeating everything I say? That's not helpful."

His breath huffs into the speaker. "Because I honestly don't know what to say. Except you have to call her. Right now. It's not like she can change your mind, and I know you're mad at her, but she's your mom. You have to tell her."

"It's not that. More like, I don't want *her* to be mad." I hate how tiny my voice is, but this is the truth. I'm scared to death of making my mom mad. Or sad. Or disappointed. Or lonely. All of it makes my stomach sick, and I know when I call her, I'll be doing all of that and more.

He must realize it, because his next words are soft.

"I'm on my way."

I catch the reflective flash of Micah's bike five minutes later. He rides straight to the backyard, and there's movement behind the curtains as he's removing his helmet.

James gives us a wave from the window in front of the sink where he's washing dishes and then leaves us alone, abandoning his spot.

That's it. I love being a grown-up.

"Okay. You're going to call your mom right this minute, and I will be here the entire time. If it goes badly, you won't be alone, and I promise to take you someplace after to distract you."

"On your bike?" I tease, playing for time.

In the dim glow of the neighbor's outside light, the corner of his mouth quirks. "That's how confident I am that this will be okay. But also, Frosty Snacks is close enough to walk."

I take a fortifying breath, tug out my phone, and dial my mom's number. She doesn't pick up at first, and I'm wondering if I can just say it all in a voice mail when she answers in a rush.

"Hello? Meg!"

"Mom? Hi. Yeah. It's me. How are you?" I ask. Stupidly.

"Oh, you know," she says. Which, I suppose I do. My phone-less hand clenches in the pocket of my sweater, stretching it.

"Mom, I got a job here." Might as well start at the top.

"A job where?"

"In Marquette," I say. My teeth chatter, and my stomach feels like it's turning inside out. "At a coffee shop. And, um, my uncle? James? He invited me to live at his place, rent-free. It's a really nice place. He's like this genius jack-of-all-trades kind of—"

She cuts me off. "You're staying with a stranger?"

"Not a stranger. My dad's brother. He's family. My *uncle*, Mom," I repeat. Even I still can't believe it sometimes. "I met my uncle and my great-grandma, and they're wonderful. I want to get to know them. I *need* to know them. Did you know Betty has purple hair? Really purple, not like old-lady lavender? Like how amazing is that? And Uncle James is the worship leader at his church—"

My mom's laugh is harsh in my ear. "Yeah, well, your father was a worship leader, too. Not exactly a ringing endorsement for morality."

I'm pulled up short. "What is *that* supposed to mean?" I whisper, eyeing Micah, who has frozen in place. "Did he attack you? Mom? Did Andrew hurt you?"

She is silent a beat. The longest beat of my entire life before, "No. He didn't. We were impulsive and led by our hormones, but I was consenting."

I slump, relieved. "Then, I don't get it. It took two of you to make me. It wasn't only Andrew's fault."

"I don't really feel like talking about this with you, Meg. Maybe when you're older. Or married."

My mouth flaps open. "Are you serious? Even now, knowing all I know about how I came to be, you're going to refuse to be real with me? It's called *sex*, Mom. You had it. You weren't married. It's okay. Why can't you just tell me you don't regret it because it gave you me? Why do you have to be such a martyr?"

"Why do *you* insist on knowing the sordid details?"

My nostrils flare, and I surge to my feet. "I don't want details, Mom, I want answers! I want the truth! I want you to tell me that sex isn't scary and dangerous and sinful and that I'm not sullied for some husband I've never met just because I bought a two-piece and wore it cliff jumping!"

"You went cliff jumping?"

"Never mind. We're not ready to talk yet. I just wanted

to check in and tell you I'm safe and I'll be staying for a while."

"That's not a good idea, Meg. Come home, please. You can get a job here. The church is hiring someone to answer phones in the afternoons. You'd be great at that."

My throat threatens to close up, and I swipe at an angry tear. I let out a shuddering breath, staring at the stars, trying to keep my composure. Micah moves closer. Not touching me, exactly, but close enough that I can feel his warmth through my sweater. I'm so, so tired, it's as though I could melt into him and never resurface. Which is entirely too tempting.

"Mom, I love you. I'm not coming home. Please don't be mad at me." My phone falls from my ear, and I stab the End button with a shaky finger.

"Shhhhhhhhhhhhhhhhhhhhhhit," I spit out, slouching onto the bench. Micah's arm presses against mine.

We sit there in silence, side by side, for a long time before he asks, "Do you want to talk about it?"

For some reason, this makes me snort. Because, holy smokes, there is *nothing* I want to talk about less than what he overheard. To be fair, it was my impulsive idea to involve him.

"No. Thank you, though."

"Ice cream?"

"Please."

He stands and offers his hand. I take it, letting go after I stand, faking the need to brush off my shorts. Part of me wants to hold his hand forever, but another part, one that sounds remarkably like my mom, wants to lock myself away in a tower, warmed only by the heat of burned fan fiction kindling.

I'm not sure which part is winning.

"What are the odds you didn't just overhear all of that?"

"I have excellent hearing."

"Of course you do."

"My dad's in prison," Micah says, wincing in the low light of the streetlamps.

I scramble to remember what he's said about his dad, but he's only talked about his stepdad, Brian. "Whoa."

"See? Not so bad in comparison, right?"

"Did he . . ." I want to ask if he killed someone, but that feels . . . tactless?

Micah shakes his head, reading me correctly. As usual. "Not that. He was a pastor. He was living this double life and stole a ton of money from the congregation and slept with a lot of women on his staff . . . It was messy. I was only thirteen when it went down. My dad was my hero, you know?"

I do know. Until a month ago, there wasn't a person on Earth I looked up to more than my mom.

"And, like, that kind of idolatry doesn't just end when the police show up. At least, it didn't for me. I thought they were wrong. I believed *him*. I was an idiot."

"You were a kid."

He nods. "I was."

I consider his profile. His serious brow. His broad shoulders. His protective presence. "Probably not after that, though, I bet."

His head jerks to look at me, his eyes searching mine briefly. "No," he says. "Not after that. Not *since* that day."

"We're quite the misfit pair, you and me," I say. "You, the former pastor's kid who knew too much, and me, the youth group girl who knew nothing at all."

"Your mom really said you'd be sullied for a two-piece?"

"Yup."

"Is that why you bought one the first day I met you?"

"Yup," I repeat with a wry smile.

"You rebel."

"That's just the beginning. I've recently started drinking caffeine."

"Careful," he warns. "It's a slippery slope to cocaine from there."

"I'm sorry about your dad," I say. "Not about the jail part. Sounds like he deserved that. But about the part where you had to grow up so quickly."

"Thanks. I'm sorry about your mom. For what it's worth, you look fantastic in your two-piece."

"Really?"

"Definitely." His grin is secret. "You should probably wear it every day. Just to prove her wrong."

"I will if you will, water polo player?"

"Nope."

"Tight end?"

"Never."

"Heavy hitter, then."

"Maybe once, but not anymore. Keep trying."

I grab his hand in a fit of courage and smile into the inky darkness.

"I'm getting closer. I can feel it."

"Me, too," he says softly, squeezing my fingers once and leading us down the sidewalk.

10

Micah

"You know how I did that canoe tour for you yesterday? With Emily?" Duke asks me a few days later.

I swallow a bite of sub sandwich and frown. "Yeah, I remember."

"Smart move. Emily came across some photos of you on the internet."

I groan. "Fuck."

"Yeah, but, like, and I don't know if this is a good thing, but she's apparently super turned on by it."

"Gross."

"Yeah. I didn't know that was a real thing outside daytime television, but she's all about your possible record."

"I don't have a record!" I shout, exasperated, causing some people at the patio table next to ours to stare.

"I know that, dipshit," Duke says, hushing me. "Everyone knows that. I'm just telling you because if she was on the prowl before, she's super on the prowl now."

"That doesn't even make sense. My dad was a disgusting human being."

"The ladies love a bad boy."

"He was a predator and stole people's money!" Heads are turning again, and Duke raises a brow.

"And I told you, I *know*. I'm not the one sweating your rep." He takes a long drink from his Fanta and grimaces. "I forgot. There was more. She also might be sweating you because she fully believes you're seeing Meg."

I blink. "What?"

"Well, you did ask Meg out in front of Em, and you went cliff jumping with her and visit her at work and—"

I shake my head. "No. I get why she'd think that. I don't understand why that would increase her interest."

"You're unavailable."

"Unofficially, but still."

Duke's hand freezes midway to his bag of salt-and-vinegar chips. "We'll circle back to that ambiguous statement, but first, yes, Micah, it's true what they say. Absence makes the heart grow fonder or whatever, and it seems that our Emily is one of those girls who wants what she can't have."

"Not that it matters, but we were never really together. A couple of make-out sessions before she started looking elsewhere. I'm not remotely interested and haven't been for a while."

Duke leans forward on his elbows. "Good. Back to that 'unofficially.'"

I shake my head with a smile. "Nothing to say, really. I like Meg. A lot. It's easy with her. I mean"—I hold out a hand—"it's not easy. Everything is hard with both of us, personally, but when we're together, it's easy. If that makes sense."

Duke nods. "Meg is quality."

"Extremely."

"Have you told her about your dad?"

"A bit. She knows he's in prison. And why. I haven't told her about his hearing yet."

"To be fair, you haven't talked to me about it either. Though I can read between the lines in the uptick of adrenaline-filled adventures you seem to be planning."

I nod at him shrewdly. "And I've noticed you're more than willing to come along."

Duke releases a long breath, crumpling his napkin and slumping back in his chair. "It's never going to be enough for him."

"The adventures?" I clarify even though I'm pretty sure I know. The thing is, Duke is pretty quiet about his relationship with his former air force captain father. He was a military brat for ages, passing through new towns and schools every twelve months, until his dad took on a civilian job in Marquette a few years back. His sister is in California, attending college, and ever since she left, I've noticed Duke is happy to do anything that takes him away from his house.

It's not that Duke's dad is abusive in the physical sense . . . he's just not accepting of his kid. To the extreme.

"Sure. Those, too."

I wait him out. He lets me. Finally, he leans forward. "I'm not the son he asked for."

"Fuck that. You're better."

He pulls a skeptical face. "Depends who you ask."

"Duke, I wouldn't bullshit you. You're the capablest person I've ever known. If something ever went down, you are exactly the person I'd want by my side."

"He doesn't see that. He sees someone who wears 'blouses' and dyes his hair."

"I wasn't aware North Face made blouses?"

He rolls his eyes.

"Listen, fine. You're eclectic. You wear whatever the fuck you want, and while sometimes you look like my grandmother, you somehow pull it off. It's a solid, uh, Duke vibe."

His lips twitch. "Vibe?"

"Whatever. You know what I mean. I'm not really a fashion person. Meg would probably be better at this."

"She would," he agrees. After a beat: "Pretty sure he thinks I'm gay."

I suck in a breath.

"I'm not," he says in a low voice. "At least. Probably not. Guess I won't rule it out completely . . . but"—he lifts one bony shoulder in a weak shrug—"I feel like he's waiting for me to give him a label so he can figure out what exactly it is that's so wrong with me."

"*Him,*" I insist.

His eyes tear away from the table and meet mine in question.

"What's wrong with *him*. Not you. You are whoever you are, and he has one job as your dad: to love you unconditionally."

"Wow, Allen, you sure you don't want to be a therapist? You're eerily good at this."

I shake my head, laughing, the tension broken. "No, thanks. You done eating?"

Duke picks up his empty tray and moves to the trash. "I have a dock full of kayaks to return to the shed. Feel like burning off some steam?"

I consider. I have class tonight, but that's hours away. "I could be convinced."

"Think Meg would be down? It was a small tour. You and I can tow one, but I could use a third person."

"I can ask. I think she was getting off work around now."
I dial up Meg, and within minutes, it's settled. "She's gonna
meet us at the shore. She just got home."

"I like her. Have I mentioned that?"

I scratch at my neck, pretending to think. "Maybe a few
times?"

Duke starts ticking off on his fingers. "She makes amazing cookies, memorized my order, isn't afraid to give you
shit, *and* she likes musicals."

I groan. "Musicals?"

"Musicals, Micah."

"I'm going to be outnumbered, aren't I?"

"You betcha."

Dani asked Duke to cover the counter, and I have another
hour and a half before class. So when Meg wanted to know
where the ice rink was, instead of telling her, I offered to
show her.

"Can I ask you something, and you can absolutely tell
me it's none of my business?"

"Sure?" I agree hesitantly.

"Well, I picked up this kind of, um, tension? Whenever
Duke talks about his family?"

I break in. "Duke is Duke, right? Duke has *always* been
Duke. But his dad is former military and can't understand
why his kid won't just clean up and fit in."

"Duke is an exceptional human. Why can't his dad see
that?"

"If only we could figure that out. All I know is, the more
his dad has pressed, the more Duke rebels. Or maybe *rebel*
isn't the word. He's not, like, *trying* to piss his dad off. He's

just . . . I don't know. Holding on to his sanity? His sense of self? Meanwhile, his dad is doing his best to break him down. It's a mess."

"Families can be jerks," she says, and we walk in silence for a few minutes before she asks, "Can I tell you something you can't tell anyone else? It's not my secret to share."

"Sure."

"My dad—not Andrew, but my *dad* dad, *Declan* . . . I'm pretty sure . . . well, maybe not sure, but I think he might be gay." She tucks her hair behind her ear compulsively. "But verrrrry closeted. Like, married my pregnant teen mom at eighteen and lived as a straight man his entire life closeted."

"That's horrible."

"I think so, too. I don't know for sure . . . It's one of those things I suspect but haven't talked to my mom about. I'd rather talk to *him* about it, to be honest. But he's MIA and has been since the Grand Announcement. All I know is both my parents came from extremely conservative Christian families. They definitely married out of mutual desperation. It's not good."

"How would you feel if he told you he was gay?"

Meg exhales a sharp breath of air. "I'd be sad for him. Mostly. And me. Him because he felt like he had to hide his entire life, and me because I think he's been lying to me out of some misplaced fear that I would judge him."

"And you wouldn't?"

To her credit, Meg doesn't answer right away. "Not anymore. But I can't say for sure I wouldn't have a few years ago. Which . . ." Suddenly, she's swiping at her cheek. "I mean. What if I made him feel like I couldn't love him for who he is? He raised me and gave up everything for me.

What if I made him feel like garbage, spouting off untested rhetoric from Sunday school?"

"Yeah," I say. "I can understand that."

"But now, definitely not." Her mouth is set in a firm line, her posture stiff as if daring anyone to contradict her. "I'd have some thoughts for him about how he's lied to me my entire life, but that's something else."

"Of course."

"Hey, Micah?"

Our arms are loose at our sides, occasionally brushing, and the sidewalk is dappled with early-autumn sunlight. I love to run and ride my bike, but sometimes a walk is better. "Yeah?"

"Do you think we'll ever have a regular old mundane boring conversation?"

"Regular, sure. Mundane? I hope. Boring? Not possible with you."

"You're very sweet, you know."

I grimace. "Don't tell anyone."

"Oh, I won't. Believe me. I fully intend for your brooding to scare the other girls away."

My cheeks grow warm, so I change the subject, flustered. "What's your favorite memory of something not including your parents or church or anything dramatic?"

She tilts her head. "I once scored near-perfect marks on my technical at Junior States. I'd debuted my triple lutz and added this super-complicated sit spin at the end that earned me top marks. Teddy bears covered the ice. It was big-time, major amazing."

"You're a figure skater?"

"Former. Though"—she gestures to the giant dome looming blocks ahead of us—"I hope to teach."

"I bet you'd be great at that. Kids love you."

She beams. "Mostly because I'm the same size as they are, I bet. How about you? Favorite memory?"

"Know Cash?"

She clutches her hands to her chest theatrically. "Love-of-my-life Cash?"

"Yeah, Cash. Well, I found him, or maybe he found me. Either way, one night, I was running along the lakeshore and it was too cold to listen to my phone, so I was without music for once. And I came up on a bunch of brush and heard this whimpering. It was Cash, all alone and half-dead. I put him in my shirt and ran all the way home with him against my heart. I had to bottle-feed him for weeks, but he made it. The crazy part was everything was a mess for me at the time. I was completely alone. I hadn't met Duke yet. Everyone was ostracizing me at school. My mom was doing what she could, but she was so overwhelmed . . . and it was like here was this gift. This animal who needed me as much as I needed him. We've been together ever since."

"That's a good memory," Meg says.

"One of the best."

"Tell me something else. What is your favorite song?"

"'Pieces' by this band called Red?"

Meg nods. "I know them well. That's a very telling song, Micah."

I scratch at my neck. "Probably too telling. What's yours?"

"It's an oldie. 'If You Wanna Be Happy' by Jimmy Soul."

A surprised laugh barks out. "The one about finding an ugly wife?"

"I can't believe you know it! That's the one!"

"It's so sexist!"

She shrugs her slim shoulders. "It makes me happy."

"Me, too, actually. It's impossible not to be happy listening to it."

"My mom and dad loved it. We would dance around the house to it when I was really little."

I think about this for a quiet moment. I know things are bad for Meg and her parents now, but they haven't always been. I'm glad for that. She has lots of nice memories, at least.

"Favorite season?" I ask.

"Winter."

"Really?"

"Absolutely. I love mittens."

"It's my favorite, too, but not because of mittens."

"Least favorite food?" she asks.

"Salmon. Yours?"

"Peas."

"Because of the texture?"

"Because they make me puke."

"Noted."

"Are you planning to make me dinner?" she asks with a cheeky grin.

"What if I were?"

"Then I'd volunteer to bring dessert."

"Brownies?" I ask, hopeful.

"Maaaaybe."

Meg's hand swings close to mine, and I grab it. She bites her lip, looking away.

"Is this okay?" I check.

"I'm very new to this, Micah. I've never . . ."

"I know. Is this too much?"

"I don't think so."

"I really like you, Meg."

She turns her face to mine. Her eyes are wide and searching. "I really like you, too. Probably too much for how little I know you. But I can't help it. Every new thing I learn makes me like you more. That seems ridiculously lucky, doesn't it?"

"It does."

"But that doesn't mean it's not real."

"I don't think so."

"I like when you hold my hand."

"Okay."

"I might want to kiss you, too."

I swallow. We stop at the edge of a lakeside park, under a copse of trees. Meg licks her lips. My mouth waters.

"I've never kissed anyone before."

"What if I kiss you? Would that be better?"

"Do you want to?"

"God, yes."

She nods, and I step forward, reaching my hand to cup her face, letting my fingers tangle in the hair at the nape of her neck. Her skin is so soft and her eyes are so blue and her breath is so sweet, and before I can overthink it, I lean forward and press my lips to hers, taking her top one in between mine for a beat of one, two, three, before stepping back and checking.

"Was that okay?"

"More than. Can we do it again?"

"Anytime you want."

She leans forward. "One more. For the road." This time, she presses her lips to mine.

11

Meg

MEG: VADA.

MEG: Oh my gosh WOMAN WHERE ARE YOU.

MEG: I AM HAVING A MOMENT.

MEG: Okay, fine. I'll be here, dying because a boy kissed me and I kissed him and he is very handsome and has real live pectoral muscles and tell Luke to stop macking on you for one stupid minute so I can freak out about it for the love of . . .

VADA: Holy Jesus I'm here. Reading back. Slow your roll.

MEG: Thank you. Jeesh. I'm having an existential crisis here.

VADA: Hold on. How do you know about his rippling pectorals? You move fast!

MEG: They actually *do* ripple. But I only know because of cliff jumping. I don't move that fast.

VADA: But you kissed! You kissed him! Your first kiss! You utter badass. I can't believe you waited to do all this when I am on the other side of the country and can't hug you!

MEG: Ann Arbor didn't have Micah.

VADA: Apparently not. So how was it?

MEG: *swoons* The sweetest.

VADA: Sure. But like, was there tongue?

MEG: No.

VADA: Bet you wanted there to be.

MEG: MAYBE.

VADA: Next time?

MEG: He's moving slow. For me. Which is very, very appreciated. But also, HOW DO I MAKE HIM FRENCH ME?

VADA: *snickers* Luke is reading over my shoulder and said (and I quote): "Just slip it in, Hennessey."

MEG: Oh my gosh. I don't know if I can do that. What if he doesn't want me to?

VADA: This is Luke: HE WANTS YOU TO I PROMISE.

MEG: Hello Lukas, I miss you. But for real, what if I suck?

VADA: (still Luke) It's not possible. But you could always ask him to teach you. I had to teach Vada and look how that turned out.

VADA: LUKAS AARON GREENLY YOU BIG FAT LIAR.

MEG: Ohhh kay. Settle down, guys. I have to go. I'll call later.

VADA: You'd better facetime. I miss your face.

MEG: Deal, babe.

James and I are early for church the following day, and I'm a nervous wreck. I wasn't ready to go to church yet. For lots of reasons, but mostly because I'm not interested in exploring this new caustic relationship I have with the institution. Which is bananas, because I have never once in my life been anything but comfortable walking into a house of God. Call it my heterosexual white girl privilege (*I* do), but I've never had a reason to feel like I didn't belong.

Truth is, it's because I've never done anything wrong. At least biblically. I mean, sure I've sinned. That itty-bitty menial white-lie kind of sin. Like that one time I told Vada I hated Fleetwood Mac, too, so I didn't have to hear why Stevie Nicks sounds like a chain-smoker for the one millionth time.

Otherwise, I'm pretty boring. I've never drank or experimented with drugs. I'm a virgin. I never cuss. I've never stolen so much as a cookie off my mom's counter back home. I cover my shoulders to keep men's thoughts pure. I always donate to the Salvation Army bucket at Christmas.

But that was before Marquette. Before Micah and James and Dani and the truth about my parents came to light. Since, I've worn a two-piece, said *fuck* out loud, kissed a boy, thought about more than kissing a boy, and lied my pants off to multiple people about the state of my heart. I've had terrible, mean-spirited thoughts about my parents, and while I haven't dabbled in alcohol, the thought did cross my mind late one night that a drink might take the edge off whatever this heartache is that I'm feeling.

With all this sinning going on, I'm halfway scared the church doors will go up in flames when I pass through. Will they be able to tell I'm different? Can they read the conflict on my face? The doubt? The insincerity?

A lot of churches say, "Come as you are," or "We are an imperfect people," or "Sinners welcome," but I feel like it's mostly a line. Not that I've had reason to question it, personally, but this is why: sinners are welcome in the door. They're encouraged, even. But if a known sinner wants to volunteer in any capacity, they are turned down. I've seen it again and again. If you are a recovering alcoholic, you can volunteer. You're a sinner, but you aren't acting on that sinful impulse. You're not a sinner on the outside. Only in your heart.

But say you slip? Something terrible happens and you have a drink? Or a photo surfaces of a drunken night out years before? Or someone sees you sitting at a bar with a questionable glass in front of you and they report you to the pastor?

The following weekend, you're no longer allowed to be a greeter in the lobby, passing out free coffee coupons. Because the uncomfortable truth is, while the church loves sinners in their pews, they don't want them in front of a crowd. It's the difference between acceptance and tolerance, and it might catch on.

God forbid.

I don't know what the answer is. I don't. But now that I'm aware of it, I'm having a hard time moving past it. Before Marquette, I was only a sinner in my heart. Now I'm . . . out there. Like toothpaste all squeezed out of the tube. I can't be put back in. And I don't think I want to be.

If kissing Micah is a sin, why did God invent kissing? Why did he create this desire in me to *want* to kiss him? Why did he create this boy who understood me so easily and has Popeye forearms, which is something I never knew I'd like but apparently really, really do?

So, yeah, I'm a ball of nervous energy crossed with raging hormones. Not really the image you want to project walking into your long-lost uncle's church for the first time. But here I am.

The honest truth is I couldn't say no. Saying no would be a giant, flashing arrow pointing to my face with the words CONFLICTED AND ALSO FEELING GUILTY ABOUT FEELING CONFLICTED.

And I don't want to talk about it. In comparison, sweating through a single church service is easier.

Typically, James is on the worship team. He's usually early to prepare and late to stay because of multiple services. He found a replacement this weekend so he could introduce me around. I can tell right away that James is loved and respected at this church. He's comfortable here. Betty arrives with a kiss to my cheek, and I make room for her next to me. That helps. *She* helps. Being near her feels like acceptance. Honestly, everyone seems kind and genuine, but I don't have time to formulate much of an opinion. Within minutes of sitting down in a comfy beige chair, front and center, the music kicks to a start, and I'm lost in the worship.

Because even when I'm not sure about me and my place in it all, I am certain about *this*. Right here. Music has always been very personal for me. Something between me and my Creator. My offering. My heart. Where nothing can get between me and my God. Not even the church.

I close my eyes and open my hands, faceup, at my sides.

Remarkably, I'm ready for this part. Starving for it. I shut out the world only to take in the universe. The simple opening piano chords are familiar to me. My skin tingles in anticipation like little live wires dancing across my surface. A chemistry found only in the divine. How do I know God is real? Because of *this*.

Peace settles in my bones, grounding me to the earth. Love paintis me top to bottom in grace. Joy overwhelms my doubts. I don't know how else to explain it but R-E-A-L. So very real.

My voice pours out, but I don't even hear it. Lost in a sea of voices, we're together in this moment. Our purpose is singular and unified. If you're using all your voice to worship, there's no breath left for anything else. Maybe that's why I've always felt so in love with this part.

After three songs, the instruments fall silent, and I open my eyes to the friendly smile of the lead singer, James's replacement.

"Good morning, church!" he says, holding his guitar pick in one hand and the mic stand in another. He's wearing a pair of Dockers and a polo and looks exactly like a dad who used to play in a band. After everyone responds with a hearty "Good morning," he smiles.

"I know you aren't used to seeing me up here these days and are probably wondering why, if James is in the front row, he's not leading you, but it's temporary, rest assured."

Laughter.

"For those of you who don't know me, I'm Brian Lundgren. I'm usually behind the soundboard on Sunday mornings, but James asked me to tune up my old guitar and take his place so he could bring his *niece* to church this morning. But I'm not going to spoil that story. I'll let James share, and then he can lead us in prayer." He looks to James for confirmation, and James looks to me.

"I'm sorry, I didn't think to check with you. Do you mind?"

I shake my head, touched, and James squeezes my shoulder, hopping up the three steps to the stage.

James looks at home onstage next to Brian. He's dressed in a casual plaid button-down with the sleeves rolled up to his elbows and a pair of jeans. He's not as flashy as Betty and me. His beard is neat, and I don't see any visible tats (though he has one for Andrew on his upper arm that he showed me one night while watching TV). But he's wearing a pair of cardinal-red Vans that I can dig. A touch of whimsy. Like my wings.

"Many of you know my story, but to summarize . . . when I was barely sixteen, I was in a terrible car accident. My big brother, Drew, was driving my girlfriend and me home from a concert, and he was intoxicated. Drew died instantly. Candace died on the way to the hospital. I walked away with a broken arm and a scarred soul.

"I battled depression and survivor's guilt for years. Started drinking and getting into trouble. I missed my brother more than I could bear. Four years older than I was, he was my hero. I worshipped the ground he walked on. I'd just started dating Candace when I lost her. Our relationship was all butterflies and sweetness. Drew died because he chose to drink and get behind the wheel. Candace died because of me. Or," he says grimly, "that's how I felt.

"Every year, on the anniversary of the accident, I go cliff jumping. It started off as a way to honor my brother, but by my junior year of college, it had started to look like an escape. You see, I was about to turn *twenty-one*." James runs a hand through his short hair and scratches at his beard. "I was about to be older than my brother for the first time. That"—he releases a shaky breath—"felt impossible and wrong. So, on that day, I decided to skip Black Rocks. Instead, I went to Dead River Falls. Which no longer technically exists, so that gives you an idea of how old I am."

A few people laugh at that. I can't. Not because I don't know the place he's talking about but because this isn't funny. This is raw and horrifying. This is gut-wrenching, and I'm not sure I want to know what happens next. That he is standing in front of me, whole and safe, is the only reason I stay with his story.

"I hiked to the top in the snow. The water was still flowing from the falls, but it was icy. I knew people jumped off there, but never in winter. It wasn't a clear jump like Black Falls. That night, it was empty. I sat there at the edge, smoking, for a long, long time. So long I was shivering and achy. My clothes were soaked through from the snow. I was exhausted of living and knew without a doubt that if I went in, as cold as it was, I wouldn't be coming out."

James turns and looks at Brian. "Then, I heard a voice. He said—" He pushes the mic in Brian's face.

Brian grins, but his eyes are red rimmed. "If you jump, I jump."

James shakes his head, lost in the moment. He turns back to us. "And I stood up and went home with Brian."

I take a closer look at the man next to my uncle. Brian? Best friend Brian? That must be Micah's stepdad.

James continues, "I couldn't bear the thought of another life ended because of me. I never went back. That spring, Dead River flooded, and the falls dried up. But it didn't matter. By that time, I was going to a weekly Bible study with this guy and falling in love with the life God meant for me."

James straightens. "A life that includes all of you and this place. And it's been a great one so far. The last fifteen years have been infinitely better than the previous twenty. I never knew I could need anything else. That was before Meg showed up." He gestures to me, and I blink through my tears at him.

"Meg is Drew's daughter. All this time, I've been missing my brother, and now I've been given such a gift because he was alive in his girl. If I had died in the accident, I wouldn't have been around to tell Meg about her dad. And if I'd jumped off that cliff that night, I wouldn't have gotten to look into my brother's eyes again."

He shakes his head, pressing his lips together before continuing in a low voice, "I can't begin to understand God's reasons for how things happen or who lives and dies in this life. But I can say with one hundred percent certainty that God sends us exactly the right person at the right time. He sent me Brian all those years ago, and he sent us Meg this past week. I am very blessed. Thank you."

James hugs Brian as a round of applause rings out. I watch them through my tears, my mind whirling out of control, one question circling round and round, making no purchase.

If God brought my parents together that one time, just to make me, and if it was a blessing planned by God, how could it be a sin? Are sins just blessings being played in God's long game?

12

Micah

It's Eve's fault. She texted me from Sunday school in a panic because she was supposed to go straight to work at Panera after church and forgot her apron. She knew I was home, likely asleep—of course I was—and asked if I could drop it off before the service started. But then she asked me to walk it in because she was stuck late in the nursery with a baby whose parents were serving in the elementary teaching room and the parents of those kids were late and it was this whole ripple effect.

There I was, holding an apron and trying not to be noticed, when I heard the music start up. I knew right away it wasn't James. Which was weird. As far as I knew, James led worship every week.

Recognizing my stepdad's voice, I snuck in the back door and sat in the last row next to the ushers, listening. It's been years since Brian sang. He used to sing every Sunday before he married my mom. But once they were married and she became pregnant, he stepped down because of the stress it caused on Sunday mornings. It was hard enough getting three kids to church on your own, let alone six.

I like Brian's voice. It's mellow and crisp. Very Vance Joy, if you know what I mean. And soon enough, it's over. I'm standing to grab up Eve's things when I hear Brian announce James and say something about his "niece" being there. Meg's here? At church?

And there's this weird feeling stirring in my gut. Like, I don't know, jealousy? But not quite. Feeling left out, maybe? Which is stupid because I could not care less about this church or any church.

But then James is getting up and he's got the mic and he's telling the story about Andrew and Candace, and before I know it, I'm sitting again. Frozen in place, barely breathing, as he talks about being on the cliff at Dead River Falls and Brian's role in saving his life.

I've never heard this part of the story. I had no idea. I knew they were close, but not this. Not "You jump, I jump."

You jump, I jump.

Holy fuck.

My breath starts panting out of me, and I can feel heat behind my eyelids. The edges of my vision get darker, and my stomach clenches.

You jump, I jump.

I'm taken back to the day when I stood with Meg on the edge of the cliff. When I jumped off first and she followed right behind me. Her expression determined, trusting.

It's too much. This story and the implications, all of it. And James is talking about how God sends exactly the right person at the right time in our lives, and I'm thinking about where the fuck would I have been if my dad hadn't gotten caught? Would I be following him blindly? Would I still worship the ground he walked on? I always think about how our family would still be involved, beloved, respected, but that's all bullshit, isn't it?

What would *that* kid have done if faced with Duke? Would he have treated him any better than Duke's dad, demanding a label of him in one breath and condemning it in the next? How would that kid have reacted to Meg, the result of a one-night stand? Neither was something they could control, but would that have mattered to Old Micah?

Did my dad's fuckery *save me*? Did his getting caught change my life for the better? My mom's life? Because then she could marry Brian and know a real marriage? Was Meg sent here to find her family, but also to find me?

It's too much. I can't process it all. This right here is why I don't go to church. It's a spiritual mind fuck every time.

I watch James and Brian tearfully embrace and James look down at Meg in the congregation with nothing short of familial affection, and I have to go. I have to get out of here.

If what James says is true, and bad things are part of God's blessings in our lives, that means God planned on my dad hurting my mom. On hurting me. He planned on everyone turning their backs on us and for all those people to get hurt by my father. And for what?

What good could come from that? And how could I possibly be worth it?

The following morning, it's fall. Sounds crazy, but that's the UP. Labor Day passes, and suddenly, it's straight-up autumn. The leaves are still green, but it's a matter of weeks before they glitter and fade to the ground.

"It's officially sweater weather," Duke says, cheerfully passing me something awesome smelling in a Styrofoam cup. "Lighthouse Gifts is giving away free cider and cookies. Might be my favorite day of the year."

"Where are the cookies?"

"Sorry," he says, not meaning it. "Ate 'em on the way in."

"I'm surprised you didn't drink all the cider," I say, taking a hearty sip.

He makes a face and heads to the back of the store to clock in. "I hate cider."

"How can you hate cider?" I ask, finishing the rest of the cup and tossing it in the trash.

"It's just hot apple juice, man."

"It smells like heaven."

"That's why I picked it up. Smells good. Tastes like hot apple juice. Be grateful. You're benefiting from my aversion."

"Thank you for hating cider. Anyway, you're early. Meeting's not for another twenty minutes."

"David would say if you're on time, you're already late." There's an edge to Duke's voice that speaks louder than words. He folds his frame onto a stool and picks up a display of organic goat's milk lip balm to organize.

"Okay."

"And furthermore, if you want to make the right impression, you really should stick to muted colors and responsible-looking hairstyles. Dress for the job you want, not the job you have."

"What exactly is responsible-looking?"

Duke jabs a balm so hard that it bounces off the top of the plastic canister and rolls under the counter. He picks it up with a frustrated grunt, muttering, "The opposite of whatever the hell I look like."

I retrieve another rogue balm in silence, passing it to him. He mumbles his thanks. This is par for the course. The hair shit, the blouse comments, the professionalism pep talks. What isn't typical is Duke being bothered by it. At least, not until recently. And not in the "aggressively restocking goat by-products" kind of way.

I really don't want to get comfortable in the role of therapist, but after a third balm hits the floor, I can't help asking, "Do you want to talk about it?"

"Nothing to say," he says. "I started to tell my parents about my promotion to crew leader, thinking that would be something David might be happy about. Me, supervising a crew of outdoor guides. It's an accomplishment."

"Absolutely. Dani didn't make the choice lightly."

"Right? But," he continues, "before I could get the words out, he started in on the teal hair and when was I going to be dyeing it back to normal?"

I grimace, and he swipes another batch of impulse buys off the counter and dumps them out. This time, hundreds of handmade buttons that read SAY YA TO DA UP, EH

"When am I dyeing it back to *normal.*" He spits out each word between his teeth. "Subtext being, 'When are you *going* to be normal, Duke?' The answer being, 'Never the fuck enough for him.'"

He finally looks at me, shoving his hair off his forehead, his eyes dark and hurting. "I gotta get out of this place. I can't live like this anymore."

"Where would you go?" I don't bother trying to change his mind. I don't think he's wrong.

He shrugs. "I'm not sure. I was thinking of applying to U of M, though."

The corner of my mouth twitches. "You, down in Ann Arbor?"

"It'd be like an unofficial exchange program with Meg. If she can come to the UP to find her family, I can go south to escape mine."

"Is nine hours far enough?"

"Barely," he concedes. "But it's farther than Traverse City, and my grades are plenty good enough. Not to mention, they have a similar outdoor vibe to this place. Only bigger and more . . . accepting."

"I like it."

He looks relieved. "You do?"

"Of course I do. Who knows? Maybe in another year, I might want to check things out downstate, too. Just to see."

His grin is wry. "Just to see, huh?"

"I hear they have a decent canoe livery there," I say. "About a hundred and fifty city parks."

"You just happen to know that, huh? Off the top of your head."

I might've googled it recently. It's actually 163 parks, but Duke doesn't need to know that.

"Point being, it would be a good move for you. Lots of North Face."

"A big queer population, too," he says quietly.

I nod, knowing that's as close as Duke may ever get to identifying himself. "That, too."

"Speaking of Meg from Ann Arbor," he says, changing the subject as people start arriving for the meeting. "I happened to see something very interesting on my way to the harbor last night."

I immediately feel my face flame right as Em saunters up to the counter. "Oh, me, too!"

I narrow my eyes at Duke and his shitty timing. He winces apologetically. "Right. We were on our way back with the kayaks and saw you and Meg. In the park."

"Your tongue was in her throat. I doubt you noticed us," Emily says shortly. Which is rich coming from her.

"I don't think it was quite like that," I say. Because, one, it wasn't. There have been zero tongues in anyone's throats, or even mouths, at this point. I'd remember. And, two, I don't like Em's tone.

"Looked pretty cozy, if you ask me," Em says. "At least we found a dark spot to hook up. Your new girl seems to be a bit of an exhibitionist."

"Em—" Duke warns.

She smirks. "If I knew public places were what you needed to get off . . ." She trails off, brightening. "Speak of the devil."

My heart stops as I take in Meg's ash-white pallor. She's holding a plate of freshly baked muffins from next door and looks like she wants to cry. Or puke. Or bathe in holy water, more like.

Fuck.

I jump to my feet, but Duke is even faster. He takes the tray from Meg's trembling hands and beams at her. "Meg, love of my life! These smell incredible!"

"Dani put in the order special for your meeting. I made a double batch since I know how you need at least seventy-five grams of white sugar to get you through."

Duke smacks a kiss on her cheek, and Meg freezes, backing up. She gives him a small apologetic smile before spinning to leave. I am a half step behind her when Dani comes to the door.

"Oh, good, the muffins. You're a lifesaver."

Meg brushes past her to the exit without a word, and Dani narrows her eyes at me in concern. "Sorry, Dani, is it okay if I—"

She shoos me away, and I sprint after Meg. By the time I catch her in the kitchen of the coffeehouse, she's leaning against the counter, hands pressed to the surface, shoulders trembling. It occurs to me that I've rushed here but have zero idea what to say. Thankfully, Meg saves me the trouble, shaking her head, a sob breaking free.

"What are the odds," she asks, "that your ex would catch us kissing the third time I've kissed anyone ever?" She raises a hand, shaking her head. "Don't answer that. We were kissing in a public place. I *was* being an exhibitionist. I deserved that."

"First of all, no one deserved that. That was Emily being spiteful with me because she thinks I chose you over her. Which, to be fair, I did."

"I didn't realize you two were serious."

"We weren't. Not in that way. Friends with benefits at best."

Meg's dewy eyes widen, her face pale. "I . . . should have . . . I didn't think. I . . . Of course you've . . . I mean. Just *look* at you . . . Your biceps are like magic . . ."

"Meg." I have to cut her off, but I'm as red as a tomato at her biceps comment and my stupid mouth. "*I'm a virgin.* It was only an expression. A tactless one. I didn't mean that we'd, um, had *those* kinds of benefits. Not for lack of trying on her part, but it didn't feel right."

Meg's lips form a silent *oh*.

"Which is probably why she's being terrible. She's actually very nice, normally. I think my rejection paired with turning around and kissing you on a park bench was a slap in her face."

"Oh my word. Do I need to apologize to her?"

"What? Why?"

"For rubbing kissing you in her face?"

"Ah." Oh wow, *that* would be something to see. "N-no. Better to let it go. I think she said her piece. If I know Duke, he's letting her have it right now."

Meg looks conflicted, and she bites her lip, which does nothing to keep me from wanting to kiss her for being so sweet and thoughtful.

And beautiful. God, she's beautiful.

"He doesn't need to do that. I'm okay."

"Are you?" I check. "Because you don't look very okay."

Her expression is wry. "It's just . . . the guilt is strong. I thought I would burn at the stake walking into church yesterday."

My stomach sinks. I was afraid of this. "For kissing me?"

"For kissing you, sure." She spreads her hands wide. "For thinking about kissing you all day and night, more like."

All the blood rushes out of my brain. *Easy, boy.* This conversation has me all over the place.

"But you didn't burn," I say, trying to redirect.

"Apparently not."

I move closer to her, taking her shaking hands in mine and trying to will some calm into her. "Meg, I can wait for you. However long you want. Even if nothing else ever happens, I'm okay. You know that, right?"

"I think so." She nods. It's timid, but it's there.

"But I also don't believe we've done anything wrong."

Her navy eyes widen the slightest bit. But she remains firm, her hands steady. "I . . . am coming around. It's hard to change the voice in my head."

She moves closer, and I swallow hard. I drop my hands to my sides, not sure what to do and not wanting to push her.

"Okay," she says. "I want to kiss you."

"Anytime," I say even as she's inching closer and closer. I glance at the doorway, and she gives me a wobbly smile.

"I'm off the clock. My last job was to make the muffins for Dani." Her eyes search mine. "I want to know what you taste like, Micah."

I swallow again, but my throat is dry as wallpaper. "Okay."

She takes my face in her small hands and presses her lips to the corner of my mouth, dragging them across to my cheek and my ear. I bite my tongue to keep from moaning and scaring her. Her hot breath does things to my insides, and I surreptitiously put distance between our lower halves.

Her tongue darts out to taste the space between my ear and collarbone, and my hands clench at my sides to keep from grabbing her hips and pulling them against me.

Meg pulls back, her eyes dazed and hungry. "I've never . . ." She swallows. "I want to be good at this. Will you help me?"

My brows rise. "Absolutely. But believe me when I say you are very, very good at this already."

She tugs my face to hers, and this time, my hands find her waist. She presses her full lips against mine, each time softer than the last until finally her tongue reaches out.

She tastes delicious.

At first, I hold back, letting her lead. Letting her tongue dance with mine and take me where she's comfortable going. That lasts a hot minute before my hands circle her back and fist at her shirt, tugging her closer. My mouth caresses hers until I can't tell where she stops and I begin.

For once, I forget to be careful, and it's the most fantastic moment of my life.

When we finally pull apart, she beams at me, flushed and dazzling. I am pretty sure my heart stops.

"I could kiss you forever," she says.

"Except I'm supposed to have a meeting."

Her eyes widen comically. "Oh my gosh. You look thoroughly mussed."

"Mussed?" I ask, smirking.

"Thoroughly. If you go, they'll all know we were frenching." I move to swipe at my lips and she grabs my hand, stopping me with a smile. "I think . . ." She shakes her head and takes a deep breath. "Let them. I'm not ashamed."

"Even Emily?"

She shrugs, playing at casual, but I know better. "Especially Emily." She cringes. "Oh, wow. That sounded petty."

I laugh. "It sounded normal, and it's more than she deserves for her snark. I'll call you later."

Meg blows me a kiss and slinks out the back door, but I'm still leaning against the counter five minutes later when Duke comes to fetch me, a knowing expression painted across his face. He grunts, rolling his eyes.

"Come on."

13

Meg

I don't know what's wrong with me. I've literally never had addictive tendencies in my life. Give me one Lay's potato chip, and I'll give you half back. Like, I can always, *always* eat just one.

But one taste of Micah and I'm losing my dang mind. I'm Angelica Schuyler the first time she matches wits with Alexander Hamilton . . . I'll never be satisfied.

Even the whole Emily thing has me all tossed up inside. Not because she upset me. Not anymore, anyway—but because I have this very weird compulsion to brand Micah as mine in front of her. Like, the park bench kissing was totally accidental, and I will definitely not be acting on this new impulse to publicly claim him because, for real, that's stupid—

But I get it now. I get *wanting* to, and that's a whole thing I never anticipated.

Feelings make everything complicated.

I'd heard that before and witnessed it firsthand with Vada and Luke last spring. But to experience it live and in person is pretty ridiculous. I can't help wondering if this is how it always feels to like someone or if Micah and I are special. I mean. We aren't. But why would you settle for anything less than this? Less than electrically charged glances and earth-quaking butterflies in the region of your heart? Less than static touches and full-fledged swoops in your belly?

What would even be the point?

I sometimes wonder if he's ruined me for anyone else. Which, admittedly, is pretty effed up. One, we're days into our unofficial relationship. Slow your roll, Hennessey, and all that. And two, the entire idea that a single person has that much power over you, that they could ruin you forever, taint you and stain your existence with only a kiss, is disgusting.

No one can do that. I once saw a tattoo on a girl's arm that read WRECK ME, and I immediately wanted to take her to church. That girl needed Jesus stat. No, ma'am. No wrecking will be happening here. Don't be stupid. That's the opposite of romantic, if you ask me.

So yeah, I put that whole "Has he ruined me?" idea to bed and tucked it in forever. He hasn't ruined me for anyone.

But I still hope with all my hopes that I won't ever have to find out for certain.

Which is surely why I am hiking up a mountain in the middle of the night armed with only a flashlight.

It's got to be true love. There's no other plausible expla-nation for this madness.

I trip over a tree root, and Micah steadies me with a warm hand on the small of my back.

"You all right?"

"Peachy," I huff out. "How many stairs?"

"Another half dozen sets," he says. I swear I hear amusement in his voice. His very-clear-and-not-at-all-out-of-breath voice. "We're about halfway up."

I let out a squeak as I trip again, this time on the bottom step of the next set of wooden stairs leading up the side of Sugarloaf Mountain. Which Micah assures me is a misnomer. It's not really a mountain. Just a really, really big hill, roughly a thousand feet above sea level. Easy-peasy mac-n-cheesy.

"I told you, you're better off without the flashlight," he reminds me. "The moon is plenty bright once your eyes adjust, and you won't trip on every root that creeps up on you."

"Pretty sure the best way to avoid tripping on tree roots is to hike in the daylight," I grouse.

"Come on, Meg, where's your sense of adventure? Isn't this your gap year?"

"You just *love* to remind me of that, don't you?"

"And you love to complain when I do."

"Listen, LeBron, we aren't all star athletes like you and your point guard friends."

"First of all, LeBron James is a star forward, not a point guard, and not that it matters, but I never played basketball. I'm a terrible shot."

"Whatever. You're not even breaking a sweat back there, are you?"

"*You are?*" he asks incredulously. "It's forty-five degrees out, figure skater."

I don't think a response is necessary. Though my lack of fitness is embarrassing and something I vow to rectify starting tomorrow.

We finish a set of stairs before winding around a few boulders and pine trees and finding ourselves at yet another set of stairs. It's never ending. I decide to concentrate on my foot placement and manage the last four climbs with my head down and my breathing not quite steady, but at least I've stopped panting so loudly. The ice rink said they could definitely use me next session, which means I have less than a month to get back in shape or I'm about to make a fool out of myself in front of God and all my new students.

When we get to the top, Micah steadies me against the urge to fall backward and takes my hand holding the flashlight. He clicks off the light and passes it back to me while tugging me along to the viewing deck.

The breeze up here is chilly and lifts the sweaty hair stuck to the back of my neck, cooling me. Micah brings me to the railing, and we look out over the inky, moonlit silhouette of Marquette and Lake Superior. Lights glitter from downtown, but they're nothing compared to the zillions of stars winking overhead. I've never seen a night like this. It's unbelievable.

"Holy bananas, this is pretty," I say.

"It's my favorite," he says, his breath puffing out in front of him. I rub my arms, and he removes the backpack he's been wearing. Unzipping it, he takes out a stocking cap and pulls it over my ears, kissing the tip of my nose as he does. Next, he takes a scarf out and wraps it around my neck so many times I can barely move. But it smells like him, and I decide I don't really need to move anyway. Just write SHE DIED HAPPY, HER LUNGS FULL OF GOODNESS, THE END on my headstone.

He turns me gently, gesturing to a couple of nice wooden benches built into the deck, and we sit, cuddled together, listening to the wind blow. After a moment, he reaches into his pack and pulls out a thermos, unscrewing the cap. "Hot chocolate?" he offers.

"How are you even real?" I ask as I reach for the cup.

"You're always drinking hot chocolate, Meg. It wasn't a reach."

"Shhh," I say. "Let me believe you are perfect."

"Far from," he says.

"Getting closer every minute, then." I close my eyes as the hot chocolate coats my tongue.

"Only to you, I swear, and even then, I'm convinced you only like me for my muscles."

I swallow another sip before passing it back. "And your hot chocolate, of course."

A ghost of a smile catches in the moonlight, and I bump him with my shoulder. "I'm not interested in perfect, Micah. I can't possibly keep up with perfect."

"You're scarily close, Meg."

I laugh. "Only to you." I throw his words back at him. He wraps an arm around my shoulders, and I sink into him. It occurs to me that at this minute, I'm completely alone with him. I don't mean physically. That, too, I suppose. But more mentally. Or emotionally. It's only us up here. No parents, no friends, no church. Just Micah and Meg, and I really, really like it. This feels comfortable and easy. The urge to "leave room for the Holy Spirit" is there, still, deep, deep down, but I ignore it. Because putting space between me and this boy feels wrong.

"My dad's parole hearing is coming up."

I sit up straighter to look at him. "Are you going?"

He shakes his head but says, "I don't know. My mom is going, and Brian asked me to go with her. James says I shouldn't have to, though."

"If you go, do you have to speak on his behalf?"

"No. I don't have to speak at all. But me being there . . .

seemingly in support of him, after all this time, would say more than words to the press and the families involved."

"Then don't go. You don't owe him that."

He looks at me, his eyes stark. When he speaks, his voice is low. "But what about my mom? Do I leave her to face him alone?"

I exhale. "Dang. But . . ."

"Yeah?"

"Well, I guess I just don't understand why it has to be *your* job to hold the adults together? Your mom isn't alone, Micah. She's got Brian. And Dani, and friends, and a new church from what I saw on Sunday."

"Yeah?"

"But also . . ."

"Also?"

I consider my words carefully. "But also, maybe you *want* to face him? Maybe you have things you need to say to him, and this is your chance."

"Like forgive him?"

"Not necessarily. I mean, sure, if that's what you need to do. But more like confronting him about how he hurt you and your family with his choices."

He releases a long breath, his head falling back to stare at the sky.

"I don't know if that's a good idea."

"Why not?"

"I'm not sure any good could come of me being honest after all this time."

"Bullshit," I say, channeling Vada. He snorts, looking at me with surprise. "Yeah. I said it." The darkness hides my red face, but I continue, "I can't think of anything better than you being honest with that man. He was your hero.

And he let you down in the worst possible way. Micah, you stopped going to church because of what he did. That's some biblical stuff right there. Like, 'Heaven help the hypocrites for they shall inherit hell,' or whatever. His actions not only drove a wedge between one of his so-called flock and God but between his only son and his son's faith. As his son, and as a man, you need to set him straight. I don't know about forgiveness. In my mind, he should be the one asking for that, and maybe you grant it, or maybe you don't. That's your choice. But you owe it to yourself and to him to speak your piece."

"I don't want to upset my mom," he says quietly.

"Yeah. I get that. But again. Not your fault."

"I've been wondering if it bothered you that I don't go to church."

"Not really. My feelings about church are complicated. I'm more concerned with your feelings about God."

"I'm good with God," he says.

I can't help the smile that spreads across my face. "Me, too."

"But I don't like church, and I'm not sure I ever will."

I release a long breath. "I'm not so crazy about it these days either, to be honest. Ironically, James asked me if I'd be interested in leading a teen girl Bible study."

"What did you say?"

I shrug. "I said yes. Because I am a perpetual people pleaser who overcommits when it comes to Jesus."

"How does that mesh with the conflicting feelings?"

"Guess we'll find out. Honestly, I'm not sure James has picked up on my conflicting feelings. Mostly because I haven't told him or anyone else besides you and Vada."

"What does Vada say?"

"About the Bible study thing?"

He nods. "Yeah. And the rest."

"That I'm playing with fire."

He stares ahead at the horizon. "Maybe. Maybe not, though. Maybe you're the exact person those girls need. I don't know much about what goes on in those small groups these days, but maybe you coming in with your eyes wide open will make a difference to them."

"You mean like when I go in there all 'Hey, you should totally make out with boys, it's the beeeeeest.'"

"Weeeeeeell. I was thinking more like, 'Hey, sometimes boys will see your shoulders and have lustful thoughts about them, and that's not your fault; it's on them. If it's hot out, tank tops are a viable option.'"

"Huh."

"Or something like that."

"Are you saying you have lustful thoughts about my shoulders, Micah?"

"Hell yes, I do. Again, though, that's on me. My sin, not yours."

"You think it's a sin?"

He exhales a long time. "I think we all sin all the time. I think God knows this about us and still allows us beautiful things. So, we accept the grace that God offers, despite that. And it's a for-life kind of deal. One and done. You accept that grace, and it covers you completely. God knows about every lustful thought I will have before I'm born. No take backs. I don't think I'm tainted because of it. It's not going to send me to hell. It's already been forgiven."

I nod. "Back home, two of my friends, Cullen and Zack, have been in love for years. They are some of the best humans I have ever known. Their love is the healthiest love I've ever seen. It can't possibly be sinful."

"Speaking of Ann Arbor, Duke said he was going to apply to U of M. He needs to get out of here."

"Ann Arbor would be better with him in it."

Micah reaches two fingers out, placing them under my chin and tilting my face to his. "Marquette is better with you in it."

"Ugh. Fine. I guess I can forgive you for dragging my butt up to this stupid-beautiful place in the middle of the night." I'm smiling when my lips meet his.

MEG: Hey, Dad. Or Declan? I'm not sure what to call you, exactly. But hi.

Delete.

MEG: Dad. Hi. I miss you. Well, I miss the old you. The you who gave me fairy wings and danced with me in the living room. The dad from before you started to work late and hid away from

Delete.

MEG: Hi, Dad. I miss you. Which is weird because I'm not sure I really know you. Not the real you. Am I crazy for thinking you've been keeping secrets

Delete.

MEG: Hey, Dad. Are you gay? If you are, that's okay, I just

Delete. I exhale in a rush. *Meg, you can do this.*

MEG: Hi, Dad. I just wanted to tell you that I love you. And you can tell me anything. About yourself. And I will still love you. Even if you like men. That kind of thing. Oh my gosh, this is awkward. Just . . . know that I love you and miss you. I'm still mad at you and Mom about the lying thing. But anyway. I love you. I'm in Marquette, getting to know Andrew's family. I'm sure Mom told you. Write me back. Or call. I promise to pick up even though I hate talking on the phone.

Sent.

14

~~~~~~~

Micah

It's not unusual for my parents to invite James over for dinner. He's been coming around for years, if for no other reason than to ease my mom's conscience that he's not starving on his bachelor diet of frozen pizza and Fanta. What is unusual is his bringing my girlfriend.

Not that my mom and Brian know about Meg and me. Or James, for that matter, though his eyes followed me when I dropped her off the other night, so he suspects something.

I'm sure Dani knows. She's picked up on things at the café and the shop, but I don't think she's told anyone. Which is all making my attempt to play it cool while also inviting myself to dinner at my mom's table very difficult.

I probably should have said something earlier. But with the impending probationary trial and wrapping up my search-and-rescue training with Cash . . . well. I've been preoccupied.

Plus, I didn't want to put a label on things yet.

There's also this whole thing that some more conservative Christian families do when their kids graduate high school, which is to try to marry them off before they can get into too much trouble. My mom mostly knows better than that. She married my dad right out of high school, and look how that turned out. But old habits run deep, and Christianity runs back a couple of thousand years. Sure, eighteen and nineteen are super young to get married, but what's a few years when compared to premarital sex and underage drinking?

My parents are very different from Meg's, and I would never compare the two situations. But in a few ways, they are the same. For a hot minute, I consider not joining them for dinner. It seems like asking for added pressure on an already-charged relationship.

But I can't stay away, and I can't bear the thought of leaving sweet Meg to deal with my family, so here I am, holding a store-bought apple pie in each hand and tapping the front door with the toe of my gym shoe.

One of the twins, Rachel, opens the door. "What are you doing here?" she asks, looking up from her phone with an appraising smirk.

"Dinner. I brought pies." I shove the baked goods into her arms and hurry past her, leaving my shoes at the door next to Meg's. James and Meg must have turned up while I was showering after my run.

"Mom?" I call out, heading straight for the kitchen, where I hear voices, abruptly stopping when I see Meg, head bent close to Lizzy's. The two are giggling, thick as thieves, and suddenly, I feel like I should leave. A hand slaps me on the back, and I look up into the amused eyes of James.

"Good to see you, Micah." I feel Meg's eyes on me, but I don't look.

"Yeah." I scratch at my wet hair. "I was hungry." I don't know why I'm explaining myself. I live here. Sort of.

"Well, I'm happy to see you, sweetheart," my mom says, kissing my cheek. "Hm," she says. "You smell nice."

"Just soap," I insist, probably sounding defensive. "I showered after my run."

"And he brought dessert," Rachel says, placing my offerings on the island.

My mom raises her eyebrows. "Really? Well, that's great. Full house tonight. Micah, have you met James's niece, Meg?"

"Yeah," I say, finally looking her way. Meg's cheeks are pink, but her eyes are laughing at me. "Meg works at the coffee shop next door."

"And you two are dating, so there's that," Brian says, entering the room.

I nod slowly. "And that. Yeah." I glance at Meg. "Sorry. I didn't want—"

"To out us to your entire family in one fell swoop?" Meg laughs, shaking her head, her black hair down, her magenta stripes bold and fun. Just like her.

"Yeah. I wasn't sure if you were ready for all that."

She shrugs, pink under the attention of everyone's eyes watching us. "Uncle James didn't know we hadn't told anyone," she says simply.

"Ah," I say. James looks a little sheepish, and I punch his shoulder lightly. "It's cool. I was going to tell them tonight anyway." Probably. "Everyone, this is my girlfriend, Meg Hennessey."

"Meg." I turn back to her, wave a hand expansively, and take in a calming breath. "This is my family."

Dinner is mostly fine. No one mentions a dowry or asks for Meg's testimony of how she came to be a child of Christ or anything, so we have that going for us. And only my sisters give me shit for the pies.

"Weird how you just happened to have these pies lying around, Micah," Rachel says as my mom pulls them out of the oven and starts slicing them into equal pieces to distribute.

"He was saving them for a rainy day, obviously," pipes up Evie.

"Neither of you need to have any, if it's an issue," I say. Rachel mimes zipping up her lips. Evie's slice is already in front of her, and she pointedly takes an enthusiastic bite.

"Apple pie is my favorite," Meg says softly from next to me.

"It is?" I ask.

"Yep. So, thank you."

"Mine, too, not that it matters," says James dryly.

"I prefer pumpkin, if you're taking requests for next time," says Brian, looking far too pleased with himself.

"I'm not."

After the pies are demolished, Brian and James offer to take the younger half of the family outside to play a game of H-O-R-S-E in the driveway. I get up to join them, when my mom clears her throat. "Micah, I've been meaning to talk to you. Mind staying back a few minutes?"

I glance at Meg. She stands, scooting out her chair. "I'd better go help my uncle."

I get up, too, grabbing some dishes to help clear the table. "Sure, Mom."

Once everyone is out of the kitchen, she turns to me, leaning a hip against the countertop, smiling. "Meg is sweet."

"Yeah."

"She seems to have a good head on her shoulders."

"I think so. She works for Maria and Dani. They said she's been a godsend in the coffee shop."

My mom turns to the sink and starts the faucet to wash the dishes. I grab a rag to dry, moving to stand at her shoulder. It feels very familiar and also weird. Familiar because this is where I always stood after dinner. Every night for years and years, beside my mom. But now it's weird because when I turn my head to the side, I stand a whole head taller than she is. Tall enough to notice the first little starts of gray mixing with the dark brown waves at the crown of her head.

"She's been good for James," my mom says. "He dotes on her. It's been healing for him, I think."

"Mmm-hmm."

"Speaking of healing," she says, passing me a plate. I groan, and she turns off the faucet, facing me fully. "I don't need you there. Brian thinks I do, but I don't. Not for my sake. I'll be fine."

"Okay." I know there's more.

"But I do think you should go for *you*, Micah. You need to speak with your dad. Man to man."

"I don't think so."

"You need to confront him about what he put you through." Her words are eerily similar to Meg's.

"What he put everyone through, you mean? It wasn't only me, and I don't feel like being the mouthpiece for the long list of people Dad fucked up."

My mom flinches at my cuss, and I bite back another groan. "I'm sorry, Mom. I don't mean to get angry. Especially with you. I'm just so tired of being the responsible one who turns the other cheek and takes it all like a man.

Because that's *really* what you're asking me to do. You aren't asking me to confront him. Not the way *I* want to. You're asking me to walk in there, with all those people watching, and swallow my anger so I can stoically tell that asshole I forgive him for what he's done to everyone I love. You're asking me to be the better person."

I don't want to say this next part. It will hurt. But after five years, it needs to be said. Maybe I am ready to confront a parent, just not the one everyone wants me to. "And I think that's *your* revenge. You want him to see that you raised me better, so you can rub it in his face. It kills you that I don't go to church, because what you would love more than anything is for me to be a model Christian. You want to feel like you still won. Don't think I haven't noticed the pamphlets you've left around for Bible college the last three years. I'm not your chance to do it better, Mom. I'm not Dad with the glitch fixed. I'm broken. He broke me." My words cut off, and silent tears roll down my mom's cheeks.

"I'm sorry," I say. It feels inadequate.

She shakes her head quickly, pressing her tears dry. "No. I'm sorry. I'm *so sorry*, Micah. I—" She starts to reach for me but pulls back. Something inside of me fissures. "I can finish here," she says. "Go on outside and save Meg from Brian and James."

I don't say anything more. She's sniffling, and I'm not sure what I *can* say to make this better. I don't regret what I've said, but I don't feel good about it. My entire body is clenched. As if I've turned to ice, my molecules have drawn in on themselves and hardened. One more strike and I'll shatter.

I slip on my shoes and step out the front door. Meg is

sitting on the stoop and turns to face me, her smile slipping when she takes in my expression. She stands quickly.

"Micah? What happened?"

I shake my head and nod toward my apartment. She doesn't ask if I want her to follow me. She just does.

A few minutes later, I'm sitting on the floor, my back against the couch. Meg's curled up on one side of me, and Cash is on the other, his chin resting on my lap while Meg strokes his ears.

Meg asks if I want to talk about it, and I tell her, "Not tonight." We stay that way until the darkness chases the shadows from my walls and there's a soft knock on the door. It's James, seeing if Meg wants a ride back.

"Do you need me to stay?"

I shake my head. I don't want her walking back in the dark. "I'll be fine."

She kisses me once on the lips and leans down to stage-whisper to Cash, "Take care of him."

Which strikes me as a really nice thing to say because I'm not used to someone caring for me. But that's what Meg has done tonight. By not saying a word, she took care of me.

A few days later, my dad is released on parole. His lawyers argued that he's rehabilitated, and *of course* he's the picture of remorse, so no longer a threat to society. Cured or whatever. The victims tried their best. My mom spoke her piece, too. In the end, it didn't matter. To be honest, I wasn't surprised. He can be very convincing. His job was words. The man knew how to talk a room into heaven, so it stood to reason that he could just as easily talk himself out of hell.

I didn't attend the hearing. Brian tried one more time to convince me, this morning, presumably on their way out. I didn't even come to the door. Cash barked and barked, and I rolled over and pulled my pillow over my head until he stopped. After I heard the car pull out of the drive, I got dressed for the woods. I drove out to Mount Marquette and spent a few hours trying to get lost and another few finding my way back. Sometimes I ran. A few times, I kicked at moss-covered logs in my path. What I didn't do was sit in the silence and reflect about what was happening a hundred miles away. It was hard enough chasing the memories all over the Northwoods; I didn't need to add the confirmation that it was all for naught—that he was going to be back in our lives like nothing had changed. Well, like *most* things hadn't changed. Obviously, my mom had moved on. Obviously, we were older. I could choose not to talk to him. But would I turn him away when he showed up? Was I strong enough to do that?

Worse. What if he didn't show up?

I fucking hate myself for that last part.

By the time I get back, it's starting to get dark. My stomach is rumbling for dinner, and Cash is ready for his pillow. My phone is perpetually lit, messages coming from my family and Duke, and I don't want to talk to any of them.

MEG: Heard the news. I'm off at 6.

MICAH: Sorry, I was in the woods. I just got back.

MEG: Figured you might be. Want to come over?

MICAH: Maybe?

I want to see Meg, but . . .

MEG: James is out. I'm making my special quesadillas.

MICAH: I'll be there in twenty.

And then I exhale, all the way, for the first time today.

I leave my bike parked against their stoop, letting James know I'm around whenever he returns. Meg opens the door with a blinding grin. "He's out on a date!"

That shocks me out of my stupor. "With whom?"

She smirks at me meaningfully.

"*No.*"

"Yes," she says, pulling me in by the arm. "In fact, I think this is their third or fourth date."

"What? Seriously?"

"Seriously. He's being very coy about it, but he was whistling on his way out tonight, and he had flowers! So cute."

"Flowers?" I've never brought flowers for Meg. Or anyone, for that matter. Should I be bringing Meg flowers?

"Gerber daisies in weird colors, but still. It's the thought."

"Do you like flowers?"

Meg moves to the stove, holding up two packs of shredded cheese for me to choose from. I pick Monterey jack, and she sprinkles it all over a sizzling flour tortilla. She tops it off with some precooked chicken and plops another tortilla on top before turning back to me, her lips crushed to one side. "I do, and I don't. I mean, I don't have a ton of experience in these things."

"Right."

"Right," she repeats with a bob of her head. Her hair is pulled up off her neck in a high pony, with strands falling all over the place. "I don't think I really care for showy signs of affection. They feel pretentious. Not like James is pretentious. He's older. It fits the whole charming older bachelor thing he has going on. But I'd rather have something spontaneous."

"Stolen flowers?"

She snorts lightly. "Definitely. Picked right out of someone else's garden, if possible."

"Noted."

She returns to the quesadilla, flipping the entire thing and leaning her hip against the counter. She crosses her arms while still holding the spatula, nailing me with a look.

"We don't have to talk about it."

"Thanks."

"But if you want to, I'm here."

"Not tonight, but thanks. I know."

She studies my face before turning back to the pan, flipping off the heat and grabbing a plate from the cabinet. She slides the quesadilla on it and holds it out to me. Then she grabs her own and we make our way to the small breakfast nook. Meg cracks open a package of premade guacamole and salsa and passes it to me.

"Special quesadillas, huh?"

"Very secret recipe. You tell anyone about this, I'll have to kill you."

"Wouldn't dream of it."

Meg takes a bite, her cheese stringing out. She's wearing a chunky blue knit sweater that brings out her eyes, and it slips off her shoulder as she tilts her head to the side, trying to catch all the melty goodness. Which leaves her ear, lined with piercings, neck, collarbone, and shoulder all bare. It's not sexy. *It's not.* It's totally innocent. I should eat. I'm hungry.

"Aren't you hungry?" she asks, noticing my staring.

I pick up my dinner and start eating, shaking off my racing thoughts. After a bite, I'm suddenly ravenous, and I finish my quesadilla in silence. I take a long drink of water and tell her how delicious it was.

She smiles, collecting my plate and putting it in the sink. "Good. I'm very talented at frying things with cheese. That's about the extent of my culinary skills, though, I'm afraid. I'm far more interested in baking."

"What's with the knock-knock jokes?" I ask, noticing the whiteboard on the fridge.

Meg turns pink, but she laughs. "It's completely dorky, right? Dani gave me the board when I moved in to help smooth over the awkwardness of being adult roommates who are related to each other. We're supposed to leave notes about where we are headed and stuff, but we mostly use it for nerdy church-dad jokes."

"I like it. It fits. How's it been living with your uncle?"

"Good. Simple. Fabulously freeing." She's moving toward me, her shampoo or perfume or something wafting around her, and it's so good. She holds out her hands, taking mine and pulling me up with her. "We have a few hours until he gets back." She tucks a loose strand of hair behind her ear. "And I have no idea how to work the complicated TV remote he's got in there. Maybe you want to sit on the couch or something? Stare at the walls? Play charades?"

"Charades? With two people?"

"How good are you at feigning surprise?"

"Not very." I'm smiling. She's somehow got me smiling. This girl is a miracle.

"Well . . ." She trails off with a fake huff of indignation. "You don't want to talk. You can't pretend to be surprised. That leaves staring at the walls . . . or . . ."

My eyebrows raise. "Or?"

She walks backward into the living room, leading me. She falls back on the couch, tugging me down with her. "Or," she says with a nervous smile, "we could practice kissing on this couch."

"That one. I choose that one."

She laughs at my enthusiasm before wrapping her hands around the back of my neck and pulling me closer. "I thought you might."

OCTOBER

15

Meg

I wake up to the house smelling like apples and cinnamon, and the day stretches out ahead of me, all mine. It's Saturday, and I don't have work. I make my way to my bathroom, splash some water on my face, brush my teeth, and throw on a bra since I hear James moving around the house, awake and baking something yummy.

Except, as I shuffle my way to the kitchen, I realize it's not only James in the kitchen. He's got a guest. A very adorable, petite, blond guest. And he's not just keeping her company, he's standing between her legs and kissing her with enthusiasm as she sits on the counter. I freeze, mid-step, my mouth gaping.

Dani's eyes widen over my uncle's shoulder, and it snaps me from my stupor. "Oh, wow." I hold up a hand, blocking my view and spinning back to the doorway. "I am so sorry! Nothing to see here. I'm going back to my room."

"Meg!" James pulls back from Dani. But other than being a little rosy under his beard, he doesn't seem to mind being caught, smitten kitten that he is. "You don't have to go," he says, reaching for a steaming mug behind Dani and taking a sip. "Dani stopped in to bring us some breakfast." He gestures to a tray of bagels.

"Just some breakfast, eh?"

He smiles, leaning back against the counter, holding his mug. "Yeah. I'm supposed to be at worship practice in twenty minutes."

"Noel is still at my mom's," Dani says, smoothing her hair. "And the house gets too quiet without her."

I wave off her awkwardness. "I was following my nose," I admit. "Are you baking?"

Dani straightens. "I am! Or I was. I made an apple crisp to bring to the church potluck tonight at Stomp's Apple Orchard. My oven is on the fritz, so James offered yours up. Are you planning to come?"

I glance at James. "I hadn't heard about it."

He startles. "You haven't? That's my fault. I thought you knew. Tonight at 6:00 p.m. Bonfire and hayrides. Kind of cheesy—"

Dani slaps his chest, and he grunts weakly. "Not cheesy at all," she says. "It's my favorite day of the year, and it's supposed to be perfect fall weather today. Want to come with us?"

I get a little giddy thinking of hayrides and bonfires. I wonder if I can talk Micah into coming. Maybe even Duke. "Is this like, a super church thing? Or can anyone come?"

"Anyone," James insists. "It *is* a church thing, but there won't be any preaching or anything tonight. Just fellowship and food."

I nod. "That sounds . . . cool. Very cool. Can I let you know about the ride? I might see if I can talk Micah into coming."

The corner of James's mouth lifts in approval. "That would be outstanding. I'm sorry I didn't think of it. I haven't been very good at inviting Micah to things."

I pull a chair out from the table and sit down. "I don't think he feels left out since he's cut himself off from church, but he really looks up to you. I think it would mean a lot if he knew you wanted to see him around. Not that he's said that, but I'm guessing so."

"Noted. I'll send him a text this afternoon, reiterating your invite."

"Good."

It gets quiet, and I stand. I get the impression that I'm getting in the way of their kissing. "Maybe I'll see you two tonight," I say, throwing a loaded look over my shoulder.

This is not something I anticipated when I left my old life and decided to find my family. In a few short months, I've moved in with my uncle, I've gotten a job, I've met Micah. Who I spent a good hour kissing on the couch the last time I saw him. Just kissing . . . but, well. We're pretty good at it. So good, in fact, that while his hands stayed in safe places the entire time, it *felt* like they were all over me. When I walked him to the door at the end of the night, I felt as wobbly as a newborn unicorn. But like, a unicorn who turned into fire. Like a mythological fire unicorn. Burning from the inside out.

Obviously, I know what it's like to be turned on. I've read about it. But I've never, like, *lived* it. It's a bit agonizing. And *very* consuming. It took me a lot of hours to fall asleep that night. I desperately wanted to text Micah and see if he was suffering as much as I was . . . but then I wondered if that would be considered sexting and decided I wasn't ready for that.

Then I thought about reading my Bible. But that felt like something my mom would have suggested. Feeling tempted? Read Lamentations until you forget what it is to be human. Repress, repress, repress. And I didn't *want* to repress because the incredible truth was that I felt alive. So alive and crazy about a boy who seemed just as crazy about me.

Instead, I tried a cold shower (since that's what the female protagonists always do in alternative universe fan fiction), which did not help. Until it did. Via the massage setting on the shower nozzle.

Problem solved. I slept like a baby after that.

But here it is again. This morning, walking in on that (admittedly pretty PG) moment between my uncle and Dani has me all distracted. If that's all it takes, I'm in trouble. I wonder if being so carefully sheltered has actually back-fired. If I hadn't been kept from seeing any physical affection growing up (on-screen or off-), maybe I wouldn't be so sensitive to it after a single night of couch kissing.

Well. Too late now, I suppose. My body flushes with heat, and I decide to tie on my old running shoes and go for a jog. I don't make it very long, but I feel better when I'm done. Wrung out and more myself. Every mile is one I didn't have to do but did, and maybe if I keep this up, I won't embarrass myself next time Micah drags me on a hike. James is pulling out of the drive as I walk up panting and sweating. A glance at my watch tells me he's going to be late for worship practice. I'll be shocked if he doesn't propose before Christmas. According to Micah and Betty, he's pined after Dani for at least five years.

Dani's car is still in the drive, and she pokes her head out the front door. "You can come back now, Meg! Don't think I couldn't tell you were hiding. Besides, I have another batch of apple crisp baking that needs testing."

I walk up the stoop and pass through the door she's holding. "Listen, I didn't want to infringe on my uncle's game."

The door closes, and Dani moves to sit on the couch, gesturing for me to join her. I toe off my shoes and go to the carpet instead. I'm not mega-sweaty, but I don't want to sit on the nice furniture. Plus, I have a feeling sitting on *that* couch would bring me right back to where I was pre-run.

I stretch out a leg, and Dani leans back, cradling her mug in her fingers and tucking her feet beneath her. "I don't think it's possible to mess with his game. I'm hooked on that man."

I throw my head back. "Finally!"

She giggles. "You've only been around a few months."

"Oh, I know. But Betty has filled me in on the years and years of loaded glances and over-the-top thoughtful gestures."

"He's very sweet."

"He's in love."

"He's not alone," she admits, blushing.

"That's fantastic news, Dani."

"After my ex . . . did what he did, leaving me after Noel was born and disappearing off the face of the earth, it took me a long time to trust another man in our lives. James has always been solid, but I wasn't ready."

"He waited for you," I say.

She nods. "I made him wait too long, I think, but he didn't give up. Thank God."

I change legs, stretching the other. "I doubt he'd say it was too long. He had a lot to face on his own. You were both becoming the people you were meant to be."

"That's a very wise thing to say, Meg."

I tilt my head to the side. "Is it? I'm mostly making it up as I go. But I think it's true."

"Is that how it feels with Micah?" Dani puts her mug down in her lap. "I don't mean to pry, but I noticed you've been together a lot."

"Since I walked in on you kissing this morning, I suppose it's fair. Sorry about that, by the way. I should've knocked."

She waves me off, skin pink. "Technically, this *is* your house, Meg. I should be the one apologizing."

"But you're not," I notice.

She shakes her head. "Unless I offended you, I won't apologize for kissing someone I love."

I chew on that a minute and let it soak into my brain for later. "I'm not offended in the least."

"Good. We women apologize too much."

"How it feels with Micah," I say, backing up, "is a little like we are helping each other become who we are meant to be. Not fixing each other, but pushing each other. He gets me, and I get him. It's like our garbage perfectly matches up."

"Is he your first boyfriend? You're pretty young."

I pull in both legs to a butterfly sit and bounce my knees. Dani means well, so I don't allow myself to be irritated. She knows, more than anyone, what can happen if you fall for someone too early and too young. "He is. And we *are* pretty young. And I definitely never thought this would happen when I got to Marquette. Or even when I imagined going on this whole gap year. I set out to find myself, and I found him."

Dani presses her lips together, and I know what she's about to say.

"But," I say, cutting off her good intentions, "he's shown me parts of myself I didn't know existed. Parts that I don't know I would've found without him there to stir them up. If that makes sense?"

"Perfect sense, actually. And don't misunderstand me. I didn't mean to imply what you are feeling isn't real. I just meant that you have lots of time for more garbage, as you say." Her face flickers in amusement.

I groan. "Please, Jesus, spare us. We've had enough garbage already for one lifetime."

Dani laughs out loud. "Amen, sister. At least you have each other."

"Twice the garbage," I mutter.

"Twice the strength, though, too."

Surprisingly, Micah agrees to come to the bonfire. Even more shocking, so does Duke. It may or may not have something to do with the spiced applesauce muffins I made this afternoon and bribed them with.

I'll never tell.

But Duke has eaten four.

There are several bonfires set up all over the farm, and hayrides are going in a constant cycle. I've made my rounds, visiting with a few of the youth group girls I've been introduced to and saying hi to their parents. I wasn't super sure about leading a small group of teens, but the girls are sweet, and their families are pretty welcoming, likely because I'm James's niece. One mom asked me about my life before coming to Marquette, and when she heard I'd been homeschooled, you would have thought Jesus himself had ordained me worthy.

I didn't bother correcting her.

The weather is crisp enough for hats and mittens with our sweaters, and it's already dark out. I'm sitting on a log, nursing a too-hot hot chocolate, as Micah teaches James how to properly chop wood.

It's no hardship, watching that boy, that's for sure.

Duke nudges me gently with his shoulder, careful not to slop my hot cocoa. "He's a good guy, right?"

"The best," I admit.

"Not unfortunate looking either."

"Nuh-uh."

"You'll take good care of him when I leave?"

I meet Duke's eyes in the firelight. He's genuinely worried.

"I will. I promise. You're really doing it, huh?"

"Going to Ann Arbor?" he checks. At my nod, he says, "Yeah. Applied last week. I have to get out of here. But . . ." He winces. "I feel like a coward. Micah and I had this unspoken contract that we'd stay. He had a shit dad, and I had a shit dad. But we could handle them together. Then you came . . ."

"And I messed it up."

"No!" Duke shakes his head. "Not at all. I was going to say, you came, and now Micah can handle anything with you. And I'm free to escape because I can't handle *anything* here."

"Okay, but you know we're here or there . . . wherever you need us. Like, I don't know if I'm staying here or moving back to Ann Arbor next year, but we're with you."

"I know."

"And if and when you decide to come back here and confront your dad, we're with you then, too."

"Okay."

"And if you decide to never come back, we're still with you."

"I notice you keep saying *we*."

"Do I?" I smile, sipping my cocoa.

"You do. I know we only just became friends, but I'm going to miss you, Meg."

"And I'll be praying for you, my friend. Will that bother you?"

Duke seems surprised but shakes his head. "I don't think so?"

"I'll be praying that you find exactly who God made you to be."

He holds up his Styrofoam mug. "Cheers, Hennessey."

Since I'm on the fence about attending any sort of church regularly, I've started joining Betty's card games every Tuesday afternoon so I can see her. Let me tell you, these ladies don't mess around with their Uno. I know. I was surprised, too. I always figured they played bridge in retirement homes. Or, at the very least, euchre. But Betty explained that the brightly colored cards were easier to follow and kept them sharp. After I am soundly trounced by Mabel, an eighty-nine-year-old Southern belle with better lipstick game than I have, Betty invites me to have tea in her apartment. I confess this is why I come. I think it's why she invites me, too. Betty is easy. Sweet and hilarious and very quick. Or perhaps I'm just an open book. She likes to tell me my dad wore his emotions all over his face, too . . . which makes me feel a little better.

Well, actually. A lot better. I didn't come to Marquette

to learn about Andrew. I told myself I wasn't really interested. But, somehow, through Betty's stories, I've become curious about this man who was barely older than I am now when he left this earth.

"He had a type," Betty says, sipping her Darjeeling and smirking. "We used to tease him because he was such a sucker for petite, dark-haired beauties."

I grin around my peanut butter cookie. After I swallow, I say, "That fits. My mom was a tiny thing with long black hair to her waist back then. I've seen pictures. She probably knocked him on his butt when he first saw her."

While a lot of things about my parents still bother me, I'm starting to feel like I can relate to them a little after falling for Micah.

"Yes. I imagine he would have been instantly smitten."

"Would have to have been, Miss Betty. They barely had more than a day or two together."

"Isn't that something?" She sighs. "It's all very romantic, honestly. A whirlwind romance." She laughs at my expression of disgust. "You don't agree?"

"Not really. Maybe. It's hard to imagine. My mom is the least romantic person I've ever met. She's so . . . so . . . ." I search for the word.

"Practical?"

"Strict," I finish. "Composed. Legalistic."

"Well, I imagine so. Think of it, Meg. You follow your heart for the first time in your life and end up alone with a child. Surely, she wasn't always like that. Had she been, you might not be here eating all my cookies." Her tone is mild, even as she passes me another two cookies. These have M&M's added.

"You're holding out on me, Miss Betty," I accuse her.

Her eyes twinkle, and she laughs, exposing her fillings. "Go on with you. I wanted to make sure I had enough to send home with you to share with your uncle."

I chew in silence, thinking of what Betty had been saying. I wonder if it's true. If my mom wasn't always as conservative as she is now. If her choices, and the fallout of those choices, resulted in who she is today.

That makes sense, and if that's the case, it would make her not so much hypocritical as . . . cautious.

"Maybe she wasn't always like that," I concede. "But she is now. And she has been since I was a baby."

"Have you spoken to her lately?"

I shake my head. "Only to tell her I'm staying. It didn't go very well."

"I imagine not," Betty says kindly. "She's being left out. Mothers love their children. They never like it when they move away."

"She kept me from you for years. Aren't you a little mad about it?"

Betty's cup is midway to her mouth, and she puts it back down. "Not mad. Maybe a little hurt. For me, but also for James. Andrew was charming, but he spent a lot of time in trouble as a kid. Nothing serious—until the end, of course—but there was a lot of contention between big brother and little. Sometimes I wonder whether, if James had gotten to be a part of your life growing up, it might have healed his hurt a little. But," she says, straightening, "it doesn't do any good to think that way. What's done is done, and you're here and the healing can take place."

"You're more gracious than I am. I'm mad," I admit. Aside from Micah, Betty is the only person I've been able to be completely honest with about my anger with my parents. After my little outburst the first time I met James, I've been careful to mostly keep my bitterness to myself. I think that's another reason why I like our weekly visits so much. It's like I can be real here.

"It's still new for you, Meg. But you will have to talk to your mom eventually. And your dad, for that matter."

"I guess so."

Betty sips her tea and gestures for me to do the same. "Enough of this. Go grab that deck behind you. We need to practice. Mabel is impossible when she wins at Uno."

16

Micah

Days after my dad's release and I'm still waiting. For what, I'm not even sure. Maybe for the other shoe to drop. Maybe for random strangers to stop writing speculating articles using my picture. Maybe for my dad to reach out. Maybe for my mom to stop looking so wounded around me. Maybe for Brian to stop "checking in" every morning. Nothing is resolving, and I'm stuck in this fucked-up stasis of wanting things to happen and hoping they never will. So, I finally go to church.

To my drums. They're in the auditorium from yesterday's services, but beggars can't be choosers. I turn on the single stage light over my throne and make my way down the carpeted aisle. It's not late, but the church is deserted. Church folk tend to take Mondays as their Sabbath. I pull out my phone and scroll to some music with a heavy beat and turn it up loud in my earbuds. Then I turn it up that much louder. My hands grip my sticks with too much force. This song starts off with a soft piano intro and the slightest kick drum. Which I am feeling just fine. I'm feeling more disciplined than ever. Wound tightly. Almost afraid to let loose, because when I do, I don't know what will come out. I sing along under my breath for the first time in half a decade. *I never, ever sing.*

Because I have this feeling, bubbling up inside of my chest, that when I open my mouth, the scream I've been holding in will let loose and never come back.

But this isn't for anyone else. It's for me.

Well. Maybe it is for someone. Maybe it's for God. Maybe I need him to hear this. Maybe I'm finally ready to talk. Scream. Whatever. It's time we have it out. Because while I always love God, I don't like him much at the moment.

Another light comes on, and James is making his way, determined, to the stage. He's holding his guitar. Not his acoustic. His electric. He doesn't say anything, just plugs in. He gestures to the live mic in front of me with a nod. I recognize the opening chords immediately, and my stony composure breaks.

I guess we're doing this.

James starts with the first verse, and it occurs to me that he's been waiting for this as much as I have. I think about the last few weeks and everything that has happened, and, well, knowing he needs this, too, helps. It helps to know I'm not alone.

The drums are heavy in this song. Abusive. It takes all my core strength to contain the rhythm. It's sharp and reckless at once. As James moves into the chorus, his voice melodic and furious, I realize my part in all of this. We're building and building and he's whining and growling and then I'm screaming. I'm screaming my *fucking soul out.*

Screaming and screaming, "*Just let go!*"

The words burn in my throat and rip at my vocal cords.

They tear from inside of my chest, and my shoulders are vibrating with the effort. Tears pour down my face, unchecked, as the chorus comes again. And again.

I scream again and again.

James slows it down for the final verse. It's meant to be pretty. In the original version performed by the metal band Red, it's all symphonic strings. But in our version, it's only James. His heartache and his chords and my complicated drumming. His tone is desperate and shattered against my furious wreck of a meltdown.

He sings about not being afraid. About changing. About finally giving up and moving past it.

Not me. I'm accusatory. I'm used up and broken. I'm taking myself back. I'm done. I'm letting go. Of my dad. Of my heartbroken thirteen-year-old self. Of always being the responsible one.

I'm not passing it off; I'm throwing it out the fucking door.

I scream the final verse over and over as James sings his version to the rafters. I'm choking, and he's mourning. We play through the end until all that's left is ringing silence. Neither of us offers to play another.

We don't need another. It's over and done. That was the end.

James puts down his guitar, and I stand from my throne. He holds out a hand, and I shake it.

"You did it," he says.

"What?" comes out in a barely audible croak. My throat is scratched to hell.

"You gave it up."

I let out an incredulous huff. "I guess so." I clear my throat. Or try to at least. "How'd you know I'd be here? Wait, let me guess. Brian?"

The corner of his mouth lifts. "No. Just me. Although Brian is struggling to know how to be there for you. Your mom, too, but you already know that."

I nod, and he gestures to the end of the stage. We sit, our legs hanging.

"I'm not a parent, and I didn't really have parents around growing up, aside from Betty," James says. "But . . ." He glances sideways at me. "I have to assume it's the most painful thing to watch your kid suffer."

"I'm not suffering."

"Okay."

I huff out a breath. "I'm not asking them to fix me."

"Of course you aren't."

I glare at him, and he raises a brow in challenge.

"*Of course* you don't want anyone to help you. I suspect you think you're unfixable. But even if you weren't, because you *aren't*"—he emphasizes the word—"there's no way you'd ask for help. So. Let's try this. We've already covered that parenting is outside my wheelhouse, and besides, you don't want a parent to help. So how about you lay it on *me,* and if I think you're damned, I swear I'll tell you."

"You just cussed in church."

James looks around theatrically. "And yet we're still here. Guess our conversation's been blessed."

The corner of my lips twitch, but I swallow my smile down. "He hasn't come to see me." James's head bobs once, and I continue. "Which is messed up, because I don't want anything to do with him. I *don't.* He ruined my life and messed with my mom and sisters, and I finally might be starting to hate him for it.

"But he's been out for almost a week and hasn't made

any effort to speak to me. To see me. He has no idea what I'm like now. The things I've done. The person I've become. You would think, after being in prison for almost six years, checking in on his kid would be his first priority. We were best friends, James. I wanted to be him. I loved everything about him. And he hasn't even called."

My voice chokes off on the last word, and James swallows hard, his Adam's apple bobbing.

"Wow," he says after a minute. "That's not what I thought this would be about."

"You thought I was angry."

"I confess I did."

"I am," I admit. "But mostly I'm . . ."

"Hurt."

I sigh. "Yeah. And I can't tell my mom, because it would kill her. She wants me to be different from him, and I am. I know I am. He's a mess. He's disgusting and manipulative and a liar. But I'm not the opposite of him. She wants me to be the opposite of him. She *needs* me to be, and I can't. I'm not perfect, and there are parts of him inside of me, still.

"And Brian is the best guy I know, but his priority is my mom and their kids together. What if he decides I can't be around them? What if you decide I'm not good enough for Meg? Oh God." I stare up at James's face, mine draining of color.

James is already shaking his head. "Okay. Hold on. This is where I step in and tell you that you aren't damned. Right here. You are not your dad, and his mistakes aren't yours."

"I know that, but—"

"You aren't condemned because you want to see him. Micah, he's your dad. You don't think I would give anything for one more minute with Drew? The guy who ignored me growing up and accidentally killed himself and my girlfriend? The guy I've spent decades grieving? One minute." He laughs, self-deprecating. "Just one minute to hug him and tell him I love him."

"My dad isn't dead, though. He was in prison. He messed up a lot of lives."

James nods. "Yeah. It's a mess. And I'm not saying he's worthy of you. Because, to be clear, he's not. But that's not your fault."

"And the videos are still circulating on the internet."

James doesn't ask which ones. Everyone knows. "They are, it's true. But you aren't that kid anymore."

"I'm not ready to forgive him," I tell him.

"You already know how I feel about that."

"I might hit him."

James cracks a smile. "If I had *two* minutes, I would most definitely kick Drew in the balls."

"You're not a very good pastor," I say.

"I keep telling them that. I think worship leaders slash youth pastors willing to work for nothing are hard to come by."

"Are you going to marry Dani?" I ask, changing the subject.

"Are you dating my niece?" he fires back.

"As long as she'll have me."

He grins. "Me, too."

He gets to his feet and holds out a hand. "I have to get this stuff cleaned up. Why don't you head over to my place; Meg will be worried."

"I thought you said Brian told you?"

"No, I told you he didn't. But Meg did. Saw your bike."

"So she sent you?"

"So she *mentioned* it, and I left. I know. I'm not as cute as my niece, but she can't play guitar."

"Actually, she might. I've never asked. But she sang for her worship band back in Ann Arbor."

James freezes. "Really?"

"Easy, Pastor. She may not like that I told you that. She's not ready."

He scratches his neck. "I might have picked up on the hesitation."

"Have you?" I waver over saying more, but all these exposed emotions have got me feeling protective. "Listen, James. However hesitant she seems to you, she's probably a hundred times more than that in actuality."

James looks thoughtful but doesn't respond.

"So, what are you going to do?"

I shake my head. "Nothing."

"You could always reach out to him."

"I don't think so."

James's expression is pained. "Maybe he's afraid to reach out. Of you rejecting him."

"Maybe. But I'm worth that much, you know? I'm not chasing him down."

"Fair enough. Can I pray for you?"

He means right now. He means for us to sit in a pew and bow our heads together. I move for the doors and open the first, still facing James, and slip on my sunglasses, palming my keys. "Sure," I say. "Thank you." And I walk out.

17

Meg

"Okay, but did Jesus have a girlfriend?"

"Um, no."

"What about Mary Magdalene?"

I smother a smile. "Just how many times have you read Dan Brown's collective works?"

Carolyn rolls her eyes in the way a fourteen-year-old girl does. I pass her an Oreo.

"Here. Take this instead. A peace offering for a ridiculous question."

"I thought there were no ridiculous questions in youth group," Maddy pouts. I pass her an Oreo, too.

"There aren't," I agree, but I hold up a finger. "Except ones I've already answered a hundred times."

"You've only known us a month," Nichole reminds me with a flick of her long red hair. My heart gives a little twinge, missing Vada.

"Which is why it's bananas to have answered that question so many times. Besides, we're not talking about that today. We're talking about the book of James. My fave. And while Jesus didn't have a girlfriend, as far as I know, he did have a brother. Which, can you even imagine?" I ask the girls. They surround me, sitting on worn sofas, their faces open and ready to learn. "Your sibling is the mother-loving son of God? I'm sure that went over splendidly at the Passover meal every year."

"I barely tolerate my brother," Maddy mumbles under her breath. I smirk.

"James was the same way at first. In fact, he didn't actually believe Jesus was the son of God until after Jesus was crucified. We talk a lot about Doubting Thomas, but James, Jesus's own half brother, was one of his biggest skeptics. It's why I love his Gospel so much. He doesn't pull any punches. He's pragmatic and real and blunt as all get-out. He went from unbeliever and naysayer of his own flesh and blood to one of the major leaders of the early church. And he believed so hard and so completely, he allowed himself to be martyred for it."

I skim my notes. "What else can I tell you about James? Oh!" I pull out my well-loved and much-marked-up Bible. "Turn to the book of James 1:19. Favorite verse time. 'Let everyone be quick to listen, slow to speak and slow to anger.'"

I close my Bible with a slap. "Like. Come on. That's good stuff right there. Just your basic 'how to be a decent human' kind of thing. What say you four?"

"I'm not very good at being slow to anger," Nichole admits. "My mom says I have a hot temper."

"Same," agrees Carolyn. "Sometimes people are stupid. I like to tell them." The others chime in with assent.

I raise a finger. Man, I love teenage girls. They're so frigging honest. And these four, Carolyn, Maddy, Nichole, and Becca, are darlings. Precocious and verging on mean, but they love with their full hearts, and I can't get enough of that. I'm still not attending church regularly, but I haven't missed a week of youth group. This small group of girls is giving me life.

"Hold up. I think you're proving my point, though. Well, mine and James's. Don't answer, but think back for a second. Have you ever gotten angry with someone before knowing all the details? It's like reading a headline but never clicking on the article. And what happens when you retweet or share that article without reading? And then you comment on it and someone else reads it without getting the full scoop and they're angry, too? And pretty soon, you have a whole lot of livid people ready to take up arms against a stranger?"

No one is meeting my eye. Excellent. It's hitting home.

"But what if, *instead*, we were faster to listen? To hear them out and get the full scoop . . . provided they are willing to give it to us?" That's where my mom went wrong. She's not ready to share the full story about my dad. Either of them.

"What if we were slower to speak? What if we heard some gossip, by accident, and instead of pulling out our phones to text it to someone immediately, or even—shocking, I know—maybe we checked the facts? Or left it alone because it's none of our beeswax? Because we're aware of the power our voices hold. Because we know the damage that could happen if we spread a lie."

"But it doesn't matter, Meg. Even if we don't share it, someone will. Shouldn't we find out the truth to help the person out?"

I smile sadly at Maddy. "Who made us the gatekeepers?"

"God."

I raise a brow. "God told you to fact-check gossip?" She doesn't respond, and I press on gently, "Or God told you to mind your own beeswax?"

"Mind my own," she grumbles with a small grin.

"Ever hear the saying, 'The road to hell is paved with good intentions'?"

They nod, a little shocked at my saying *hell*. I don't roll my eyes in exasperation. It's not their fault. Someone will report me, though, I'm sure of it. James told me a mom was concerned that I had a boyfriend and that the boyfriend was named Micah Allen.

James told her to mind her own beeswax.

Solidarity, Uncle.

"Well, that saying is pretty appropriate for this conversation. You might mean well. You might even feel like you're justified because you love Jesus and he's on your side. And he is. But that doesn't mean it's a good idea to meddle. Or"—I make a face—"maybe *meddle* isn't the right word. You should always, always stand up for others. Love them. Offer what you can. But no one needs you to perpetuate the cycle of hurt. Take a seat. Take a minute. Take a breather. Weigh the consequences.

"James didn't say, 'Don't speak.' Or 'Don't get angry.' He said, 'Be *slow* to speak. Be *slow* to anger.' See the difference?"

"Take a chill pill."

I laugh outright and ask Becca, who'd been silent this entire time, "Who taught you that?"

She lifts a shoulder. "Saw it on a T-shirt, maybe?"

"That's it. Next week, we're making matching tees that say that."

This gets their attention. If there's one thing eighth graders love, it's making tees.

There's a knock at the door, and it's James. I glance at the clock. "Oh! We're out of time."

The girls groan, and I smile, secretly pleased. We collect our things, and I stack the Bibles up on the end table, snatching one off the top. "Becca! Hold up a sec!"

James leads the rest of the girls upstairs to the lobby, where their rides await them, but I hold the Bible out to Becca. "Do you have one of these yet?"

She shakes her head. I grab a yellow marker from a coffee can on the floor and highlight the verse in James we talked about. Then I pass it to her. "Yours. To read, to mark up, to study, to hold. Whatever. Humans will fail you. Church will fail you. *I* will inevitably fail you. This, though? It won't. God won't. Bring it to him. All of it. The messy, angry, disgusting things, even. He won't mind. Deal?"

Becca smiles shyly, tucking it under her arm. "Is it really okay to write in it?"

I nod. "The biggest mistake we make is trying to keep God tidy. He created the skunk, for goodness' sake. He doesn't mind a mess. He finds messiness beautiful."

Becca impulsively reaches out to hug me, and I squeeze her for a moment longer. "Now, hurry upstairs before your mom thinks I kidnapped you."

I'm only half kidding. Becca's mom is the one who asked about Micah. She's also the one who wanted to know if my hair color was permanent or if I could dye it back.

I told her *technically* I could.

"Knock, knock," my uncle says. I finish clearing the room and smile at him to come in.

"What is it this time, boss?"

He rolls his eyes and plops on the couch. "Mrs. Sanderson."

I plop across from him, even as my phone buzzes with a text. Micah, letting me know he's in the parking lot. It's not that he's afraid to come in, but after I told him about Becca's mom, he got all quiet and told me he'd wait in the car from now on.

Which is stupid.

"Apparently, the high school is holding a safe-sex talk for incoming freshmen, and she wants to know when we will be covering abstinence in youth group."

My breath catches. "How about never?"

"Meg."

"James. No. I'm not doing that."

"We have to address the biblical view. The girls love you. You've been brilliant with them."

"James, I mean it. I can't. I hate the way churches portray abstinence, and I'll be honest, I'm not entirely sure how I feel on the matter these days."

James slumps back in his chair. "Do I need to give *you* the abstinence talk?"

I ignore that. "I can't do it, James. Not the way Mrs. Sanderson wants, anyway. I won't tell those girls that they are the sole bearers of purity and virginity and innocence in their relationships. I refuse to comment on their clothing and the sin it is causing in the boys, or girls, around them."

"What would you say? Hypothetically?"

I release a puff of air that lifts my bangs off my forehead. "That their bodies are a precious gift from a God who loves them and to treat them as such. But there will be no pictures of aborted fetuses, no used-up metaphors, and zero shaming."

"What if they ask you about sex before marriage?" He raises a hand at my protest. "I have to ask, Meg. I trust you, but they are going to ask, and you need to be prepared. They look up to you and will want to know what *you* practice."

I feel my face flame. "I will tell them the same thing I just said. That my body is a precious gift from a God who loves me, and I treat it as such." My throat tightens, and I can't continue right away. After a moment, I stand, grabbing my bag. "And that they have to decide for themselves when to share their gift with someone special to them and who that special someone is."

James, realizing I'm through, stands. "Okay."

"Is that enough?"

He hesitates and then sighs. "I think it has to be."

The tears are edging back in by the time I make it to Micah's car. The evening air has a bite to it. My breath is frosty and I'm trembling, though I'm not convinced that's not from the conversation I just had.

Micah jumps out and opens the door for me, and that's all it takes for the tears to spill over.

He stares at me, alarmed. "What happened?"

I shake my head at first, feeling stupid. "Nothing. It was going so well. But Mrs. Sanderson"—Micah lets out a sound like a growl—"asked James when we'd be addressing abstinence and I told him I wouldn't do that, and it just brought up all these icky feelings and I don't know!" I wail.

Micah seems uncomfortable and unsure how to proceed. After a second, he puts the car into gear. "This isn't the place for this conversation. Let me get us out of here."

The only sound in the car is my occasional sniffling.

Instead of my place, Micah takes me to his. He leads me up his stairs and unlocks the door. "Give me a minute. I need to walk Cash." He gestures to his apartment. "Make yourself at home. I'll be right back."

He closes the door behind him, and I hear his and Cash's footfalls on the steps. I pace around the small space. In the last two months, Micah's slowly added furniture. A coffee table and a couple of lamps. Some blankets on the couch. A small flat-screen TV and DVD player. His queen-size bed is made in the corner. His place reminds me of him. Tidy, no fuss, smells good. I head to his bathroom to splash some water on my face. I look at his deodorant and toothpaste. Just noticing.

I turn off the bathroom light and make my way to my usual spot in the corner of his couch. I kick off my shoes and lean back, grabbing the single pillow and plopping it on my lap right as the door opens and Micah and Cash enter. Cash heads straight for me, and I'm quick to nuzzle his head, giving him lots of baby talk. He gives me the smallest lick and plops on the rug at my feet.

Micah makes his way to the sink, pulling out a couple of glasses. Without asking, he fills and carries them over, offering one to me. I take a sip, grateful, and put it down on the coffee table, on a coaster. Because Micah is the exact kind of nineteen-year-old guy who buys coasters to protect his thrift-store furniture from rings.

"Okay, so let's back up. They want you to give an abstinence talk to your youth group girls." A small part of me warms at how Micah refers to them as my girls. Because that's what they are.

"Right. And I told him I wouldn't do that. At least, not

in the traditional sense, which, believe me, is exactly what Mrs. Sanderson wants. All fire and brimstone and licked Oreos."

"Licked. Or— Wait. What?"

"Oh, you know. The whole 'lick an Oreo and pass it on / would someone want it now? / that's what having sex before marriage is like / you're ruined for your husband' talk."

Micah straightens. "You're serious."

"Completely. You've never heard that?"

"No. But I stopped going to church in eighth grade. Maybe I missed it."

"Actually, my mom told me that one. That was my sex talk. Ruined Oreos for me for a bit. Thankfully, I've recovered. Brought them tonight to share, even. Minus the saliva."

"That's . . . wow."

I lean back into the couch, tucking my feet under me. "That's what she heard, and her mom before her, I'm sure. Not that I'm condoning it. I'm trying to stop the cycle. But it's difficult when I hardly know what I think about all of it."

"It being . . . ?"

I wince. "Sex."

"Right." He waits. I sigh, picking at the pillow in my lap.

"It's just that I've always thought it was wrong, and that's a difficult mindset to change."

"That sex is wrong or sex before marriage is wrong?"

"That's the thing," I say. "It was always sex. I thought. But I've realized I was tying the two together in my mind. Sex and premarital sex. Until like three months ago, I called it *boinking,* Micah."

Micah snorts, and I feel the ghost of a grin tease my lips.

"Vada used to tell me my homeschool was showing."

"Duke calls it *borking*. Close enough."

"I knew I liked him." I pause, carefully planning what I want to say. "I really like kissing you."

"Same," says Micah easily. "But I'm okay if that's all you want. I get it. I can wait for you."

"I think there's something wrong with me," I whisper. "Because it's not all I want, but I'm afraid to do anything else. I told James tonight that I would tell the girls their bodies were a gift from God, and they should protect them as such and only give them away if and when they were ready to share that gift."

Micah exhales softly. "That's a good way to say it."

"But I'm afraid to believe it myself."

Micah leans forward so his face is only a foot away from mine. "Can I tell you something, with you bearing in mind what I just said about being willing to wait for you? Because I meant that, but I need to be honest with you."

"Okay," I whisper.

"I think God created sex, so it's a good thing."

"Okay."

"Still with me?"

"I think so. Is there more?"

"Does there need to be?"

"No. But you haven't had sex?"

"Not yet. But I'd like to one day. With you, even. Still okay?" he checks.

I press my lips together to keep my heart from jumping out of my mouth and nod.

"I don't know if I want to have sex before I'm married. The thing is, my parents are divorced. So, while I believe in marriage, a hundred percent, it doesn't always mean the same thing it did in biblical times, and even then, it wasn't great for women. Marriage, as a finish line, has never made sense to me."

"That's fair. My parents' marriage was a sham."

"I guess I'm not waiting for marriage as much as I'm waiting for the person God has planned for me."

I bite down on my lip, but it doesn't keep my heart from leaking out of my eyeballs.

This boy.

"And I feel like you're that person. You're my person, Meg."

My tears are in full force now. Micah wipes them, pulling me close. I tuck into the space between his chest and his neck and listen to his heart, trying to get a handle on my emotions.

"You're my person, too."

18

Micah

Days go by, and the leaves change and fall to the ground. The air crisps to frozen overnight, and it's taking longer and longer to defrost each morning. Soon it won't at all. The holidays will come and go, and I'm looking forward to seeing how Meg glows in the Christmas lights. Cash and I graduate from search and rescue in a week, after eighteen arduous months of training.

Time passes, and some things pass with it. But some things are permanent.

Meg is making her mark count. She told me about her fairy wing collection at home. Her "touch of whimsy," she called it. I can imagine them perfectly. I also see why she left them behind. It's sort of like me moving out of my parents' house all those months ago. It was time to leave behind the room I grew up in. Time to put on my grown-up shoes.

Which brings us to the tattoo parlor this bitterly cold fall afternoon, along with James. When we walk in, the girl behind the counter smiles at me first. "Micah! Finally ready to commit?"

Meg whirls around to face me. "Commit to what?"

I shake my head and gesture to Meg. "I'm here as a support, actually."

Meg gives me a look but pulls her sketch out of her bag. "I spoke with Joshua earlier this week. I have an appointment."

"Right! Meg! I'm Alex. Welcome!" Alex pulls out a tablet preloaded with consent forms. "I'll grab Joshua, but you can start on the paperwork. I'll need a form of identification." She turns to me and passes another tablet over. "In case you get brave. Your sketch is on file, Micah. Today's the day, my friend."

Alex walks away, and Meg points at my chest. "What?"

I stare at the tablet, not touching it. "I've been in here a time or five since I turned eighteen. Never pulled the trigger."

"Micah! You never said anything. What are you getting?"

"I *wanted* to get a compass. One of those really intricate, old-fashioned-looking ones. On the inside of my forearm." I trace the spot.

"Are you afraid of the pain?"

I shake my head. "Not really."

"Can I see the sketch?"

"Easy, Meg, if he doesn't want to . . . " James says. "It's forever," he reminds me.

And for some reason, this rankles. Well, for a good reason. Because I want to say, "So is fatherhood." But I check myself because that feels like a conversation meant for someone else.

Instead, I reach for the tablet and sign the dotted line because doing something permanent with Meg feels exactly right. And maybe it's time I commit to something for once in my life.

It's just some ink under my skin, but it feels like more than that.

A minute later, Joshua is coming forward to shake Meg's hand. "Good to see you again. Ready for this?"

"Ready as I'll ever be," Meg says, bouncing on her toes. It's as if she's already gotten wings. This is just the physical manifestation of her personality, really. I can't wait to see them.

"We're going to duck behind this curtain for privacy," Joshua says, looking at James, who is staring him down.

"Perfect. Uncle James? There's a coffee shop around the corner," she says, shooing him away. I have a feeling he's going to sit in the waiting room the entire time she's in there with Joshua. Meg turns to me, kissing my cheek. "See you in a few hours, Micah. Good luck."

A few minutes later, my artist, Ryder, comes up to the front, a big smile on his face. "Finally! I didn't think you'd ever come in."

"Well, I came with my girlfriend, actually." I jerk a thumb to the curtain where I can already hear the buzzing of the needle. "But since I'm here anyway . . ."

Ryder smirks. "Sure. Well, I've been looking forward to this for a year. This sketch is a thing of beauty." He raises it in the air. "Let's do this."

I sit down on the reclining chair, and Ryder pulls an armrest up between us to support my forearm. He peels off the back of the printed sketch and checks with me before carefully placing it on my skin. "I took the liberty of adding the wording we discussed last time, but I realize I should have checked. Before I put ink on it, why don't you give it a look?"

I take it in. The tattoo stretches to cover the underside

of my forearm completely, facing away from me, so that the *N* for north is closest to the inside of my elbow and the *S* is nearly to my wrist. Eight points reach out like a starburst from the center, each connected, a large circle intersecting them all. The original design had rivets at regular intervals along the circle. Almost like the cogs of a clock. But instead of rivets, I wanted in small, precise print the Hebrew words *Jehovah Jireh,* which translates to "the Lord will provide."

No matter what happens, no matter who lets me down, no matter where I end up, no matter what mess I get myself into, God will provide a way out.

He's my compass.

I release a slow breath, surprised at the emotion constricting my throat at the image on my skin. I nod, coughing a little. "It's perfect."

Ryder slaps my shoulder. He and I go back a little bit. We were in high school at the same time, though he graduated when I was a freshman. He used to be my youth group leader back when I went to church. Back when we both did. Which is why I went to him with this. I knew that out of everyone, he would get it. And for some reason, that felt important.

Even if I kept leaving without doing it.

But I'm not leaving today. I lean my head back against the headrest as I hear the needle turn on. Today, I'm making my mark.

The following weekend, it's Halloween. I don't go out on Halloween as a rule. But Emily is having a house party at her new place, and she invited all of us to come. "Costumes only, Micah," she insisted. "Don't you dare come in your North Face and try that whole 'I'm a Coloradoan hipster' thing again."

What? It was a good costume. Everyone got it, and it was free.

Anyway, it wouldn't have mattered. Meg has never celebrated Halloween in her life, and for that reason, Duke and I decided that we had to do it right.

"I can't believe you never dressed up for Halloween," Duke says, sitting on my couch and yelling through the door of the bathroom, where Meg is changing. He's wearing a neon purple zoot suit that clashes with his teal hair and is polishing a pair of pointy black-and-white wing tips.

"When I was in third grade, our church did a trunk-or-treat in the parking lot. I got to dress up as one of the fruits of the spirit!" she yells. I am buttoning up my dress shirt and trying to figure out the superlong, super fat tie that comes with the costume but am brought up short by her announcement.

"Which one?"

"Is this a church thing?" Duke stage-whispers. I nod, grinning.

"You get three guesses," she says, opening the door with a flourish. Duke lets out a low whistle, but I . . . can't move. I've forgotten what words are at the sight of Meg in a shimmery, short, silver flapper dress. She does a little old-fashioned twist, causing the layers of glittery fringe to swing around her, and pops a hip out, fluffing her short hair with her hand. She's wearing a black headband with a gaudy feather on it but somehow manages to make it look good.

All of her. Every part of her looks good. I cross the room to her, palming her cheek and placing a small kiss on her ruby-painted lips.

"You're beautiful."

"So are you," she says with a wink, cupping my biceps in my shirt. "Who knew you boys cleaned up so well?"

Duke slips his shoes on and does a little tap dance. "I could get used to these."

"Not much use on rafting trips," I say.

The corner of his mouth lifts. "But I feel like Gene Kelly."

"Who?"

Meg and Duke roll their eyes at each other as if to commiserate about how uncultured I am. I don't mind. Duke takes Meg's hand and spins her out so her fringe flares again, her wings on full display due to the sheer back piece covering her shoulders.

They are every bit Meg . . . whimsical and powerful, delicate and bold, fluttering and steadfast. They make me ache.

"Self-control," I say quickly.

"Hmm?" Meg says, twirling to face me. Duke smirks over her shoulder.

I roll my eyes, rubbing absently at my chest. "The fruits of the spirit. I bet you were self-control. Though I have no idea how you would dress like that."

Meg laughs. "Oh. Right. Yep. You guessed it. My mom made me this costume that looked like a giant game of Operation, except the patient was me and I was completely dressed. There were all these 'temptations'"—she surrounds the final word in air quotes—"like lying to get chocolate and eating too much candy and not brushing my teeth. It was terrible. I had to carry around a buzzer and buzz anyone who tried to touch the costume or give me candy. Everyone thought it was hilarious."

Duke and I stare at her. Finally, Duke flops back on the couch. "Fuck. I need a drink after that. That sounds terrible. To be fair, though, David would probably love that." I mouth the word *dad* to Meg, whose mouth forms a silent *oh*. Duke fumbles around in his bag, pulling out a bottle of something clear and a Gatorade. "Anyone else need one?"

"No, thanks," I say.

"What is it?" asks Meg.

"Vodka and fruit punch Gatorade."

Meg shrugs, and Duke pours them each a small glass. Meg takes one sip and grimaces. "Is it supposed to burn?"

Duke drinks his in one gulp. "If it's done right, yes."

Meg puts the glass down on the table in front of her and looks at me. "You don't drink?"

I shake my head. "Not really. I did one time. It wasn't my thing."

"Micah doesn't like to let loose," Duke says, pouring another glass. This time more vodka than fruit punch.

"Type A, remember?" I say, pointing to myself.

Meg grins. "It's your fruit of the spirit!"

"Usually, though that dress has me thinking otherwise."

Meg's face turns pink. "Really?"

"Uh, yeah. Which is another good reason to stay very sober."

Meg finds her way to the couch, sitting so close to me that her knees meet mine. "I'll stay sober, too, then."

But I can see that she's not sure. "It's okay," I insist. "If you want to drink, I promise to behave. And I'll be around to keep an eye on you both."

Meg's teeth find her bottom lip.

"It's your choice. No pressure."

Meg grabs her drink, taking a larger gulp and wincing. "Is there anything better than this available?"

"Nope!" Duke admits. "Cheers, Meg!"

"To self-control," she says dryly, tapping his glass with hers.

I think I'm going to like Halloween this year.

19

Meg

I have to admit, this is waaaay more fun than the trunk-or-treat in third grade. I'm still not super sure about Emily or her motives, but she's been friendly tonight in the rare moments we've crossed paths. But her basement is kind of dark and filled to the brim with people in confusing costumes, so I haven't had the time to miss her or feel uncomfortable.

Plus, Duke's concoction improves upon further sampling. Emily's roommates also have a keg in the corner where people have been milling all night. Every now and again, a bunch of shouting and cheering will come from that corner as various people play drinking games with the tap.

I'm in the cozy space between not caring that all those guests are putting their slobbery mouths on the same piece of hardware and being absolutely certain that I don't want anything to do with it.

If pressed, I would call myself *tipsy*, because I accidentally dribbled red fruit punch down my front.

One thing I didn't know before this party was how much Duke likes to dance. And how much I would want to join him. His happiness is infectious, and this feeling of not caring—of not needing to hold myself a certain way or protect others from myself or whatever—is really something. Is this why Jesus drank wine? Did he just need to loosen up at the end of a long day of performing miracles and putting up with the Sanhedrin's baloney?

If so, I get it.

I'm fanning my face and talking with a girl named Amelia or Amanda, who is dressed up like Cleopatra. I give the girl props. So many of the costumes here are just (*insert title*) (*but make it sexy*), but I feel like Possibly-Amy really tried to embrace the history of her character.

Also, Cleopatra is already sexy, so she didn't have to stretch the truth.

"I love your tat," she's saying, tracing the wings on my back.

"Me, too," I say.

"And your fringe," she points out.

I shimmy a little. "Thanks. It's not as cool as a toga, though. I'd kill for a blanket down here." Maybe-Alexis tips her head to the side, causing her wig to slip, and I reach out to straighten it. She slurps her drink. "I'm going to get a refill."

"See ya," I say, even though I probably won't. Was-it-Annie? is the fourth girl I've talked to tonight, and as soon as each one guzzles down her drink, I never see them again. Making friends at a party is far trickier than I realized. One, I keep forgetting everyone's names, and/or I can't hear them over the music. And two, basically zero people have boundaries. Except my boyfriend, who is not drinking.

"They feel safe with you." His warm breath sends shivers

along the back of my neck as he presses in close to be heard over the music.

I spin to look at his face. "You think?"

He shrugs, stepping back a little. "Sure. You're approachable and don't have an ulterior motive."

"Not the boys, I've noticed. They're steering clear."

He rubs his chin, subtly covering what I am certain is a smile.

I step closer, tracing a fingertip along the back of his hand. "You seem very pleased with yourself, Micah Allen."

He wraps my fingers in his giant, warm ones. "I haven't said a word."

I nod, smirking. "Of course. Just letting those biceps do the talking for you?"

He seems to fight with himself a moment and settles on insecure. "Would you rather I take a lap? Give you some space?"

I'm shaking my head before he even finishes the thought. "Please don't. *You* make *me* feel safe."

He presses a relieved kiss to my forehead. "Good."

Suddenly, my arm is yanked. "They're playing our song, Hennessey!"

I grin at Duke's antics and take a little sip of my drink before handing my cup to Micah. "Be right back."

Last week, while I was couch-bound and waiting for my shoulders to heal, I convinced Duke to hang out with me one afternoon and binge-watch movies. Turns out, he has a bit of a thing for the Killers, so when Cameron Diaz lost her mind to "Mr. Brightside" in *The Holiday,* he pulled me off the couch and insisted we dance like maniacs right there in the living room.

I can't say I minded one bit, even if my shoulders felt sunburned the rest of the night.

Duke leads me to the middle of a crowd of strangers and spins me around, hopping up and down with the intro beat. We're screaming the lyrics and bobbing our heads and swirling this way and that. When we get to the chorus, we stop dancing and shout the words, pounding our chests and feeling the lyrics as if they were written about us. Duke spins me under his arm and pulls me in, one hand around my waist and the other held in his. I beam up at his carefree face. This kid deserves to feel this way all the time. Something snags his attention, and he surges through the crowd, pulling Micah in with us. Micah laughs, punching Duke in the arm lightly, but stays and dances. We're in the middle of a mob of dancing kids, everyone screaming the lyrics and feeling alive. My cheeks hurt from smiling so hard, and when the song ends, it's bittersweet. Something slow and hip-hop comes on next, and a girl is offering a drink to Duke, who winks over her shoulder at me as he starts to talk to the pretty redhead.

I press my lips together, pleased, watching them before turning my attention to Micah, who says, "I left your drink behind when Duke pulled me in to dance . . . Would you like me to get you another?"

"I'm good," I say. "My belly is plenty swoopy for one night."

We stand on the edges, my back to his front and his arms loose around my shoulders, watching Duke dance and flirt and have fun. Mostly. I would be lying if I said I wasn't hyperaware of Micah's body pressed against mine. The music slows down, and I can't keep myself from swaying along, brushing myself against him and letting the friction buzz in my blood. I'm distracted and a little dizzy, and I can't be sure if it's him or the alcohol.

I think it might be him. Which . . . yowza.

Some beautiful person puts on Hozier. My eyes slip shut, and I turn in Micah's arms to face him in one quick movement. It's like my body is acting without my brain. Pure feeling. I just want to feel this. Feel him. I press forward, and he hits the wall behind him with a quiet gasp. He leans down the moment I lift up, and soon our lips are touching. Soon every part of us is touching. His hands are fire on my skin and through my dress. His body is unyielding underneath mine, and every soft part of me aches for more contact. In an instant, he's spun us, and my back is against the wall. He's kissing me, and I'm devouring him. My knees slide apart, and in no time he's there, pressed against me. My hips rock forward, and he groans against my mouth, pulling back a little, his forehead resting on mine as he catches his breath.

"Meg." He swallows, his eyes shutting as if in pain.

"I know. I know. Too fast."

"Too something," he mutters. His tongue slides along his lower lip, and my eyes chase it down.

"Just a little more," I say and press in, my fingers tangling in the hair at the nape of his neck and tugging him down to my mouth once more.

"If you insist."

I haven't drank since before our kiss, and by the time we're dropping Duke off at his house and watching him gracelessly stumble up his front porch, I'm feeling back to myself.

Mostly. The alcohol has faded from my system, but I still

feel a little drunk on Micah. His fingers wrap over mine, and he holds my hand against his thigh as he drives me back to James's. He pulls into the drive and parks next to James's truck. It's nearly midnight, and all the lights are off except the porch light.

"Want to come in?"

Micah stares past the steering wheel, considering. "I don't know if James will like being woken up."

"I have my own entrance," I remind him.

He takes a deep breath and seems so conflicted that I start to backtrack. "It's okay. I know it's late—"

"It's not that," he interrupts quickly. "It *should* be that, but it's not."

"Oh."

The corner of his mouth quirks. "Yeah, okay. I'll come in."

My heart tap-dances in my chest. "Yeah?"

He slips the keys out of the ignition. "Yeah."

We're careful not to slam the car doors. Or to rush around the house to my entrance. Almost like we are working really hard not to appear overeager or guilty or whatever. Or at least I am. I unlock my door, swinging it open, and flip on the light. Right into my bedroom. Like, bam! Here we are. Where my bed is. Right there.

I never thought about it before, but I don't have any chairs in my room. Which is decidedly awkward at this very moment and also convenient.

I clear my throat. "So, here's my room."

Micah's voice is a little strangled when he says, "It's nice."

"I have to pee. So . . ." I gesture to the bed. "Um. Be right back."

I make a beeline for the bathroom and turn on the water full blast, staring at my reflection. My eyes are wild and wide, my skin is whiter than white except where bright pink has infused my cheeks, and I can almost see my pulse throbbing in my neck. I shake myself and use the bathroom before washing my hands extra well. I splash cool water on my face, over and over, and dab it dry. I smooth on some ChapStick, my image blushing even more furiously when I remember why my lips are so dry.

"Be brave," I whisper to my reflection, and open the door. Micah is sitting on my bed and looks ready to bolt, but he's taken off his shoes and suit jacket. So maybe not.

I slip out of my shoes and move to sit by him, curling my feet under me. He's holding a framed picture.

"Vada?" His voice is low. James's room is on the opposite side of the house, so I doubt he can hear, but it still feels a little like sneaking.

I nod, pointing. "That's Vada. And next to her is her boyfriend, Luke. Me, obviously. And behind us are CullenandZack." I say, running their names together in a sing-song way. "Cullen and Luke are twins."

"Those are the wings you were talking about?"

"Yep. I have a whole collection back in Ann Arbor."

Micah traces them with his finger and looks to me. "I like your new ones better."

I trail my finger along his forearm where his compass is hidden beneath his shirt. "Me, too."

He puts the frame back on my nightstand and rubs his hands down his thighs like he's waiting. For me. Always. I take his face in my hands, scooting closer, and he sucks in a breath. I skim my fingertips over his eyebrows, smoothing them and drawing them along his cheekbones down to his lips. I trace his lower lip with the pad of my thumb and follow it with my lips. At first, I'm tender, pacing myself and holding back against the wall of hormones surging inside of me.

He returns my kiss, careful to keep his hands on his legs, but I've already tasted this man, and I don't want to be in this alone, so without second-guessing myself, I draw one knee over his lap until I'm straddling him.

Oh yes. *This* I love. Micah's hands cling to my hips as if to push me off or pull me down. I don't think he knows which. I don't think I do either. He squeezes me in his grip, and I fist my hands in his hair, pressing myself against him, letting out a very uncool squeak when I feel *him* against me *there*.

He freezes, and I bite my lip. "Sorry," I whisper.

"Don't apologize. But maybe we should . . ." He gently removes me from his lap.

I try to cross my legs under me again, flustered at the heat radiating from my core. Micah doesn't look much better off. He's flushed and trying valiantly to cover any evidence of his enthusiasm. I'm torn between feeling proud and mortified.

"I didn't know it could be like this," I start, gesturing between us. "This is kind of intense. Right?"

He chuckles low. "Understatement."

"I mean. Is this how it always is?"

He shakes his head. "I don't know. No? I don't have a lot of experience, but this feels different. You have this effect on me."

My stomach sinks at his words. "I do?"

He's still not looking at me, lost in thought. My fingers itch to touch him, but I can't. Is this my fault? Did I push him too far?

Suddenly, every youth group speech is filtering into the clouded mess of thoughts in my head. *Keep your body covered. Protect the eyes of your spiritual brothers. Don't lead boys into temptation. Guard your body. Save it for your future husband. Don't drink alcohol; you'll lose your morals. Don't spend time alone with boys. Don't let boys into your bedroom. If you are ever alone with a boy, stay vertical; nothing good can come from being horizontal.*

Kissing is the gateway to sex.

Suddenly, I'm on my feet. "I don't know how to apologize, Micah. I am so sorry. This is my fault."

His head whips up, shock evident on his face. "What?"

I shut my eyes, too embarrassed to look at him. "I led you astray. This stupid short dress, and I was dancing provocatively, and then I pushed you against that wall and kissed you, and—"

He swears under his breath, and I open my eyes, expecting to see him angry. But instead, he's . . . understanding.

"Meg, please sit down."

As soon as I do, he turns his body to face me.

"When I said that you have this effect on me, I meant it. But not in the way that I feel like you're tempting me into something sinful and dark."

"But I did do those things, and you *did* respond."

He rolls his eyes lightly. "Yeah. Obviously. You're very good at being you. And I'm attracted to *you*. It doesn't matter what you wear or how you move or what you drink, I'm going to respond to you."

I want to cry. "This is hopeless."

"How so? I feel like it is the exact opposite of hopeless."

"I'm leading you to sin."

"No, you aren't. I'm a sinner with or without you pushing me into dark corners and kissing me. That wasn't sinning, Meg. That was *loving*."

I don't know what to say to that.

He picks up my hand and starts to play with it, sending frissons of electricity through me. "This feeling between us isn't a bad thing."

"Are you sure?"

He releases a breath, and his dark eyes pierce mine. "Pretty sure."

"But the Bible says premarital sex is a sin."

The corner of his mouth lifts. "Who said anything about sex?" He pretends to look around us. "Did someone have sex tonight? Wasn't me." His eyes are wide and comically innocent, and I can't help giggling.

"Me neither." I sober a little. "I felt like maybe I could have, though."

Micah flops back on my bed with a groan. "Stupid Hozier."

Another small giggle erupts past my lips, and I sink down next to him, facing the ceiling. "Stupid Hozier," I agree.

Micah raises up on one elbow, his expression serious and full of something new. "I have an idea, but I don't want you to feel pressured."

I cover my eyes. "If you're going to advocate for the pull-out method, don't."

He snorts. "Um, definitely not."

I press my fingers to my warm cheeks. "I can't believe I said that. Sorry. What were you thinking?"

"Do you trust me?"

My voice is tiny when I say it, but I do. "Yes."

"I want to show you that things between a guy and a girl

can be amazing, even without sex. I want to do something for you. If you can trust me. To touch you, I mean."

My heart literally stops. I swear it pauses beating for a full ten seconds. I don't breathe. I don't move. But on the inside, my brain is whirring. Could I do that? Could I let him touch me?

I close my eyes, blocking out the tenderness in his. I need to think.

The thing is, the Bible doesn't lay out the rules for this part. Sex, yes, but touching? Or maybe it does, but not in specific detail, and maybe I need details. Or maybe we're meant to presume from the outline of standards that this is off-limits, which was fine Before Micah, but now I find I am verrrrrry interested in the logistics. Can a man and woman touch before marriage?

Probably not. Right? But also, people were marrying strangers, and women were basically sold off to the highest bidder, and didn't King Solomon have, like, seven hundred wives? And like, three hundred mistresses? So, was that the ancient workaround? Can't have sex until marriage? Marry them all!

Ugh. This is very complicated. I want to turn my brain off. I want to forget all the things I've been told and just live. For once in my life, I want to *be*. Why does everything have to have eternal consequences? What kind of bullshit is that, anyway?

Without opening my eyes, I make a choice. I lean toward him, wrapping my fingers around the back of his neck and relishing the softness of his hair. "Yes," I whisper. I place a kiss on his lips, savoring the sweetness there, before pressing closer and opening my mouth to him for the zillionth time tonight. This I like. This I've gotten better at, if his enthusiasm is any measure. Micah's hands find my hips like before and squeeze. With my other hand, I find his heart under his dress shirt. It's racing as fast as mine, and that's what causes me to pull him over on top of me. We lay there a long time, kissing and feeling. Exploring each other's mouths. Tasting and loving.

Because I do love him. Maybe I'm not ready to tell him yet. It feels early and scary to admit it after only knowing him a few months.

But I show him with every exhale and lick and whisper. And he shows me. His sure hands cupping and caressing me over my dress. His body, firm and strong on top of me. This time, unabashedly pressing against me *right there,* causing us both to gasp over and over with every brush.

And when his fingers dance along the hem of my dress, and his eyes seek mine for permission, I lay my hand over his and lead him underneath.

20

~~~~~~~~~

Micah

I'm in love with her, and this is the best way I know how to show her.

Please, please, please, for all that is good and holy and right, let her *feel* it.

21

~~~~

Meg

It starts with tiny breaths and fluttering lashes
Rolling hips and whispered pants that build and stretch
Until
Trembling
Shaking
Quaking
Gasping
Singing
Praying
Stars and fire and lightning strikes
Blink and wink and glitter and fade
Until
All my shattered pieces fuse back together around him
Him
Him
Forever him

NOVEMBER

22

Micah

I've been running a lot more lately, and for once, it's not because of my dad. Well, mostly. I'm still being stupid over the fact that he hasn't sought me out. And my sisters insist on sending me the articles popping up online, recapping the entire fucking debacle, weeks later. It's been a month since he was released on probation, and I can't wait to forget he ever existed.

No, I'm running, sometimes twice a day, because of Meg.

I imagine this feeling will go away eventually. Probably after our last kid graduates from college. I'm considering taking up running ultramarathons. What's a hundred miles, give or take?

Duke thinks it's hilarious. Like right now. When Meg stops by the Outfitters on her way to work, she's wearing high-waisted jeans and a cropped sweater with a pair of brand-new Columbia boots. Objectively, the least sexy outfit ever.

Except I can't stop staring at her. Her hair is piled on her head, black bangs tucked back, drawing all my worldly focus onto the delicate shell of her ear. Today she has half a dozen tiny hoops glittering, and it's driving me out of my skin.

Which only proves the whole modesty argument really is bunk. She could be in a potato sack and I would find something to obsess over.

So, yeah. I'm in a near-constant state of hot and bothered. So much so that I am using the term *hot and bothered*.

"Did I tell you Vada is coming?" Meg asks, startling me out of my staring.

"Best friend Vada is coming?"

"And Luke! They are flying in for Thanksgiving. James said they could stay with us."

"Flying in where, exactly?" I ask. We're hours from the closest major airport.

"Green Bay."

I raise an eyebrow, and Meg bats her eyelashes. I didn't know she knew how to do that, but man, she's good at it.

"Hey, Micah," she sings.

Duke sniggers from behind the rack of down jackets he's organizing.

"Yes, Meg?"

"Can we road trip down to Green Bay to pick them up in two weeks?" Part of me still does a mental fist pump whenever she talks in future tense. Even if it's only weeks in the future. I mean, I obviously have her Christmas gift already picked out, but it's nice to have it reciprocated.

I pretend to be annoyed. She bites her lip, smoothing a finger in between my so-called grouchy eyebrows that she loves so much.

"Please?" she asks softly.

Duke groans. I let the corner of my mouth quirk. "I

suppose. But get me the date so I can make sure Dani doesn't schedule me."

Meg raises on her tiptoes and gives me a quick kiss on the cheek before a glance at the clock behind the register has her rushing next door for the start of her shift. The store is quiet, and for a full minute, it stays that way.

"Do you need to take a break?" Duke asks mildly.

"I'm good," I bite back.

"I can cover if you need to go for a little jog."

"Thanks, I'm fine."

"Did Meg get a new cartilage cuff?" he asks, gesturing to the tip of his ear. "Right here? I swear I haven't seen that one before."

"Fuck you."

Duke barks out a laugh, shaking his head. "Does she know about your earring fetish?"

"It's not a fetish."

"It's something."

"Aren't you supposed to be on a tour?"

"Canceled due to the snow."

I look outside to the dry street. "What snow?"

Duke pulls an outlandish orange down coat off the hanger and slips it over his shoulders. "The cold front that's supposed to start this afternoon. Don't you watch the weather?"

"I haven't gotten an alert yet." I pull out my phone and glance at the screen. I have weather alerts set up as notifications. Part of the deal post-graduation from search-and-rescue training is being on call at all times and part of *that* deal is always knowing what the weather is doing.

"Wait. You're right. There's a weather watch. I put my

phone on silent." Last night. My mom and Brian asked me to babysit for them, and Meg and I were texting all night.

I also have a call from an unknown number and a voice mail. Leaving Duke in charge of the counter, I head to the back before pressing Play. I listen three times through before I can comprehend it, and each time, I feel a little differently about it, cycling through fury, annoyance, and a little bit of curiosity. I walk to the front, and Duke is still arranging coats. Business has been slow all afternoon, likely due to the coming snow. Fat flurries are beginning to fall on the street.

"Anything wrong?" Duke's stopped with his fussing and is watching me with a speculative stare.

I slump onto a stool behind the checkout counter. "I don't know. The weirdest thing happened. I got a phone call for an interview from a guy who writes for a progressive Christian magazine."

"Progressive how?"

"Progressive like they seem to genuinely want to interview me about the aftermath of my dad's downfall, about how our church abandoned us and left us to rot. They aren't afraid to represent all sides of a story. They're definitely talking about church corruption here but also want to give us a chance to talk about our experience."

Duke whistles low. "That's good, right?"

I scrub a hand down my face. "I don't know."

"Worth a phone call, at least?"

"Maybe. Five minutes ago, I would have said I never wanted to talk about this again . . . that I want to let it fade away."

"But it hasn't."

"Exactly," I agree with a frustrated groan. "It's been

years, and every time I think it's finally over, another round starts."

"Okay."

"So, maybe I should consider this?"

"It's only a phone call. You aren't committing to anything."

"And it's a chance to control my own narrative."

"Definitely. If nothing else, you get your say. Micah," Duke says, his tone serious, "this could be a game changer for you and your family."

"Or it could be the worst idea ever and they're just trying to fuck with us."

Duke snorts good-naturedly. "Won't know until you ask."

The bell over the door rings, and a customer comes in, ending our conversation. But as the snow starts to stick to the windowsill, I consider what it might be like to have my say after all this time.

Later that night, Meg and I are getting off work when Duke calls to say he's at Emily's new boyfriend's place and is too drunk to drive home. Duke doesn't even really like Emily, but her friends are older and can buy alcohol. Which isn't really a thing he cares that much about. Until recently. He must be getting more shit at home.

He's waiting on the curb when we pull up, and he swings open the back passenger door, throwing his body on the seat in a beer-soaked huff.

"You sure you want to go home?" I ask. It's barely nine thirty. "Want to grab some food first?"

"Nah. Just puked up my dinner, thanks. I'm good. David and Laura are out of town."

"Ah." That explains a lot.

"Before he left, he made sure to mention that I'm not to have any visitors. Bought a fucking nanny cam. Told me he would be checking it regularly."

Meg laughs, but at my look, she cuts off. "Wait, seriously?"

Duke ignores her. "'No guests, Duke. Female *or male*. They won't be tolerated.'"

"Shit," I mutter, flipping my blinker. Meg looks stricken in the light of the passing cars.

The car is silent for several long minutes before Meg clears her throat. "Duke?" she asks softly.

His eyes are closed, and he's laying his head back on the seat. "Yes, my heart?"

Meg's lips press together tremulously, and she turns in her seat to face Duke. "I love you. You know that, right? Micah, too. You're enough just as you are."

"Too much at times, even," I say, smiling at him in the mirror so he knows I'm mostly kidding.

"I know," he says quietly, his lips curling into a small grin. "But I gotta get the hell out of here."

"I know some people, Duke," Meg says. "I hope you don't think I've overstepped, but my dear friend Luke? He and his twin brother are both away at college. They'll be home for Christmas break, but their parents? Charlie and Iris? They're used to having a lot of kids around and have been pretty lonely. They'd love to have you stay with them in Ann Arbor for a little bit."

Duke sits up, opening his eyes. "Really?"

"Absolutely."

"Okay, but, uh, are they like your mom? Are they sure? Would they need to meet me first, because—"

Meg is already shaking her head and laughing. "Not at all like my mom. In fact, the opposite of my mom. Luke is dating my best friend Vada, but Cullen, his brother, has been with his boyfriend for four years now. They are a very loving and open family. Also, Charlie used to be some British punk icon? In like, the '80s or '90s?"

"Not Charlie Greenly."

"Um, yeah?"

"Of the Bad Apples. *That* Charlie Greenly. Are you serious right now?"

Meg shrugs. "I mean. I don't really listen to punk, but—"

Duke shoves forward in his seat and places a sloppy kiss on Meg's cheek. Even in the dark, I can see the sheen of tears in his eyes.

I squeeze Meg's hand. I'm overwhelmed. She smiles at me. "Okay," she says. "I'll call tomorrow. If you need out sooner than Christmas, though—"

"No. That's fine," he says. "After Christmas is perfect. Just knowing I'm almost out of here is everything."

"I'll drive you down," I say. "So, if you need to leave sooner, let me know, okay?"

Duke nods, silent now. We pull into his drive a few minutes later, and he walks up his steps in the dark. I wait until he flips a light on in the house before pulling out.

"Well. Now what?"

"I could eat," Meg says.

"I think Burrito Grill is still open."

She moans. "Oh, yum. I love their hot sauce. It's not as good as Chela's back home, but it's a very close second."

I turn onto 41 and head for the restaurant. The snowfall from earlier has stopped, so we order our burritos to go, and instead of parking in the lot, I cut perpendicular behind campus and head out of town on Big Bay Road. After a few minutes, I pull onto a dirt road that leads to a bunch of cabins and a lake. Out here, you can nearly pull all the way to the edge of the water. It's dark, but the moon is full, and the clouds have cleared so its reflection off the still-as-glass lake bathes everything it touches in a soft silvery glow.

"You said the phone call went well?"

Meg and I haven't had a chance to talk since I told her about the reporter when I stopped in briefly on my break.

"I think so. I'm still being cautious, and I didn't guarantee them anything. I need to talk with my family first."

"What do you think they'll say?"

I release my breath slowly. "Good question. My mom and Brian might not like it. They want it all to disappear. Or at least they did. But since I talked to my mom a few weeks ago, she's seemed softer? Lately? She might understand better where I'm coming from now. So maybe she'll realize this is something I need to do for myself."

"It's incredibly brave."

"You think?" I grunt. "Maybe I don't want to do it, then."

She smacks my arm. "I just mean that you're facing down the masses. Allowing yourself to be vulnerable to strangers to get the truth out there. That takes courage."

"Yeah. Definitely don't want to do that," I joke.

"Want me to do it with you?"

I stare at her. "You'd do that?"

"I'm with *you*, Micah. Whatever comes."

"What if this goes to hell again and people start judging me on the internet?"

"They probably will. It's inevitable. Anytime someone is vulnerable, they open themselves up to strangers purposely misunderstanding them for their own devices."

"That's very . . ."

"Cynical?"

"I was going to say *accurate*."

She points at me. "Now *that* is cynical. But yeah. Last year, Luke wrote this love song about Vada. Like totally anonymously in the privacy of his bedroom. But his brother overheard it and thought it was good. And it was! Like super amazing and swoony. So anyway, Cullen thinks he's doing Luke a solid and releases the song on their podcast. But it goes viral. Like overnight. Like gangbusters, and all of a sudden, there are a gazillion strangers on the internet commenting and criticizing Luke's song."

"That sounds awful."

"Sort of. I mean, it definitely was at the time. But also, it ended up bringing Luke and Vada together. Eventually. And Luke's songs ended up saving the bar where they work, which helped Vada get this incredible internship at *Rolling Stone*."

"Really?"

Meg waves me off. "Yeah. So, while it's true that it was terrible, a lot of amazing things came out of it. Which I think could be the case here. Like, sure, there is a good chance that you are opening yourself up to speculation. But what if there are others like you? Scratch that." She shakes her head. "There are *absolutely* others like you. Think of all the garbage the church is going through these days! How many pastors' kids are struggling with trying to find their place? Stuck between their obligations to their families and the expectations of their parents' congregations? And that's not even the kids dealing with corruption."

"That's a lot of pressure."

"You have broad shoulders. You can carry it."

"Maybe," I say. "I'll think about it."

"Good." Meg turns the radio on low, scooting her seat back a bit and tucking her feet under her. She hums while we eat, and our conversation is light but comfortable.

"Poor Duke," she says suddenly. "Think he'll be feeling that in the morning?"

"Probably, but at least this time, he has something positive to look forward to." I squeeze her hand. "He does this every few months. Usually after his dad says something extra shitty to him. He'll overdrink, get sick, swear to never do it again, and doesn't for a while, but then it starts all over again."

"And you never join him?"

I shake my head. "I really don't. I rarely go to parties, honestly. I don't like the noise, and inevitably, someone will recognize me as *that pastor's kid,* and it's just not a road I want to go down."

Meg tilts her head. "Did anyone recognize you at the Halloween party? Besides Emily, I mean?"

I grin. "Nope. If they saw me, I doubt they noticed anything other than my beautiful girlfriend."

She beams a smile at me. "You're sweet. I could barely concentrate on anyone at all. Micah in a suit is like a whole new level, and I am totally here for it."

I snicker but feel my cheeks heat.

Meg crumples up her burrito wrapper, adopting a dreamy look. "All I could think about was how lucky I am to be dating a pro wrestler."

"No."

"Competitive bass fisherman."

"Not a chance."

"Hockey player."

I don't say anything.

Meg's head turns to me in slow motion, her eyes wide and full of glee. "You play *hockey*?"

"Only in a club league. We start up again next week, actually."

"You play hockey."

"And lots of other things, but technically, yes. I *am* a hockey player."

Her eyes take on a mischievous glint. "And I am a former competitive figure skater, which means—"

"Stop."

"—we are like, six degrees from my all-time favorite rom-com—"

"Don't say it."

"*The Cutting Edge*."

"There it is."

She squeals. "I'm serious, Micah! I've watched it a thousand times. Well, most of it. Of course, my mom had some bootlegged, kid-friendly version that was missing the tequila scene—"

"Naturally."

"—but, oh my word, when I saw that with Vada last year!" She slips back happily against her seat with a sigh. "I've always wanted to date a hockey player when I grow up."

"You did not."

"I have! I swear it. Cross my heart, hope to die, stick a needle in my thread."

"That's not how that goes."

"Micah! Be serious."

"I'm finding it difficult, to be honest."

"A grumpy hockey player with magic fingers," she says to herself.

I choke on air. "Excuse me?"

She turns to me, her face probably pink, but in the moonlight I can't tell. "That slipped out."

"I'm not saying I mind."

"It's just that Vada said some girls never feel, um, *that way*. At least not the first time someone touches them. That it sometimes takes a bit of practice. She said you must have magic fingers."

"Yeah?" I ask, inordinately pleased with myself.

"I told her maybe it's got nothing to do with your fingers. Maybe it's just you. And me. Maybe it's the way with us. It's magic."

I think about that. "I can't disagree." Meg tucks her hair behind her ear, earrings glinting, and I swallow hard.

"I was thinking," she continues, "maybe we could try something else and see if it works the same."

"Yeah?"

"Yeah," she says softly, biting her lip. "But this time, I want to do the touching."

I inhale sharply, and my heart thuds. "Are you sure? You don't have to."

She nods, still biting her lip. She moves closer. "Do these seats lean back?"

23

Meg

Figure skating was always a thing that my dad and I had in common. Not Andrew, obviously. Declan and me. Which, now that I think of it, is odd, since it wasn't genetic like I always assumed.

Maybe that makes it more meaningful. Declan knew I wasn't his, but he chose to share this important thing with me. I wonder if it broke his heart when I quit. It left a sharp ache in mine that I still feel.

But the rink helps. Being with these little ones and teaching them how to spin and glide and dance along the smooth expanse of ice carries a potency of healing I never expected.

Which is probably why I don't immediately lash out when I wrap up my final lesson of the afternoon and see Declan waiting in the stands. My stomach lodges somewhere in the vicinity of the center of my chest, but I paste a wide smile on my lips, skating over to where the parents are waiting. I share a few words of encouragement, confirm plans for the upcoming session, and talk to a mother about her daughter's blades, pointing her to the service booth, where they can be sharpened for a few dollars, which will most definitely improve little Cecelia's coordination on her sit spin.

At last, when the final student has left, and the concession stand flips their sign to CLOSED, I take a seat next to my father and work at the laces in my boot, loosening them.

"How in earth did you find me?"

He gestures, and I automatically lift my foot to his outstretched palm. He skillfully plucks at the laces and motions for the other when he's done.

"It took a little work," he says softly. Though, in this ginormous space, even the quietest words carry an echo. "Your mom told me you were working at a coffee shop. I started there. I met a friend of yours. Duke? Nice kid with blue hair? He told me you were here. After interrogating me, of course."

"Duke's got a thing with dads."

Declan nods solemnly. Something tells me he can relate.

"Well, you found me."

"I got your text," he says.

"I wondered. You never responded."

"That's because what I had to say shouldn't be texted. I needed to come and do this in person. And see you and make sure you're okay," he adds. "Which, from the looks of things, you are. It's wonderful to see you on blades again."

"Even if I'm not performing?"

"Even if," he agrees. "I'm sorry if you thought differently. I'm happy if you're happy. That's how being a parent works."

"Dad," I stop him softly. "You haven't been a parent to me in years. You realize that, right?"

He releases a long breath, and I slip into my sturdy winter boots, wiggling my toes at the toasty feeling as the blood rushes back into them. I feel oddly calm for this conversation. I was so overwrought speaking with my mom that I'd assumed I'd be the same with my dad. But then, things have never been overly emotional with Declan. When I was really little, things were so easy between us, and as I got older, I felt more resigned.

"I'm sorry you believe that. On the outside, maybe I haven't been there for you, not like I should, but on the inside, I've always been your dad."

I snort derisively (which I'm getting better at; Vada would be proud), turning to face him on the bench. "That doesn't even make sense."

"I didn't think you needed me." His jaw clenches momentarily, and I take in the dark circles under his eyes and the sharpened cut of his cheekbones. He's not taking care of himself.

"That sounds like bullshit."

His eyes widen, his lips pressing together. He almost looks amused, but in a flash, he's back to remorseful. "Fine," he relents. "That's fair. I can't believe you just swore in front of me, but you're an adult."

"Are you gay?" I ask, before I lose my nerve. "It's okay if you—"

He lets out a slow, shaky breath and nods. "I . . . Yes—I am."

I wait him out, conflicted. I want to congratulate him on finally telling the truth but kick him for everything else.

"I always have been," he admits. "Obviously. In my family, that wasn't allowed. In fact"—he presses his hands to his thighs—"it was basically the worst thing you could be. Next to a murderer. And you could be forgiven for murder," he jokes weakly.

"Does Mom know?"

He gives a small smile. "She's always known. She was my best friend. We knew all each other's secrets. We also knew our families and our church. We knew exactly what our secrets could do to us if they got out. So, I offered to marry her and raise you as my own."

"Why would you give up everything? I don't understand. You had your entire lives ahead of you."

His grin is sardonic. "Did we, though? Your mom was eighteen and pregnant with a stranger's baby. A stranger who she found out had died. I was a gay kid in a conservative family. I couldn't have fallen in love for real. Back then, gay marriage was illegal, so even if I had managed to fall in love with a man, I couldn't marry him and start a family. It didn't feel like such a sacrifice, honestly. It was more like an answer to a prayer for two kids in a jam. A chance at happiness, even if it wasn't what we dreamed of."

I shake my head. "But you weren't happy," I said. "You can't lie to me. I saw it. Everyone saw it. For years, you two have been strangers in the same house. I thought it was because of me. Because I quit skating."

Declan straightens. "Meg, no. Absolutely not. Nothing like that. I was sad when you quit, but only because figure skating was our thing. It was what we had in common. Maybe the only thing. And when you stepped down, I wasn't sure if it was because of church or because of your mom or because you truly wanted out. Not knowing for sure? That bothered me more than I can say. Your mother and I let church dictate our lives. I didn't want the same for you. I wanted you to have your chance. But there you were, as perfect as could be. So joyful in your love of Jesus, singing in the worship band, attending youth group lock-ins. And your mom had you dressing so modestly . . .

"Meg, it was like you wilted when you got your first period."

Oh *God*.

He laughs at the look of horror on my face. "Sorry, but it's true. You were barely thirteen, and all of a sudden, you were covering up and staying away from the rink and boys and homeschooling double time, and it just . . . felt like you were repeating our mistakes. It made me sick inside."

"Why didn't you say something?"

He settles back on his elbows, stretching his body between two rows of bleachers, and grimaces. "I don't know. I guess I didn't feel like it was my place. Your mom was doing the best she knew how to keep you from following in her footsteps. In all honesty, it wasn't healthy, but who was I to talk? I've been hiding my true self for decades."

"So, you just let her? You fell off the face of the Earth and let her have free rein?"

"I did try, once. A few Christmases back. Your mom showed me the card from your great-grandmother, and I told her we should let you meet her before it got to be too late. I said if Betty passed away and you found out afterward that you could have known her, you would never forgive us."

I grunt in approval. He sighs.

"Which worked out anyway, obviously. But not in the best way. At the time, however, your mom refused. She didn't want you to know about her getting pregnant out of wedlock. She was afraid you might act out and repeat her choices."

"And that was enough for you to keep quiet? Wow," I

sulk. "You guys don't have a whole lot of faith in me, do you? No offense, but I know about birth control. Something she clearly did not."

"Stop. That's enough. I hope you're only being flippant because you're angry. Because that's way oversimplifying what your mom went through at an age younger than you are now. And no, that wasn't enough to keep me quiet. She also reminded me that coming clean about her past meant coming clean about mine, and I wasn't ready. It was selfish of me, but there you are."

"Because of me or because of you?" I ask.

"Hmm?" he asks mildly.

"You weren't ready because of you or because of me?"

"Both," he admits. "I've been living as a miserable straight man for thirty-six years. I don't know how to be gay. Or happy. And it did cross my mind, every day, twice a day, that you might not approve of my sexuality, which happens to mean more to me than the grand total of the world's opinion." He pins me with his gaze, his dark brown eyes warm behind his glasses frames. "You might not be my biological daughter, Meg, but you are my girl. You have been since the first time you opened your eyes and saw straight into my soul."

"You aren't the first gay person I know, Dad."

"But I'm the first gay *dad* you know. It's different. What happens if I bring someone home to meet you one day? How would you feel about that?"

"I get what you're saying," I admit. "And a few years ago, I might've been uncomfortable. But I might not have been. No matter what I learned in youth group, you supersede that. You always have. Same with Mom. And if my parents had trusted me with their truths, how much sooner could I have figured out mine?"

I shake my head. "You chose for me, and I'm sorry, but I think you chose wrong. What's worse is, I think you *knew* that. You knew how awful those choices made you both feel—you knew everything you'd been forced to put aside and give up, and you chose to let me do the same. Like, do you realize how cruel that is? I had to move ten hours away to figure it out!

"And you did it to protect yourself. And I get it. I do. I can't begin to understand how painful this has been for you. I get how messed up you've been over it, for decades, even. That's unreal, and I'm so sorry. I'm sorry if I made you feel like you weren't worthy of my love, because that's just not true. But, Dad—Declan . . ." I hear the pleading in my voice, but I'm proud of myself for not crying. It seems I'm always crying. I'm tired of crying. "You have to stop this. Today. I'm not saying you need to out yourself. That's your decision, and I can't make it for you. But you need to stop living a lie."

"Your mom signed the divorce papers. We're no longer married."

I shouldn't be relieved, but I am. As much as I wish it weren't this way, it's the only way that's survivable for everyone. The only way that's real.

"Good," I say.

"I found a place outside town. In downtown Dexter. It's a rental, but it's cute and affordable."

"Okay."

"And . . . I met someone. Just online, but we've been talking a lot. Both recent divorcés. Mine more recent than his, obviously. We're taking things really slowly. This is a first-time thing for us both."

My smile is quick and genuine. "That's great, Dad. Truly."

He shrugs, his head dancing on his shoulders. "Maybe. I don't know." Declan leans forward on his knees, his hands clasped together in front of him. He rubs at the vacant spot on his ring finger.

"I'm sorry, Meg."

I lean forward to match him. "Thank you."

"Everything you said is right. I've been selfish."

I shake my head. "You've been scared."

"You are worth bravery."

I glance sideways at him, the corner of my mouth lifting. "I've been working on growing my own. It's not a terrible thing." I take in the empty ice in front of us, struck with an idea. "What are you doing after this?"

Declan catches on. "I was hoping to spend time with my kid. I booked a room for a few days. My schedule is wide open."

"Fantastic. Let's get you some skates."

"I haven't seen your wings around . . ." Declan trails off, with every appearance of nonchalant-ness, as he flips through the giant menu at the family diner we're sitting in. We're meeting Betty and James here, along with Micah and Dani. You know, just to get all the awkward introductions over with in one fell swoop. We're early, though, because Declan, despite recent complications, is too much of a dad to be late. The place is loud and clang-y and has an unusual collection of old-fashioned fenders affixed to the walls.

Which I'm not noticing right now, because I'm purposely not looking up from my menu, not wanting to meet his eyes. "I left them at home. Or, well, at Mom's place, I guess."

"All of them?"

"Yup."

"Is this a 'growing up' kind of thing or an 'I'm sad and can't bear feathers' kind of thing or 'my new boyfriend won't approve of wings so I'm changing for him' kind of thing?"

"Woooooow."

He raises a brow, the corner of his mouth lifting in a faux severe smirk that can be interpreted as "You wanted a dad, so you've got one, Meg" plain as day.

I raise one right back, closing the menu with a *slap*. Well, a *slap, slap,* since it's a trifold of epic and confusing proportions. "It's a combination of the first two. But in reverse order. At first, I was too sad and angry. Then, I decided I was probably too old for wings and it was time to leave them behind. My boyfriend, *Micah*," I say, enunciating his name over several extra syllables, "has only seen the wings in pictures, but took them in stride."

"Well, I'm a little sad to see them go, but I suppose it's your choice."

"Actually, and I'm only telling you this because I'm eighteen now and you're not my real dad anyway"—I wink, and he rolls his eyes—"I got wings tattooed onto my shoulders."

"Ah." Declan schools his features, but he's struggling with a response. "When?"

"A month or so ago."

"A tattoo is permanent."

"Wait," I deadpan. "It is?"

"Well, okay, then."

"That's it?"

"Are you waiting for me to ground you? Can I see them?"

I pull one shoulder of my sweater down, and he takes in the ink with a soft gasp.

"It's lovely, Meg."

"Thanks."

He shakes his head. "Your mom will murder me when she finds out I saw them first and didn't ground you." He winces at the thought. "But I've always wanted a tattoo, actually."

"Really?"

"Yeah. Of course, mine wouldn't be some misguided attempt at teenage rebellion." His scoff is teasing, but I glare at him.

"Not a thing. If I wanted to rebel, I wouldn't have told you about it."

"Oh. So, you've told your mom?" he asks, tracing a finger in the condensation on his glass of iced tea.

"So she can judge me and tell me that baring my shoulders to a tattoo artist will only lead to fornication? Or that vanity is a sin? Or that needles carry hep C?"

"She's not that bad," he says. But it comes out uncertain, so I don't bother arguing. Besides, I've been wondering about something else.

"Before everyone else gets here, can I ask: What was she like before me?"

"You mean at seventeen?"

I nod.

"She was the kind of girl who radiated happy. Fearless and a flirt, if you can imagine."

The corner of my mouth twitches. "I honestly can't."

"Beautiful and kind. She practically forced me to be her best friend, much like you did to poor Vada back in the day." His eyes hold a hint of teasing. "She fell head over heels for your dad. She likes to play it off like they were these strangers who barely knew each other . . . which is true, truer still in her memories. But meeting him lit a spark inside of her.

That weekend they spent together was her romantic ideal for years. Maybe still is, since she doesn't have anything to compare it to."

I play with my napkin, unfolding and refolding it. "This is sort of surreal, talking to you about this. But nice. Thank you. Were you there when they met?"

His eyes soften. "Actually, yes. They were like two magnets. Completely absorbed from the very first. I watched her watch him during the show, and she was enamored. I'd never seen her so fixated. Afterward, he sought her out and introduced himself. They were making out by the end of the evening, making all of us sick. There was no going back for Amanda once she met Andrew. That they lived so far apart and really only had one weekend to explore each other made it all the more exciting, I think. She gave everything she had and didn't regret it one bit."

Declan leans in as I spot Micah at the entrance. "Don't forget that part, okay? Your mom never regretted what happened with Andrew, and she never regretted you."

24

Micah

Seeing Meg with Declan was an education. It's this glimpse into who she was before she came to the UP and crashed into all our lives. Meg strikes me as someone who has no problem speaking her mind, but I now realize it's a recent development. At least when it comes to her parents. From what she's told me, I can see why, but it blows my mind how far she's come in such a short time.

Seems like it's blown Declan's mind a bit, too. But in a good way. I wasn't sure what to expect from Meg's stepdad. Not a lot, truthfully. She's barely talked about him, whether it was because she was hurt or ambivalent. Turns out, she was definitely hurt by him and his disappearing act, but unlike some people I know, she is ready to forgive and move forward.

Mostly.

There's this underlying tension that speaks to how fresh and raw it still is. Things have yet to marinate and settle down. Declan had to return downstate this morning, and

Meg hasn't talked to her mom yet, but I think she's found a little more peace.

"Want to get dinner after work?" I ask, dropping her off for her shift.

She shakes her head. "Sorry. Can't. Uncle James said he needed to talk to me about something youth group related."

"Okay, I'll text later."

She presses her lips to mine in a lightning-swift move and closes the door behind her, hurrying through the heavy snow to reach the back entrance before I can pull away from the curb. I drive around the block to park in the public lot, and since I have twenty minutes before I'm supposed to start, I pull out my phone right when the alert comes through.

Fuuuuuuuuck.

0900 EST Monday—Missing person report filed for recent parolee out of Manistee, Michigan. Suspected runaway. Silver alert. Has connections in Marquette County. Missed check-in with parole officer. After follow-up, it is suspected man ran away of own volition but might be in danger. Looking for assistance in Pictured Rocks National Lakeshore and surrounding vicinity. Weather advisory. Rapidly decreasing temps and heavy snowfall/high winds expected. Canine rescue preferred.

I jump out of my car, running to the store and whipping open the front door. Duke regards me with startled eyes but is thankfully in the store alone because all I can say is, "Fuck! Fuck that fucker!"

I reach for the landline with shaking fingers and dial

into headquarters, reporting in. My training officer, Cliff, answers on the first ring.

"Micah Allen reporting in." I hear the rustle of Duke coming alongside me. I pass him my phone.

"Micah. I wasn't sure if you were working—"

"It's my dad, isn't it?"

"Yeah."

I swallow down the curse sitting at the back of my throat. "They're sure he's up there?"

"He left a note."

"Goddamn it."

"You don't have to do this."

"Cliff. Cash and I are ready now. How many other canine teams do you have ready?"

"Just you. Jake and Daggett went down to Green Bay for a training exercise."

I shake my head. I don't want to do this. "I'll be there within the hour. I have to swing by home and pick up my gear and Cash."

It won't take long. I have a go bag for this kind of thing. This is my first time out on my own, though. I can't tell if the stakes are higher or lower because it's my dad.

Probably both.

I hang up and turn to Duke. "Go on," he says, having pieced together the situation. "I can watch the store. I'll give Dani a call, but it's gonna be slow as hell with the snowstorm."

"Thanks, man."

"It's really him?"

"It's really him."

Duke hugs me. "Go save his unworthy ass."

I glance next door. "I don't really have time . . ."

"I'll tell Meg where you went. Text her when you get there. Keep us posted."

The snow has started sticking by the time I get home. Cash is antsy when I let him out to go to the bathroom before our drive. We get our assignment and all the paperwork at headquarters before hitting the road again and driving straight to Pictured Rocks to check in at the ranger station. By the time we arrive, there is a solid four inches of powder on the ground, covering all easy leads to my dad. Or anyone.

But that's okay. Cash is the best. We graduated top of our class two weeks ago and are more than ready to prove ourselves. I buckle Cash into his jacket and snow gear, including protective booties to save his feet from getting torn up in the frozen brush.

I triple-check my pack to make sure I have plenty of supplies for both Cash and me, and I layer up. Hiking will warm us up, but I don't want to risk sweating and flash freezing when the weather drops or I get stuck somewhere.

Before we head out, my phone pings.

MEG: Stay safe. Give Cash a hug for me. I'll be praying for you both!

MEG: I love you.

MEG: Ugh. I wasn't going to say it and then I *had* to say it because what if something happened but NOTHING is going to happen.

MEG: You totally don't have to say it back.

MEG: I'm rambling.

I'm smiling so hard, my face hurts. I lean down, giving Cash a hug, and then write back.

MICAH: You're totally rambling.

MICAH: I love you, too. I'll call you tonight.

Five soaking and miserable hours later, I'm about to give up. It's freezing, and I'm tired. Ranger Cade had to return to the station for his shift change. I said I'd follow him in but wanted to check the Blue Dash trail before I came in for the night. It's starting to get dark, and while the snow has stopped, the wind is bitter as ever. Blue Dash is barely a mile-long loop. If I were running from my responsibilities and the police, I would definitely pick something longer and more complicated.

But my dad preemptively mailed a letter to his probation officer. One that made it seem like he was looking for a quiet place to fade away. Permanently. He's unstable, and that, paired with the cold temps, could mean he's not thinking clearly.

If nothing else, I can check this off my list of places to try in the morning.

But three quarters of a mile in, Cash hits on something. I follow him off trail into the brush another several hundred feet, and something bright catches my eye. Cash barks and points, the way he's been taught, and I lean over to look. It's a dark knit hat. With the recent snow, and this hat resting on top, it has to be my dad's, but it's alarming that it's not on him.

I straighten, making a full circle and scanning the woods for any clue as to what direction he might have gone in. I squint, my breath making clouds around me as Cash's hackles rise. I whip around at the sharp sound of his bark when a blinding flash of pain throbs at the back of my head and everything goes dark.

I open my eyes to blackness, and for a panicked moment, I think I've gone blind.

Cash whines and licks my face, and finally, I see a dull flicker of light on the ceiling. I blink a few times. I'm in a cave.

My skull feels like it's going to split in two, but I raise myself on my elbow, groaning. And there he is. My father. Fanning a small flame that's more smolder than light. He looks terrible. If I didn't know it was him, I'd have never picked him out in a crowd. He's older, and smaller looking somehow. Shriveled. Sunken in on himself as he's hunched over his pathetic fire. My dad was never much of an outdoorsman.

"What are you doing?" I croak. "You're going to kill us. There's no air vent in here."

"Ah, he's awake."

I rise up the rest of the way and squint against the sting of smoke.

"Where's the vent?" I ask. Hacking.

"It's there right above our heads. It's only smoky because the leaves are wet. I had a hell of a time getting the fire to catch."

I prod the back of my head and suck in a breath sharply as my stomach swoops in pain. I swallow back bile and pull my fingers away to see blood. A lot of it. My stomach roils again. This isn't good.

"Did you hit me?" I ask, incredulous.

"I told them I didn't want anyone to come find me."

"Yeah, well, apparently, 'Leave me alone with my feelings'

isn't a federally approved excuse to miss your probation check-in."

His eyes narrow, taking me in fully. I swallow against another wave of dizziness, my breath caught in my throat. Can he tell?

"I wasn't skipping out on my probation, I wanted to be left to die. Who are you anyway? Your coat says *Search and Rescue*. With what agency?"

"You seriously don't know me?"

He blinks in the growing firelight, clearly uncomfortable. This is definitely not how I pictured this going down, particularly since I suspect my dad is the reason my skull feels like it's been cracked open.

"I've been in prison, kid," he scoffs.

"Yeah. I know. For nearly six years. You missed my baseball tryouts."

His grizzled jawline jerks in recognition.

"Micah?"

I nod, squeezing my eyes shut against the pain.

After a long pause, he shakes his head. "Unbelievable. Of all the people—" he mutters. "I just wanted to be left alone." He glances up at the ceiling of the cave as if he's praying. "Enough already! And all of a sudden, my long-lost kid turns up to save the day—"

I cut him off, fighting tunnel vision. I'm going to lose consciousness again soon, and this self-absorbed asshole is more concerned with his failed suicide mission. "First of all, I'm not your long-lost kid. I've been here all along. You were the lost one." He's cradling his arm to his chest when I focus on him. "What happened to you?"

"Your dog doesn't like me."

That makes me happy, at least. I rub Cash behind the

ears, crooning weakly, "Gooood boyyyy, Cash. Such a good boy." Cash licks my face with another whine. If it's possible for a dog to look concerned, he does. Yeah. This is not ideal. I squint in the darkness, trying to get my bearings, but my head throbs with every blink, and all I want to do is close my eyes and take a nap.

Fuck, this was a bad idea.

"I can't believe it's really you. You're grown."

"It was bound to happen."

"How tall are you?"

I level him with a look. Or at least I try to. "Where's my phone? We need to get out of here. What time is it?"

"I crushed it. Threw it against a rock."

I turn to my dad slowly, or maybe it only feels that way because of my head injury. "Are you kidding?"

"I told you. I came here to die. I don't need to be rescued."

I stare at him a long minute. The light flickering from the growing fire deepens the lines in his face.

"You're planning to starve to death?"

My dad holds up a gun. "Not letting it get that far."

I grit my teeth. "Well, you can't do that *now*. I'm here. You've already fucked me up enough. You sure as hell aren't shooting yourself in front of me."

"Then I suggest you leave. You said it yourself, you're not the lost one. What's it to you?"

I groan against the throb in my skull, feeling a warm trickle down the back of my neck. "I don't have the energy for this, Dad. I'm not here to convince you to live your life. I'm here to fucking search for and rescue you. So, let me do my job."

"You found me. You can leave now." His voice trembles,

and it's suddenly clear to me that he's not brave enough to do this. "I'm not going back to prison, Micah."

I settle back. Angry and sad and exhausted. "Dad. I can't leave you like this."

"I left you."

"You sure did. But I'm a different kind of man than you are."

"No one would blame you for walking out. Your mom, even."

"Oh, she would definitely blame me. You'd be surprised at the amount of blame I've gotten for things out of my control." The way I see it, I don't have a whole lot of time to negotiate. Best to lay it on the proverbial table. "So, you decide. I'm cold and bleeding pretty bad and probably going to die of hypothermia if I pass out from blood loss. If that happens, it will be your fault. You want to kill yourself? Then you'll have to kill me, too."

You jump, I jump, I think wryly.

"Someone will come for you," he says, but even I know he's not certain.

"Probably," I say. "But will they come in time? It's dark, and Cash won't leave me. He's no Lassie." Duke could find me, maybe. But who knows if he's on his way or still in Marquette working, thinking I let my phone die.

My phone never dies.

Duke *has* to be on his way.

"I didn't ask for you to come here."

I want to punch him, but I barely have the energy to keep my eyes open. "I didn't ask for any of this, period. But here we are." *Please, God, please don't let my dad fail me. Please get us out of here.* "So, Dad. Are you going to save me, or are you going to kill us both?"

25

Meg

I know something is wrong when Duke comes in at the end of my shift, looking . . . bland-ish.

"I don't suppose you've heard from him?" he asks.

"No. But it's still early. Barely seven."

Duke shakes his head. "It's been dark for over an hour. I have a bad feeling."

"Because Micah is the most responsible human being on the planet and would never wait this long to check in?"

He nods.

"Me, too," I say in a rush. "Maybe his phone died."

"He has extra battery power in his pack."

"Maybe he found his dad and it's taking longer to retrieve him."

Duke slumps on a stool. "When are you done?"

Maria comes out from the back carrying a rag and glances out the window. "She can be done now. It's too messy out for crowds."

"Are you sure?" I check. "If you need me—"

"You're no good to me. Go on. Check in with James or

Brian. They might have an idea how to get in touch with the ranger station nearest to where Micah was out. He's probably there."

Duke drives, and I start calling. I try Micah but only get his voice mail. Like he's turned his phone off. Which isn't likely under the circumstances. Next, I call James, only because I don't have Brian's number, and I don't want to show up at the house and scare anyone. James tells me he's going to call Brian and get back to me. Meanwhile, Duke and I decide to drive to Pictured Rocks.

It might be impulsive, and I really hope Micah is hanging out with the rangers and makes fun of us for panicking . . . but.

But.

I start praying. Begging. My stomach is sick. Duke is pale as a ghost, his fingers white knuckling the steering wheel as he works to keep his beater Subaru on the slushy road.

The car is silent. I try Micah's phone again. No answer.

"He's trained for this," I say. "Right? Like, this is his training. At the store, sure, with all the tours and everything, but also at school. This is his job."

"Right."

"I mean, if you were with him, you could survive a night in the woods, no problem."

"For sure. And Micah is in prime shape. He's completely prepared for every eventuality and the smartest guy I know."

I release a slow breath. "So, it's fine. He's fine."

"As long as he's not hurt."

"Cash would never leave him. Micah saved him. Cash will protect him."

"True."

"Duke, I *have* to believe he's okay. So, let's believe he's okay."

He nods, and I've gone back to praying when my phone rings.

"Hello?"

"You and Duke are on your way?" James asks.

"Yeah."

"The ranger said Micah never checked in at the shift change. He was checking one last mile-long trail and was supposed to come in after that. So, they have an idea of where to look, but it's dark. They are calling in another ranger and the lead conservation officer in the area, but it's going to take a little while because of the weather. Can you put me on speaker?"

After I do, I hold up the phone so James's voice echoes in the car. "Brian and I are leaving now, but, Duke?"

"Yeah?"

"You're probably the best bet for finding where Micah went off trail. You know him, and you two have been on all sorts of adventures. When you get there, don't wait for us. You go ahead and hit the last trail Micah went on. Meg?"

"Yeah?"

"Be honest. Can you handle this? I know you've been running, but the snow is going to make this hike a challenge. It won't do anyone any good if you are holding Duke back."

I work at being objective. He doesn't mean to insult me. Everyone is just worried about Micah, including me. But I have been running. Every morning, on top of teaching at the rink. I really do feel like I can handle this.

"I can do this. I promise I won't hold anyone back."

James lets out a slow breath. "All right, then. Don't stray

from the trail. Stay in contact with us. Are your phones charged?"

"Mine is," Duke says.

"Mine's plugged in now," I say.

"Okay. Are you close?"

"About fifteen miles."

"Check in with the ranger station, load up on safety supplies, and be safe. We don't need to lose two more people tonight."

"Okay, Uncle James."

"I'm praying, guys. We're gonna find them."

I hang up, and Duke and I start making plans. Which is the best thing possible. Turns out, Duke has a similar go bag to Micah in his trunk. They play in the woods so much, he's perpetually prepared. When we arrive at the station, we check in, get our directions, and head back out to Duke's trunk to load up on gear. The second ranger is on his way in, but we decide to go out without him. I get the impression that the ranger on duty thinks Duke is another search-and-rescue graduate, likely because of his gear.

We don't confirm or deny. We just hit the trail.

I used to love snow. It's so beautiful and pure. How many freaking worship songs talk about being white as snow? About how sin is wiped away by God's grace and redemption, just as snow erases any trace of darkness and dirt on earth?

Know what else snow wipes away?

Your missing boyfriend's footprints.

We could really use a rescue dog right now.

My headlamp bobs, casting wicked shadows along the

trail. I think of the night hike Micah and I took, when he told me moonlight was better than any flashlight. I trip on a snow-covered root and mutter a curse. Another reason to hate snow. Its cloud cover blocks the moonlight.

Duke's headlamp swings back to check on me. "You sure you don't want to lead? Two lights are better than one," he says.

I wave him off. "No, thanks. We'll make more progress with you in front."

"Are you warm enough?" he asks. I want to roll my eyes at his tone. I'm not the one he should be worried about.

"I'm fine. And I'm plenty sure on my feet. Figure skater, remember? Just keep going. It was only a tree root."

Duke nods once, making the light swim, and starts forward. I heft my pack. Duke has rations and camping gear in case we get caught overnight. I have the first aid gear that I really, *really* hope is only a precaution. Every moment that passes in this silent wood, however, makes that hope seem implausible. We're making slow progress, mostly because Duke is being hypervigilant. The snow dusted over the trail pretty thoroughly, but with the tree cover off trail, he thinks there's a good chance we'll see footprints or a disturbance in the powder that hasn't succumbed to the wind or new flakes.

We've been at it an hour and a half, ninety minutes to travel three-quarters of a mile, and there's no sign of anything; a few false alarms where Duke jogged off trail, only to loop back to me within a minute or so. He's started speeding up. It's like following Cash, I imagine. I can't tell if he's moving at a faster pace because his gut is telling him we're on the right track or if, like me, it's the passing of time. If Micah somehow got hurt . . .

"I'm gonna start calling out for Cash," I say. "We only have a quarter mile left."

Duke releases a sigh, his breath puffing out between us. He didn't want us to because he was afraid that would give away our position, and if Micah was in danger . . .

"It's his dad," I say softly. "I know he's a terrible human being, but I can't imagine he's going to hurt Micah. We're running out of time. If Micah were safe, he'd have turned up already."

Duke looks skeptical.

"Cash will come to me. I'm sure of it. And he wouldn't leave Micah. Just let me try. Last quarter mile."

Duke grimaces. "Okay. Yeah. You're probably right. We need a miracle. The snow's getting pretty heavy again."

I glance up at the sky, the white swirls getting bigger and closer together. Panic wants to strangle in my throat. *Come on, lungs. Don't fail me now.*

"Caaaaaaash!" I start in a singsong voice. "Caaaaaash, baby, it's Meg. Come on, puppy!"

Nothing. Duke tries. "Cash! Here, boy! Cash, Cash, Cash! Whooop!"

I spin around and try again and again and again, until Duke's arm lashes out to cut me off. He turns the way we came and yells, "Cash?!" We hear the distinct cracking of feet over brush.

"Cash! Micah! Come on, puppy! Caaaaaaash!"

He runs up wagging his tail. A sob breaks in my throat as I get down to my knees. Cash jumps into my arms, in full rescue gear, licking and wiggling and barking like mad.

Duke drops to join me. "Cash! Where's Micah? Where is he, boy? Is he with you?"

More footsteps sound, but as they get closer, my stomach drops out. It's not Micah.

Duke surges to his feet. "Where's Micah?"

The older man holds his hands out. "Easy, kid. Are you Duke?"

"Where is Micah?" Duke repeats, his tone deadly.

I'm already crashing through the woods back the way he came with Cash nipping at my heels and barking.

"He's this way," his dad says. "He's injured and couldn't make it out."

I start to run. My steps falter when I see what looks like a lot of blood on the ground and a whole ton of disturbance in the leaves and underbrush.

Duke swings on Micah's dad accusingly. "What happened here?"

"Later," the man says, looking pale. "He doesn't have a lot of time. I thought he was bluffing." He shakes his head. "Just hurry."

Cash isn't waiting around anyway, but Duke looks like he's ready to put his fist through Micah's dad's face. Not that I blame him. I'm not feeling much better.

I grab Duke's arm and shake it once. "Later, Duke. Okay? First Micah, then we can deal with the rest. Please."

Duke gives Micah's dad a final glare, promising to pick it up later, and we take off after the dog. After another few minutes of running, Cash ducks between two edges in the face of a cliff. If I hadn't watched him do it, I'd have missed it.

I'd have missed *him*.

I can't think of that right now.

I sprint into the cave, my pack bouncing hard against my back. I wince. That'll bruise. The light is dim. But there, lying on his side next to a small fire, is Micah. I dive onto the floor, barely noticing the sting in my hands scraping the surface.

"Micah. Micah!" I cry out. His eyes are shut, without even a flutter of movement. I turn to his dad. "What's wrong with him?"

"Hit on the head. He's been bleeding pretty badly but was talking until a few minutes ago. Then he went out like a light. Cash heard your voices, and I ran after him."

"He's too pale," I say. I feel around his collar and find a weak pulse. "Thank you, Jesus," I breathe. "Thank you, Jesus. He's not dead."

"I couldn't move him. He's too heavy, and I didn't want to risk him bleeding more. I wasn't sure—"

"Where's his phone?" Duke interrupts, already pulling out his own and dialing out.

"I crushed it."

Duke advances on Micah's dad, and I stop him with a screech. "Not now! Later! First Micah!" I turn to Micah's dad. "Where's he hurt?"

"The back of his head."

Duke starts explaining in a clear and concise way how to find us. We're only a quarter mile from the end of the loop, but we're probably another quarter mile into the woods, and this cave is literally invisible in the dark.

I grab Micah's pack and rip it open, listing items out loud. "Flares, rations, first aid." I turn to Micah's dad. "What the fuck have you been doing? He has a full first aid kit here."

His dad sinks against the wall of the cave, and I pass the flares to Duke. "Light these. Outside the cave. I'll see to his head wound." I turn to his dad again. "How did he hurt the back of his head?"

"I hit him. With a log. I didn't know who he was."

I gape at him. "You could have killed him."

He starts weeping noisily, and I want to throttle him.

"Useless," I mutter before pulling out the first aid materials and arranging them in front of me. "Triage only, Hennessey." I took first aid and CPR this summer to prep for the dude ranch gig, but I never had reason to use it. Now is as good a time as any, I suppose. I take a deep breath and gently prod along the back of Micah's head, careful not to apply pressure in case there's a break. My stomach heaves at how much blood is warm against my fingers. How is he even still bleeding? Nothing feels shattered, but that doesn't mean there isn't a fracture. I take gauze and gently press it to his skull before wrapping it firmly with some medical-grade tape. When I realize it's still seeping, I do it again.

I let out a shaky breath when, after a few of the scariest moments of my entire life, it starts to slow.

I unwrap hand warmers and triage blankets to pack around his frame, creating as much warmth as I can. Duke is building up the fire, and I move around to Micah's front, huddling close and wrapping my arms around his shoulders as gently as possible. Cash curls up behind him in the curve of his legs, and I choke on tears thinking how Micah once saved Cash the exact same way.

"Please, Jesus," I whisper. "Please don't take him from us." Hot tears slip from my eyes, and I just keep whispering my prayer under my breath and straight up to heaven. "Please, Jesus, please. Please, please, please." I'm in love with this boy, and I want to tell him to his face. I need to tell him. Please, Jesus, *please* let him *hear* it.

26

Micah

It begins with slow breaths and hissing curses
Roiling stomach and whispered groans
Until
Bright lights screaming
Throbbing
Aching
Sobbing
Gasping
Praying
Stars and fire behind my eyes
Blink and wink and glitter and fade
Until
I am awake
and she's there

27

Micah

When I really wake up, it's to the sound of low voices. Strained ones. It takes me longer than I like to remember where I am. The good news is I've made it out of the cave alive. The bad news is my head feels like it's been cracked open, and I suspect that's because it has been.

I try to sit up to see where the voices are coming from, but the stabbing shards of pain are so intense, I give up easily.

"He's awake! Micah, baby. We're here." I wince. *Mom*.

"Along with about five camera crews and some reporter from—"

"Shh," my mother cuts off my sister. "Give him time to wake up."

"Meg?" I ask, not bothering to lift my head this time.

"With Duke in the waiting area."

"Cash?"

"James took him back to your place. I'm sure he's getting plenty spoiled right now."

"Am I fired?" I ask.

My sister snorts. My mom takes my hand. Or at least I think it's her. "What, why would you ask that?"

"I failed my first rescue, ended up unconscious on the cave floor."

"Not that it matters, but you didn't fail, Micah. Dad's back in prison. Alive and well."

I groan. "That's not helpful."

"It's just as well you feel that way. Technically, Duke dragged his ass in."

"Rachel!"

"Sorry, Mom."

A ghost of a grin crosses my dry lips. "I wish I'd seen that."

"You would've liked the part where your tiny girlfriend read him the riot act for breaking your phone and not checking for first aid supplies in your pack."

My mom squeezes my fingers. "You have good friends, Micah."

I squeeze back. "I have a good family, too, Mom."

She chokes on a sob, and I try again to open my eyes. It takes a moment to focus, but as long as I don't move my head, it's okay.

My sister excuses herself, and my mom starts crying harder. I let her for a few minutes before my fingers tighten on her hand to get her attention. "Mom. It's okay. I'm okay."

"He could have killed you."

"He didn't know it was me, Mom."

She shakes her head. "That doesn't matter. Not really. You told me how broken you were, and I kept trying to ignore it. I figured you'd grow out of it. You'd forget about him. Instead, you ran after him and nearly died."

"It's only a head injury," I argue weakly.

"Meg told me, Micah. She told me how you've been holding yourself together for us. And I knew that. Brian said it, you said it, James said it. I knew it, but I couldn't see past my own broken heart. I let you hold yourself together and told myself you were okay. That you were stronger and better off than the rest of us. That I didn't need to worry about you."

I feel my throat thicken, but I don't speak.

"I should have paid more attention to what was real. For your sake, and Rachel's and Evie's."

My voice is barely a whisper when I say, "It's not too late, Mom. I still need someone to worry for me." I drift off to sleep on a fresh round of her tears.

The next time I wake up, I'm alone with Meg. She's reading some magazine in the chair next to me, snacking on M&M's, and I watch her for a while. Eventually, her eyes turn to me, and her lips spread in a wide smile, brightening her entire face.

"Hey," she says, reaching forward to grab my hand.

"You found me."

She nods, her brown eyes sparkling with unshed tears. "Duke and Cash did all the work."

"I heard you yelled at my dad."

She blushes. "Yeah. Well. I was a little distraught. But in my defense, you were bleeding out, and the idiot had smashed your phone."

"He didn't know it was me," I say. Meg can tell I'm not defending him. She sighs sadly.

"I'm sorry."

"I don't know what I was thinking. I guess I thought maybe if he saw me, saving the fucking day, he would be . . ."

"Proud of you."

"Or something. Anything. Instead, he was mad I crashed his suicide mission."

"He looked genuinely sorry when he came for us. He let us treat you and didn't prevent Duke from calling the police."

"I'm not sure that's enough."

"No," she admits softly. "But it's worth knowing, I think."

She changes the subject. "Cash is beside himself. I've been staying at your place, taking care of him. He wouldn't leave the bed last night. Also," she adds, turning bright pink, "I'm sleeping in your bed. I think Cash, um, sleeps better when he can smell you."

"Cash, huh?"

Her eyes glitter with mirth as she tries not to smile. "He seems addicted."

I make a face. "You let Cash in my bed?"

Her eyes widen innocently. "Micah. He's been through a huge ordeal. He saved your life!"

"He's going to be impossible after this."

"I will not apologize." I smile at her, and she sighs again. "Fine, I'm sorry I ruined your dog. I guess I'll just have to keep him."

"Or I'll need to get a bigger bed."

She looks adorably pleased with herself but lifts a casual shoulder like, *If you must.*

"How's Duke?"

"Good! You just missed him, actually. He had to go to work. You scared a good five years off his life, but he was incredible. I don't know if we would have found you in time without him. I invited him to Thanksgiving."

"What day is that?"

"Thursday. It's Tuesday now. Don't worry, I begged Duke to pick up Vada. You're off the hook. But that might mean we won't be around to get you home tomorrow."

"I get to come home tomorrow?"

"Tentatively. Now that you're awake and lucid, they can run their tests."

"Good."

"Micah?" She presses her lips together, working them between her teeth anxiously.

"Yeah?"

"I love you."

My heart speeds up, and I fall fully against my pillow, feeling my grin take over my face. "I love you, too."

"Let's not do that again, okay?"

"I think I can manage that."

"I'm gonna go get your nurse."

"Okay."

"I love you," she says again, and I give a low chuckle, a little confused.

"I love you, too?"

She gets a mischievous gleam in her eyes. "I like saying it while you're hooked up to that thing. I get to watch your heartbeat pick up."

"No fair," I say, my face growing warm.

"Just curious to see what happens if I . . ." She drags her finger along my hand up to the edges of my tattoo, tracing it, before slipping it north, along my exposed collarbone. All the while, my heart is thudding almost painfully in my chest. She presses in closer to me, her lips hovering over mine, and despite the dull ache at the back of my head, my heart races as my lips capture hers. After a moment, she steps back, breathless.

"I think you'll be juuust fine, Micah Allen. Everything's working right from where I'm standing." And with that, she skips out to find the nurse, leaving me to listen as my heartbeat slows to normal levels.

28

Meg

Today has been the best day of my life for two reasons:

1. Micah came home from the hospital.
2. Vada is here.

Having my two very most favorite people in the same room at the same time is the equivalent to my heart exploding into fireworks of more hearts. Micah's mom just left after dropping off half a dozen pizzas and some soda. Micah ended up having to stay three nights at Marquette General for observation. He's got an incredibly thick skull that thankfully didn't crack, but definitely swelled and bruised dangerously, and he needed an emergency blood transfusion.

That meant I spent three nights sleeping in his bed and taking care of Cash. My most favorite dog of all time. Every time I think about what could have happened if he hadn't heard my calls . . . if he hadn't been there . . .

I die inside.

I would have stayed at the hospital, but his mom wanted

to be there. I get that. She was first. And she's going through some stuff for sure. I can't even imagine. Her ex-husband nearly killed her son.

Micah's dad is back in the county jail, awaiting sentencing for breaking his parole and also assault and battery for attacking Micah. I went to see him yesterday. I didn't tell anyone, but I wanted him to know Micah made it out okay and was coming home. I can't say I have much love for the guy, but I thought he deserved the update after, well . . . after nothing, I suppose. Maybe he would have run for help given enough time. I want to think that's the case. Micah needs to think that's the case. But we'll never be sure.

And besides, if Duke went, he'd probably murder the guy and ruin his future and then he'd never get into U of M.

We're sitting on the couch in Micah's apartment, and Duke is asking Vada all sorts of questions about Ann Arbor. She's already offering to hook him up with a job at the Loud Lizard. I tip my head to hers. "Thanks for coming, babe."

She rolls her eyes. "Like you could keep me from jumping on that plane. I only missed one class anyway. Luke's getting the notes for me from my roommate. What you should really be thanking me for is that last forty-minute flight on the twelve-passenger death trap from Green Bay. I thought my heart was gonna fly out of my ass."

"Thank you. I owe you massively. To be fair, we had planned on driving down to get you both. I'm sorry Luke couldn't make it."

Duke snorts.

"What?"

Micah scowls at him.

"What?" I repeat.

"You should have seen the act she put on to convince him to drive down," Duke says to Vada, whose rusty eyebrows disappear under her adorable new blunt-cut bangs.

"You make it sound like I stripped or something."

Micah clears his throat. "Listen. I was going to go anyway. And she definitely did not strip."

"I don't even know what you're talking about."

"It's this fetish he has . . ." Duke says gleefully.

"Fetish?" I squeak.

Micah practically growls, but Duke laughs. "It's not a fetish," he insists.

"It's the earrings, isn't it?" Vada guesses.

Micah's face goes slack. Duke throws his head back in a cackle. I turn to face my boyfriend. "Really?"

He winces. "If I say yes, will you think I'm a perv?"

Vada rolls her eyes. "Luke has the same one. What are the odds we find the two boys in the world with the same weird ear cuff fetish?"

"Not a fetish," Micah tries again.

"It's okay," I say softly, taking his face in my hands. "I'm slightly obsessed with your forearms. Particularly"—I run a finger down his tattooed arm—"this one."

"Speaking of obsessed," Vada says, interrupting our loaded look with an unapologetic smirk. "I'm pretty obsessed with your wings. I sobbed a full minute when you sent the picture. Luke thought someone had died."

I bite my cheek to keep from smiling. "It felt right."

"It's perfect," she admits. "And your dad saw it?"

I nod. "Declan came up a few weeks after."

"And your mom?"

I exhale through pursed lips. "Mom will likely disown me. But maybe one day she'll accept me for who I'm becoming and talk to me freely about what happened, and maybe then we can be okay. Declan thinks she has it in her. Deep, *deep* down inside."

I wake up early on Thanksgiving and leave Vada snoring in my bed, her face hidden behind her tangled mass of red hair. After brushing my teeth and putting on a bra and pajama top, I pad on bare feet into the living room, switching on the Macy's Thanksgiving Day parade. I turn the volume low and ignore the pang in my chest that reminds me I normally watch this with my mom.

Slipping into the kitchen, I intend to start the coffee brewing but am surprised to find James already sitting at the island with a steaming cup in front of him. He's got his Bible open and looks . . . thoughtful.

I don't interrupt, walking straight for the pot and pouring the smallest amount in my mug before dumping in a generous amount of vanilla almond milk from the fridge to cover anything remotely coffee tasting.

I'm about to head back to the living room when James speaks up. "Have a seat, Meg. We need to talk about something."

My stomach drops at his tone. "That sounds ominous."

He sighs, closing his Bible.

"I meant to talk to you about this the other night, but Micah's accident happened. And, well, honestly I didn't know how."

I sit on the stool, putting my mug down and clasping my fingers together in front of me. "Okay."

"It's about youth group. Well, sort of. It's about your witness and youth group."

My eyes widen. My *witness*? It's been a minute since someone used words like *that* with me.

I swallow. "Okay."

"I'm not your uncle right now, okay? Or Micah's friend. I'm your pastor."

I blink, thinking that I wouldn't be caught dead in my pajamas in front of my *pastor,* but okay.

"Mrs. Sanderson came to me after Halloween. She was . . . concerned. She saw Micah bringing you home late after your friend's costume party and then staying."

I blink again, waiting for more. James watches me silently.

"Okay? He didn't spend the night. You were home, even."

James looks uncomfortable. "But he did stay for a while? In your room? In the middle of the night?"

My cheeks burn at the implications in his tone, but my mind is boggled that this conversation is even happening—that my privacy is being invaded in this way.

"James," I say, trying to keep my tone calm. "What exactly are you saying?"

He looks super uncomfortable, but I refuse to make this easy on him. "So, he did stay?"

"He did," I admit. "For a little while. We came in my entrance because I didn't want to wake you."

"I don't need details. Remember, I'm your pastor right now."

I sit back against the rest, stung. "No. I don't think I can separate the two. Clearly, Mrs. Sanderson can't. If I don't get to pick when I'm witnessing or not, neither do you."

James rubs his hand down his tired face. "I can't have you talking to girls about abstinence and not practicing it yourself, Meg. You're supposed to lead by example."

I inhale sharply. "I'm not having sex!"

"It doesn't matter, does it? You have to keep up appearances."

"It was the middle of the night! I'm sorry, but what is she doing watching me that late at night?! How did she even see us?"

"She said she was letting out her dog, but it doesn't matter. She saw it. As someone who is affiliated with the church, you are to remain above censure at all times."

I swallow back a tide of hurt. "So, you're saying that even though I did not have sex and my boyfriend did not stay the night, I am still being held accountable as if we did."

"Meg, my hands are tied—"

I shake my head, cutting him off. "No. I get it. Appearances. You said that. Thank you for reminding me. I was just starting to relax, you know?" My voice is thick with emotion. "I thought maybe it would be okay if I lived a little. Wear short sleeves, kiss my boyfriend, fall in love. Maybe I could do that *and* still share my love of Christ. Maybe it didn't have to be one or the other. I guess that was stupid. I didn't want to believe my mom was right, but she was, wasn't she?"

James looks stunned.

"It's fine," I say. "I understand, *Pastor*."

I hop off the stool and rush back into my room, slamming the door, and startling Vada awake. Before she can ask, I shake my head and head for the shower, waiting for the water to hit before I let the torrent of tears fall.

Thanksgiving is an uncomfortable affair. It's at Micah's parents', so I tell James we'll meet him there. I explain I need to stop off for some things at the grocery store, and he allows me the excuse. Vada watches warily as I layer up over my loosest boyfriend jeans and baggy sweater, throwing on an ugly knit hat that completely covers my ears.

We make it several blocks before she bites. "Okay. What happened? You and James have an iceberg between you this morning, and you're dressed like a marshmallow puff getting ready for the Iditarod. It's not even that cold out."

I shrug, shoving my hands in my pockets. "I'm comfortable."

She tries another tack. "Okay, it's a holiday. Your *favorite* holiday. You barely even acknowledged the Rockette kick line this morning. You can't lie to me, Hennessey."

I huff a sigh, my breath clouding out before me. "One of my youth group girls' moms came to James about seeing Micah and me hanging out late on Halloween."

I glance at Vada out of the corner of my eye. She appears to be thinking, and I know she's not comprehending the significance.

"They were concerned about my 'witness,' which basically means they don't think I can be a good influence anymore, because how am I supposed to teach abstinence if I'm having sex?"

Vada blinks. "Wait, you had sex?"

"Definitely not. Which is what I said to James, but it doesn't even matter. I could have. There's no proof either way, and that's the point. I'm damned by association."

My best friend scoffs. "This is like some serious Regency-era bullshit, you know that?"

"It's church, Vada. I know you think it's wrong, but it's the way it is. I knew that going into this, but I guess I wanted to forget it for a while. Instead, I just wanted to be happy and in love for the first time ever."

"I don't see what one has to do with the other."

"It does when you have young girls watching your every move."

"But *they* aren't. *They* didn't see anything. It was a mom, right? Like, in the middle of the night? You weren't fornicating in the church parking lot or wearing nipple tassels as a bathing suit, right?"

I snicker, but it's weak. "Of course not. Ew."

Vada sighs. "I know I don't go to church, but I've known you my entire life, and I've yet to meet anyone more joyful and full of love for Jesus. I can't think of a single human being I'd rather teach my thirteen-year-old about God."

"Thank you." I say, touched. "But?"

Vada's nostrils flare. "But at what risk to yourself? I've never seen you so happy and flustered and complete. Micah does that for you."

"I know," I say miserably. "I know that. But what if I messed it up? By being loose with him? What if I cursed us and God won't bless our relationship?"

"Whoa, what?" Vada's eyes narrow. "You can't actually believe that?"

"I honestly don't know *what* I believe anymore. Before, everything felt beautiful and right between us. But now I can't shake this feeling that Satan was tricking me. I feel dirty."

Vada stops. We're on the sidewalk in front of Micah's, but she doesn't let me pass. She takes my shoulders in her hands and looks in my eyes, pleading. "Meg, no. You're not dirty or used up or anything like that. What happened with Micah *is* beautiful. Truly. And the way he looks at you is so special."

I feel the sting of fresh tears, but I can't even speak. I shake my head, breaking myself from her hold, and make my way up the sidewalk to Micah's house.

29

Micah

I might have a concussion, but it takes approximately thirty seconds to see that something is wrong with Meg and maybe five more to see it's directly related to her uncle. As soon as she walks in the house, I meet her, leaning to press a kiss on her mouth, but she turns to the side, offering her cheek instead. She looks like she's in pain as I help her remove her coat and she refuses to take off her hat. I raise my eyebrow at Vada, who shakes her head, silently communicating, *Don't ask.*

James is sitting at our table, sipping a beer and talking to Brian, but when Meg enters the kitchen, her arms full of rolls and some cookies she brought, James gets quiet. It occurs to me that they came separately. Everything is strained through dinner. Meg lets me hold her hand under the table, but she barely looks at me. After dessert, I ask if she and Vada want to come up to my apartment to watch a movie or something, and she declines for them.

"Cash misses you," I whisper.

She draws back from me, misery pooling in her navy eyes. "I miss him, too." But it feels like she's trying to say something different. My little sister asks her to read an Anna and Elsa book, and Meg cuddles up with her on the recliner, leaving me alone on the love seat. Vada jumps up, offering to start the dishes, and drags me with her.

When we enter the kitchen, my mom is getting started, but Vada waves her off. "Please, Mrs. Lundgren, let me. I'm a terrible cook, so doing dishes is all I can do to show my gratitude."

My mom looks like she wants to argue, but Vada is already reaching for the dish in her hand, and that is that.

After making sure we're alone, Vada presses me into a chair. "You sit and keep me company. You nearly died a week ago." I wouldn't dare call Meg's best friend pushy, but she sure is goal oriented. She leans toward me, bright red hair falling in her face and hiding her mouth as she speaks in a low tone. "Some youth group mom saw you leaving Meg's on Halloween."

I slump back against my chair, catching on immediately.

"*Exactly,* and Mrs. Busybody went to James who in turn went and chastised Meg for her *witness* or some bullshit like that?"

"*James* did?" I ask in a strangled whisper.

"Yeah. So, my best friend, the sweetest, purest human on the planet, told me she feels dirty and thinks she's wronged the ever-loving church."

I lean forward on my elbows, cradling my head in my hands and feeling like I've been socked in the gut.

Vada tilts her head down to catch my attention. "This is bad, Micah. I've never seen Meg like this. When I went to bed last night, she was giddy and happy and so in love. This morning, it was like someone turned the light off inside of her."

Which is exactly how she seemed to me. Dimmed. Defeated.

I'm so fucking sick of this, I could scream.

I stand, ignoring Vada's protests, and we do the dishes in silence for several minutes, me tense, Vada cautious. Eventually, she speaks, her voice quiet. "I'm not a church kid, Micah. I can't pretend to understand this compulsion you guys have to hide your humanity at the risk of appearing human. I've always supported Meg in her modesty. It's different, but whatever. She was happy. Until she wasn't. It's like the bottom of her beliefs fell out, and she hasn't been able to hold herself up without them. She's scrambling back to the closest source of reality she has, and it's *fucking her up*."

The last words are spit through clenched teeth, and I stop what I'm doing to face Vada, fully appreciating for the first time how well she understands Meg. And also how fiercely scary she can be.

Well, I understand Meg pretty well, too.

"I'm not walking away. I'm not ashamed of us. She can try to put me off, but I doubt it will work." I return to the dishes, thinking, and my head falls back with a groan. Ignoring the dull ache, I ask, "Is that why she's wearing the hat inside? Is she covering her ears?"

Vada snorts.

"It's *not* a fetish," I insist.

"Thank you, Micah."

"Anytime, Vada."

As much as I want to run over to James's the very next morning, proverbial sword drawn to defend Meg's honor, I know I can't, because I'm not the boyfriend talking to the uncle in this scenario. I'm Micah, who needs to approach his pastor about his pastor's treatment of a member of his church.

It sounds bogus when I say it like that. But it's a whole thing, and I'm an adult, so I'm doing this by the book.

Which means I have to do something else first.

"You sure you don't want me to come in?" Duke asks as he passes his wallet, keys, and phone across the desk and steps under the security scanner into the county jail.

"Nah. This is far enough. Besides, you'll just punch him and get yourself arrested."

Duke grins. "Meg said the same thing."

"She's a smart girl," I say. Duke knows a little about what's been going on, but like Vada, he doesn't fully get what the big deal is because he didn't grow up in the church.

Duke takes a seat on a bench inside the waiting area, and I'm escorted to an empty room to wait for my father. I'm sitting at one end of a heavy metal table, and it's like an icebox in here.

I can't believe this is real. I can't believe I'm visiting my dad in jail. I can't believe he's *in* jail. Again. Because of me.

No. Because of *him*. I just happened to be there.

A buzzer startles me out of my reverie, and a door opens. A guard is followed by a guy in an orange jumpsuit, followed by another guard.

I know it's my dad. Logically, it has to be him. And he looks as sunken and sallow as he did in the cave. But only now, under the halogens, can I fully appreciate how much he's changed.

I stand up slowly, letting him take in my full measure. All six foot two, two hundred pounds of me. Two hundred pounds of solid muscle, and all of it because of him. Because of hiding in the dark. Because of not being able to sleep. Because of feeling like I had to defend myself against the world after what he put me through.

When I went after him—when he knocked me out—I didn't get the chance to do this. I lost the upper hand, and after all these years, I need it back. I want this to happen on my own terms.

The way his eyes widen, shock clear on his pale, haggard face, is a balm to my soul.

"Micah?"

I sit down with a loud scrape of my chair. "Dad." I gesture for him to sit. He does, far more slowly than I do. His wrists are in chains.

"I didn't think I'd ever see you again," he says.

"Didn't think or didn't want?"

He settles back with a frown that slips deep into the creases and grooves of his face. "Your mom said you were angry with me. I thought maybe she'd exaggerated."

"Mom's been to see you?"

He nods but doesn't offer anything else. I hope she gave him hell.

"I'm not angry," I lie, tapping the tabletop. I look into his eyes. They're clouded, so unlike the brilliant hazel they used to be. "I barely think of you."

His expression is mild. "Then why are you here?"

I let out a huff. "Actually, you're right. I *am* angry. I'm furious. You left me, a thirteen-year-old who worshipped the ground you walked on, to deal with the consequences of your actions. You fucked up, and we paid for it."

"What do you want me to say, Micah? They sent me to prison. I paid my debt."

"I don't think so. You hid out in there. Do you even know what you put Mom through?"

"Well." His expression is wry. "She remarried. My youth pastor, if I remember correctly, so I doubt she's been in real dire straits. Popped out three more—"

"Don't do that." I cut him off. "Don't you dare. You had sex with women on your staff while married to her."

He shrugs. "I'm a sex addict. Not that it's any of your business, *son,* but I'm in recovery."

"Fuck you."

"Micah," he says with a heavy sigh. "Is this all? You're just in here to what? Complain how I ruined your life? Fine. I'm sorry. I wasn't planning to drag you all down with me. I wasn't planning to get caught in the first place. So, I *am* sorry that you've had to suffer for my misdeeds, and I'm very sorry for what happened at Pictured Rocks. I never in a million years dreamed it was you. I wouldn't have struck had I known." Before I can say anything, he raises a hand. "That doesn't change the fact that I was willing to hit a stranger. I was ready to leave a stranger to die in the cave. I'm not a good person, Micah. I deserve what's coming to me."

I'm speechless for several long minutes. I keep opening my mouth, but nothing comes out. I had planned for defensive. I'd even planned—naively—for apologetic.

I hadn't planned for complacent. I don't know what to do with that. He doesn't seem sorry but resigned.

"If I hadn't been in that cave, you weren't ever going to reach out to me, were you?"

He shakes his head. "No. You never came to see me. I assumed you wanted nothing to do with me."

"It's not my job to come to see you. You're the parent. You're the adult. You're supposed to reach out to *me.* You're supposed to *want* to reach out to me. To try."

He doesn't say anything, and holy shit, that *sucks.* I

exhale slowly and straighten. Because as much as this hurts, I came here to say something, and this is my chance.

"I *loved* you. I—" I shake my head. "I believed you. I stood up for you. I prayed for you every night. I stopped going to church because of you. Mom went bankrupt because of you. We lost our home because of you." I stand up. "This"—I gesture to my physique—"happened because I needed to distance myself from you. To protect myself. I thought, 'Let him come and see me. Write me a letter. I'll set it on fire. Call me and I'll hang up. He rejected me, and I can't wait to reject him back.'"

"Now, son . . ."

"Don't," I spit out with a downward slash of my hand. "Do not call me 'son.' I'm not your son. I'm not your anything. *Clearly.* Enjoy your life," I say. "And every day when you wake up in your cell alone, with no wife or kids or congregation or friends, I hope you remember that it's because I loved you enough to come after you. Because I showed up when you needed me most."

I pull a piece of paper out of my pocket and slap it on the table. "I brought you something. I wanted to tell you that even though I stopped going to church because of you, I didn't stop believing in God. You didn't steal my belief. A long, long time ago, I wanted to *be* you. I wanted to be a pastor, and then you ripped that away from me and made it disgusting.

"A few weeks ago, someone reached out to me and wanted to talk about what happened. They wanted my side of the story, for once. Unfiltered. I was going to turn them down, but you happened. Again. And I nearly died. So instead, I gave them all the gory details. I wanted something good to come out of the ashes of our relationship. As of this morning, I've gotten over three hundred emails from other pastors' kids and hurting Christians, thanking me for telling my truth. So." I smile sardonically. "I guess it wasn't all for nothing. It was for me and"—I tap the printed article in front of him—"it was for them."

With that, I leave. I tell the guards, "You can have him. I'm done."

"One down," I mutter, pulling up to James's house. "One to go." Meg is at work for at least two more hours, so after I finished at the county jail, I dropped off Duke and texted James, asking if we could meet.

My knock on his door is sharp, and he opens it right away, looking grim. He gestures for me to sit, and I shake my head.

"No, thank you."

James sighs. "Micah, I didn't have a choice. The church has very clear rules."

"Bullshit," I say bluntly. "James, how many times have you stayed at Dani's until late in the evening?"

James opens his mouth, but I don't let him speak.

"How many times has Dani been here in the mornings?"

"She's never stayed the night," he says defensively.

"You know that doesn't matter. Dani is a divorcée with a little girl. Tell me that there's not some rule in the outdated church bylaws about that?"

"That's not what this is about, and I don't like your tone."

"But it is! James! Are you serious right now? My tone? You straight-up slut-shamed the girl I love! Who's your family, by the way."

"Meg knew what a huge responsibility it was before she took on this role. Those girls are impressionable, and they look up to her."

"And they still can! Meg is exactly the kind of role model those girls need. She's sweet and generous and has a heart for Jesus. She's studied the Bible and really knows it. She's passionate about evangelism. She's also fun as hell and *willing* to hang out with thirteen-year-old girls because she loves them so much."

"You didn't say *modest*, Micah," James is quiet and pained. "You have to understand the position I'm in. She's got to be upright and modest and practice abstinence."

A scream of frustration rattles in my throat. If I never hear the word *abstinence* again, it will be too soon. "Modest by *whose* standards? Who is she answering to here? Because I don't remember hearing that you or Brian ever had to get up in front of the congregation and make a pledge of abstinence when you were single."

James doesn't have a response to that. I move to the door. "The truth is, the only time churches are worried about modesty and purity is when it comes to their teenage girls. I think maybe you all need to take a hard look at why that is. Your *niece* isn't the problem here."

30

Meg

I've never been so grateful for skating. Not even when I was touring the country on the junior national team and feeling like I was on top of the world was I so thankful to have the ice.

They've increased my teaching load for the next session, so much so I had to tell Maria I need to cut back on my café hours. I've even been asked to privately coach a tiny upstart who shows gobs and gobs of promise. Livy is young, barely nine, but already has the kind of form and natural grace that makes seasoned skaters weep. It wasn't a hard choice. I've been doing some soul-searching since Declan's visit, making sure I'm not trying to live vicariously through my students, and I'm happy to report that I'm not. I did love skating. Still do. But the constant pressure of being a competitive skater isn't anything that holds my passion.

But coaching? I could really, truly love coaching. Being on the ice, encouraging and pushing someone to be better than they've ever been? Choreographing routines that I couldn't dream of nailing but that could lead someone else to their dreams coming true?

Oh yes. This has Meg Hennessey written all over it. And Livy is such a special little girl. I'm not sure what the future holds for her, but I'm honored to be invited along.

Things have been strained at James's. I came in late on Thanksgiving to him and Dani cuddling on the couch and had to physically restrain Vada before she could make any rude comments. She doesn't understand it, but I don't blame James. Not really. He's been put in a terrible position, and he's just doing his best.

And no matter what my best friend thinks, I can't begrudge James and Dani their happiness together. Even if it feels the tiniest bit like a double standard.

The Friday after Thanksgiving, Vada and I took Betty Christmas shopping in downtown Marquette. I could tell my great-grandmother wanted to address the elephant in the room, but I wouldn't hear of it. I won't have her feeling like she needs to intercede between her grandson and her great-granddaughter. Instead, we ate too many cinnamon sugar doughnuts from the bakery, and I buzzed around the small shops, buying every person I know UP-themed presents. People at home are plenty proud of their state and its Great Lakes status, but Yoopers take it to a whole other level, and I am here for it.

Vada left early Sunday morning, and I missed church to drop her off. It's not like I've been attending church regularly since I've been here, but this is the first time it felt like I was avoiding it. And James. And Micah's family. And my youth group girls.

I've been at the rink or in the café every day since, biding my time and, yeah, okay, licking my wounds. I don't think James was wrong in speaking with me, but I'm not exactly sure how I feel about it. My gut reaction was to be chastised. Convicted. Someone from the church, which has always been a trusted authority figure in my life, brought sinful behavior to my attention.

What follows, biblically, is my acceptance and repentance. And in some circles, my (public) reconciliation. I don't know how that works here. James's church is new to me, and he *is* my uncle. There was a girl in my old youth group. She was a few years older than me and a leader of sorts. She ended up accidentally getting pregnant by her longtime boyfriend, who wasn't a believer, and was asked to give our entire youth group a public apology for her actions.

It felt very . . . icky. Even at fourteen, I knew it wasn't okay. Like, that young woman was alone and pregnant and about to be a mom as a teenager, and the church was ostracizing her from the only support group she had.

What shit.

But still, that's the way it's always been.

On the other hand, what *exactly* am I supposed to be reconciling here?

Try as I might, I can't seem to feel sorry for the things that happened between Micah and me that night or any of the moments before or since. Every second is dear to me. Full disclosure, I meant what I said to Vada. I absolutely felt like dirt after James talked to me. But that feeling is fading. My knee-jerk conditioned response is slower to come the more I think about it. Mrs. Sanderson probably wouldn't approve of a lot of what I've been up to since I moved here. My tattoo, my language, my sporadic church attendance, my friendship with the irreverent Duke, my tiptoeing into underage drinking, my two-piece bathing suit, my gay stepdad. My unmarried biological parents. My teen mother. My worship-team-leader-of-a-dad who died in a drunk-driving accident.

The list goes on and on, and a girl could drown under all her transgressions when you lay them all out like that.

The rink is mostly empty since classes ended for the night. Which finds me gliding slowly in circle after circle on the ice, my earbuds in and my brain busy. The chill of the rink air frosts my cheeks, but the rest of me is burning in exertion and warmth as I cross ankle over ankle. The rhythm soothes all my aching pieces.

Vada left me with a playlist, and I've been testing out the music on the ice. Twenty One Pilots' "Addict with a Pen" comes on, and my eyes slip closed. Sometimes it's the songs about faith that aren't written explicitly for believers that can be the most meaningful—the most deep-down, gut-felt. There's a time for worship and a time for wondering. I can't help feeling like it's a lie to pretend otherwise.

I spread my arms wide, spinning myself backward and letting my broken heart lead me. The singer speaks of his pain, his desperation for water in the desert—his need for someone to fill his brittle, gaping inequities and coming up empty. Except I don't feel empty. I feel patched up. Refined. In Ann Arbor, I was this fragile Fabergé egg. My faith was pretty, but untested. And once it was tested, it shattered into a million little pieces that felt impossible to put back together.

Meeting Micah has glued my pieces back together. Betty and James and Duke and Dani. Micah's dad, even. I'm not the same girl I was, and I'm not sure the woman I am now is the kind who apologizes for something she didn't do.

A warm hand reaches for my arm, and I startle, my eyes

shooting open. Micah's deep brown eyes watch me, and it takes me a second to realize he's skating alongside me and keeping up as if he were born for the ice.

Because *of course* he is.

His face is uncertain, and I beam, hummingbirds taking flight in my stomach. His hand slides from my arm to my fingers, and I hold on tight.

"I've missed you," I say.

"I wasn't sure. Vada told me what happened," he confesses and shakes his head. "I told her I wasn't going to give up on you, but I realized I needed to let you decide that."

I spin around so I'm backward and he's forward, and with my hands to his broad chest, I slow him. "I needed a few days," I say once he's stopped and I can look him in the eyes. "But I'm not done with you, and I'm not walking away from us. I'm not sure how I feel about what happened, but I don't regret you or the things we've done."

He releases a long breath, his face awash with relief. His lips spread into a hopeful smile. "You don't?"

Using my toe pick as leverage, I press myself up, kissing him. His arms immediately circle my waist, slipping along my spandex jacket. Kissing while wearing spandex is kind of alarming, but in a very, *very* good way. His hands slide along the edge of where my jacket meets my pants, lifting it slightly, allowing a chilly breeze to hit my bare skin. That's enough to wake me from my Micah-tastes-like-everything-delicious trance, and I gently push him away, causing him to slide back on his blades. I grin at his disappointed pout.

"Later, hockey player. I've got thirty minutes of ice time and a skating fantasy to act out."

He groans theatrically but is quick to understand, catching

up with me halfway around the rink. We spend the next half hour kissing and spinning and gliding together and apart. I make him chase me, and I make it worth his time when he catches me. He makes me laugh until my sides ache and my heart feels like it's going to burst.

It's the best moment of my entire life, and I'm not one bit sorry about it.

The following morning, Micah and Cash surprise me with doughnuts and an offer to run together. We're finishing up, slowing to a walk, when I see Mrs. Sanderson out in her drive, shoveling snow. I try to ignore her, but she's watching me. In fact, when I glance over out of the corner of my eye, she's dropped all pretense and is openly staring at us.

"Is Cash even tired?" I ask, panting slightly, avoiding looking her way.

Micah laughs. "Not really. He'll definitely nap after this, but I've taken him along for bike rides where I've gone fifteen miles and he doesn't even bat an eye."

"I wonder if he was a sled dog in another life."

"I've actually thought about training him to sled race. Just for fun."

I raise a skeptical eyebrow. "Just for fun, huh?"

Micah shrugs, and I hear Mrs. Sanderson clear her throat. "Meg! I was hoping I could talk to you for a minute." My heart sinks in my chest, but Micah reaches out for my hand and squeezes it.

"Up to you."

"Don't go," I say.

"I won't."

I turn to Mrs. Sanderson, who's dropped her shovel and is crunching over the snowy drifts to address us. "Hi, Mrs. Sanderson. How are you today?"

"I've been better," she says stiffly. "I was wondering if you planned on leading the girls' small group this evening."

I swallow. In truth, I hadn't brought it up to my uncle, but I assumed that didn't matter. I shake my head. "I haven't spoken with James about it, so I'm not sure."

She presses her lips together, clearly not pleased with my answer. "Can you have Pastor James let me know? I want Becca to attend, but not until there is a new, morally sound leader in place."

Micah inhales sharply. My mouth falls open at her hostility, and the hot sting of tears presses out behind my eyelids. Mrs. Sanderson doesn't wait for an answer, spinning on her heel and walking back to her house. Micah steps to follow her, and I put an arm to his chest, stopping him. Through the curtains of the house, I see Becca watching us with a sad look on her face.

That's not going to work.

I take a deep breath, whisper a prayer in my heart, and call after her quietly. She hesitates and faces me again.

I open my mouth and another voice interrupts us.

"Excuse me, I'm sorry. I was passing by and couldn't help overhearing you insult my daughter."

My breath catches in my throat at the sound of my mother's voice. "Mom! What are you doing here?"

"Miss Betty called me. I came as soon as I heard." My heart soars. She came. My mom heard what happened and she came. She must have driven all night. Before the implications of what this means can settle, she's marching toward Mrs. Sanderson, a fierce look on her face. "Who gave you the right to judge the morality of an eighteen-year-old volunteer? My daughter loves Jesus so much she sacrifices her time to teach young girls about him, and you are not only spying on her but judging her actions without allowing her the courtesy of defending herself? Not that she needs to. Not to you or anyone else." My mom's voice sharpens and cuts through the cold air. "Please enlighten me. Just what did God look like when he came down from heaven and asked you to be his judge and jury?"

Mrs. Sanderson looks flabbergasted, and I'm not much better.

Micah, however, says, "Bravo, Mrs. Hennessey."

"It's Ms. Knudsen, actually. I've gone back to my maiden name."

Mrs. Sanderson's eyes narrow. "Yes, well, you're Meg's mom? The one who got pregnant as a teen and never told the father?" Her lips curl in a cruel way. "I've heard all about you."

Before my mom can say anything, I speak up. "Enough is enough." My voice is quiet, but rings with finality. "Are you above forgiveness, Mrs. Sanderson? Because I'm not. I'm not perfect. My mom's not perfect. You're not perfect, and your daughter is not perfect. Thank goodness Jesus didn't ask us to be perfect. He asked us to love.

"I'm not apologizing for loving Micah. We've done nothing wrong. I'm sorry you think this disqualifies me to teach your daughter. But to answer your question, no. I will not be the one leading her in youth group. Because while I know in my heart that God is love, I'm very murky on the rest these days.

"But I do have one thing to ask of you." I glance at the window where Becca is watching. Her mom follows my gaze and sees her. "Someday, maybe soon, your daughter will have questions about what it is to be human and alive and loved. I beg you: Don't make her feel as dirty and shameful as you've made me feel." My words wobble a bit. Even if she's wrong, it still hurts. "You see, I have friends and family who are there to remind me that God doesn't make mistakes, but she might not."

I hold out a hand to my mom, whose eyes are overflowing with approval. There's a lot we need to work out. Years of heartache and misunderstandings will be rehashed. But we have time for that, and I'm ready to hear her out. We walk back to my uncle's house, leaving Mrs. Sanderson gaping behind us.

"Are you able to stay for a little while?"

She nods and grins at Micah. "Nice to meet you, by the way."

"Sorry, Mom, this is Micah. He's my . . . I love him," I finish, feeling my cheeks heat. "And Cash, my favorite dog in the world."

"As I said, nice to meet you, Micah." My mom smiles warmly. "I've been praying for you for a long time."

The following morning, my mom arrives bright and early after picking up Betty. James invited my mom to stay at the house with us last night, but she declined, saying she'd gotten a hotel room. It's evident to everyone that she feels awkward around Andrew's family, and I'm trying to put myself in her shoes. Imagine meeting the fam nearly nineteen years after the fact! If Andrew were alive, she'd probably have murdered him for stranding her with strangers.

Not that there are any strangers with Betty, who has

taken it upon herself to adopt my mother. Thank God. Apparently, they've been in regular contact for the last few months. Betty was the only person my mom knew up here, so after that fateful call where I told her I was staying with James, my mom did the mom thing and called up Betty to do a background check on my uncle. Once Betty confirmed he wasn't a dangerous creep, they talked. For hours, if my mom is to be believed. And then they made plans to talk again. Every week, my mom would ring up Betty under the pretense of checking on me, but in reality, she was finally getting the unconditional love and care she'd needed for years. From the woman who raised the man who took her virginity. At a youth group conference.

Which is a bit squicky for me still, but Betty finally convinced my mom to see it as something romantic, and that means everything. It's like I'm finally able to glimpse a shadow of the girl Declan described to me: starry-eyed and adventurous and full of life. She's there, underneath. Sometimes far underneath, but hey. It takes a bold woman to stand up to the Mrs. Sandersons of the world and pull out a line like, "Just what did God look like when he came down from heaven and asked you to be his judge and jury?"

I mean. Dang. Get me that on a T-shirt.

Baby steps is what I am saying. We're making baby steps of reparation.

Betty hands over a casserole dish of baked cinnamon rolls to James. "Into the oven at three fifty until we can't handle the aroma a second longer, then pull them out and plate them, thanks."

James takes the directions in stride, heading off to the kitchen and accepting his dismissal. Things are the most awkward between him and my mom. Not to mention, Betty is giving him the cold shoulder. Dani seems torn. She was a little quiet during dinner last night, but when he leaned in to kiss her good night, she turned her cheek at the last second. James tried to hide his wince, but I saw it. I'm planning to head into the Outfitters after breakfast to talk with her. I don't want what happened between James and me to hinder things in their relationship. He's crazy about her. I'd never forgive myself.

I lean back in my La-Z-Boy recliner, listening as my mom tells Betty about her tentative plans to relocate to Marquette. She's thinking about taking some night classes and finishing her degree in social work. Betty tells her the senior living community is hiring an activities planner, which, admittedly, my mom would be great at. She loves micromanaging things.

I'm not sure how I'd like her living up here. I guess I'm not entirely sure I'm staying here forever myself. Micah has talked about us eventually joining Duke in Ann Arbor, but even that is up in the air . . . I have a lot of months left in this gap year, and I intend to use them.

Though, as long as I'm with Micah, I don't care where I am.

So, I guess it would be okay if my mom moved here. After all, Marquette has done wonders to patch my broken heart. Perhaps it can work a miracle in hers as well.

My mom glances over at me and smiles. "You look sleepy, kid."

A yawn pops out before I can stop it. "I am. You and Miss Betty kept me up late with your chitchat last night."

"More like Micah kept you up late after we left," Betty teases with a twinkle in her eyes, and I inhale so sharply, I choke on air, hacking until my eyes are streaming. Once

I've recovered, I steal a glance at my mom. Her cheeks are pink, but she's tried to school her features to resemble "accepting."

"He did not," I shoot back, rolling my eyes like the petulant teen I am. "He left minutes after you did. Ask James."

"It's okay, Meg," my mom insists. "Truly. She's only teasing. Micah seems like a very nice boy."

"He is," I say.

"I trust you, Meg."

My eyes meet my mom's, and it's like we're the only two people in the room. "You do?" I whisper.

"I do."

I release a slow breath. "Okay."

"Okay." She grins.

"I have a tattoo." I blurt the confession.

This time, my mom rolls her eyes like a teen. "Yeah, I know. Hope you don't regret *that* when you're my age."

"How did you know?" I ask, shooting an accusatory glance at Betty.

My mom shakes her head. "Declan told me. We had dinner after his visit to see you. The man is terrible at keeping secrets."

"What are you talking about?" I howl. "He's been keeping his sexuality secret his entire life."

"Not from me," she reminds me, almost smug. I gape at her. *Who is this woman?*

"Well," I say, a little sheepish. "I guess not really from me either. Maybe he is terrible at secrets."

"Within minutes, he was telling me about your wings, your boyfriend, and your ice-skating. By the end of dinner, he was pulling out his phone and showing me photos of Richard, his new online boyfriend. I haven't seen Declan that giddy since I bought him that Mark McGrath poster in the eleventh grade."

Betty chortles. "Is that the kid with the hair from that band?"

"Sugar Ray, and yes." My mom's eyes are sparkling.

"Andrew had that same haircut. Looked like a spiky blond porcupine."

My mom smiles. "He sure did," she says, except her tone is dreamy in a way I've never heard from her before.

What is happening?

"I guess you and Declan had similar taste," I say.

"I guess we did."

"This is weird," I say.

My mom sobers. "I'm sorry, Meg."

"I know," I say.

James interrupts, clearing his throat and ushering in a pile of cinnamon rolls.

"Knock, knock."

Betty presses her lips together in a line and stands to take over, but my uncle ignores her and clears his throat again.

"Sit, please, I have something to say." He starts passing the plates around.

Betty harrumphs but settles on the sofa closer to my mom. I curl up on the chair, placing a pillow in my lap for the plate to rest on. After passing me one, James stands awkwardly in the middle of the room.

"I'm stepping down from being the youth pastor."

"What?" I nearly shout. "Why?" What is *with* today?

"Good on you!" says Betty at the same time.

James shares an exasperated look with his grandmother before turning to me. "Because I don't fully buy into the way things went down with you about the whole abstinence thing." He runs a hand through his hair, frustrated. "It wasn't fair to you. There's a definite double standard in the way things are handled at the church. That said, I don't have a good answer for them or you. I'm not sure they were wrong in expecting an abstinence pledge from their young, unmarried staff. I'm not sure they were right either. It's clear that the individuals standing to lose the most are the young women in our congregation, and I can't draw a line of impartiality. I can't be a pastor and an uncle or a pastor and a friend. I don't want to do that anymore. I'll still lead worship on Sundays, but I'm done with youth group. You're out, so I'm out," he finishes.

I put the plate down and stand up, the pillow falling to the floor, before crossing the room and hugging my uncle so tight, I knock out his breath.

"Are you sure? I don't want this to be because of me. That feels wrong."

"It's not," he promises. "It's because of me. And maybe a little because of something Micah said, but that's between us. He put me straight, and I deserved it."

James backs up, his expression soft. "I should have stood up for you. You're my family, and someone was judging you and I let them. I went along with it, even. I am so sorry."

"James," I say, "I don't blame you. You did what your job told you to do. I was in the wrong. I should have acted above reproach as a leader, and I didn't."

He's shaking his head. "From the moment I first met you and knew you were my family, I was no longer a pastor. I was your uncle. Family first. And not only that, but I've been Micah's friend a long time. I've watched him hurt for years because of the way his church family treated him. I knew better. He proved that to me. Please forgive me."

"Okay," I say easily. "But I'm still not coming back to youth group."

"That's fine. They won't take you. Mrs. Sanderson is stepping into my old role."

"Oh nooo."

"Hell in a handbasket," he admits wryly.

"Maybe I should reach out to Becca, let her know I'm here if she ever wants to talk to someone who's not her mom."

James grins. "That would be awesome. Maybe I'll reach out to a few of the guys, too. Let them know I'm around."

"Maybe every first Tuesday from 8:00 to 10:00 p.m. on the front porch or something," I suggest idly.

"I'll probably drop off doughnuts and cookies those days, purely coincidentally," Betty says.

My mom groans. "Maybe I should reach out to my new friend, Mrs. Sanderson, and ask her to coffee those days. From 8:00 to 10:00 p.m. To make amends."

My eyes widen. "You'd do that?"

My mom shrugs, looking mischievous. "We all have our crosses to bear. If it means a generation of girls not growing up hating their bodies, it will be worth it."

And with that settled, we scarf down cinnamon rolls, and the secret underground unofficial monthly youth gathering doesn't come up again. Me, across from my mom, sitting next to my great-grandmother, sitting next to my uncle. I try to remember back to that day in August when all the secrets came out and I came to Marquette. I'd stood on the shore of Lake Superior, feeling empty and small and alone, hoping to figure out who I was.

I think I'm finally starting to figure it out.

EPILOGUE

~~~~~~~

Micah

SUMMER

"And you're sure this is safe?" Luke Greenly squints over the edge of the cliff to the shimmering waves of Lake Superior below. Dude is practically translucent in the hot July sun, his pale blond hair gathered at the nape of his neck in a stubby ponytail. Apparently, the pony is recent. Meg keeps calling him "beatnik," while his twin, Cullen, keeps frowning at his "blatant American aesthetic."

Guess sunny California will do that for a guy. Vada isn't bothered, judging by the sounds coming from the guest room in James's house early this morning.

Meg smirks at her friend. "Come on, Lukas. It's plenty deep. Besides, Duke, Micah, and I are all CPR and first aid certified."

Luke doesn't look reassured.

"I'll go," Zack says and, without hesitation, launches off the cliff, folding his body into an admirable cannonball.

"Shite," Cullen mutters. "Now I have to go off and do something equally impressive or I'll never hear the end of it."

"Let's go, Greenly!" Zack yells from below.

"I hate you, you impossibly handsome man-child!" Cullen yells back before executing a near-perfect swan dive off the cliff.

Vada whistles low, teasing. "Wow, Luke. Can you do that?"

If possible, Luke goes even paler.

Duke takes pity on him. "I thought Charlie taught you swimming in the Greek islands off Tommy Ramone's yacht?"

Vada snickers, and Luke rolls his eyes. "Duke. Mate. I've told you. Charlie's full of shit. Tommy Ramone wouldn't be caught dead floating a yacht."

Duke shrugs good-naturedly, grinning ear to ear, and lopes right off the cliff, relaxed in a way I haven't seen in years. Charlie and Iris Greenly have done wonders for my friend. His hair is as vibrant as ever, his clothes maybe more so. He's mentioned a few girls to me since I dropped him off in Ann Arbor seven months ago. And one guy. But when Meg and I invited everyone to come stay with us for a few weeks, Duke came alone. Which is fine. He knows where we stand. We'll take him however he comes.

Meg pretends to tap her foot, glancing at her imaginary watch. "I don't mean to pressure you, but we have a wedding to attend this evening. Think you can manage in that time, Lukas?"

Vada rubs her boyfriend's back sympathetically. She flicks a long red braid over her shoulder and pretends to read the sun as it tracks the sky. "Yeah, I'm guessing you have about four hours. Micah's got groomsman duties."

"Eh." Meg waves a hand. "James is in good hands."

"Brian's there."

Meg grins. "I meant Dani's hands. The two can barely keep from kissing each other's faces off. I've started knocking every time I enter the kitchen."

"Ten bucks says they have a honeymoon baby," says Vada.

"Twenty says they name it after Meg," I counter.

She grins conspiratorially. "You're on."

"I'm just relieved to be moving out," Meg says. "I'll miss the clawfoot tub James has at his house, but at least I won't have to wear a bra every time I leave my room anymore."

Luke chokes on air, sputtering.

I grin at Meg, looking her up and down in her two-piece suit. She's still Meg. Still modest and reserved, mostly. But not with me, and I love that.

Not with Luke either, though I suspect that's her subtle retaliation for being woken up early due to thin walls.

"Okay," Vada says, reaching out her hand. "Let's do this, Greenly. I'm with you, remember?" Her eyes are lit with meaning, and Luke immediately reaches for her. "On three. One . . . two . . ."

Three is drowned out by the refined shrieks of a very pale Brit. But they make it over.

Meg curls into my side, her sun-soaked skin soft against mine. "Should we just stay up here? It's nice and quiet."

I pretend to consider it, turning my body so my arms wrap around her completely. She traces the lines of my chest. "Did you know that you were the inspiration for my sexual awakening right here on these rocks?"

I throw back my head and bark out a laugh. "What?"

Her cheeks are pink, but she's got a sly grin on her lips. "I'm serious. I'd never seen a boy up close without a shirt on before you took me cliff jumping that day. I'm lucky

I didn't fall off the cliff, I was so distracted by all your muscles."

"I should feel cheap, but . . ."

"But you sort of like that I can't get enough of you?"

I chuckle low. "Yes, that. And it's mutual." I draw my fingertips along her wings and tip her head back to look at me. "I love you."

"I love you, too. Are you ready?" she asks, eyes dancing.

"You jump, I jump, Hennessey."

Author's Note

I've done a lot of soul-searching as I drafted this book. I'm a classic overthinker, and as an author of books for young people, I take my job *very* seriously. My intended audience is teens, and that carries a lot of weight—I get to shape *hearts* as a writer. It's an incredible feeling. But yeah, I think about that a lot before I set fingers to the keys, and this was a tough one.

I've worked with kids and teens all my adult life. And one night, when I was in my early twenties, I co-led a junior high / senior high girls small group (similar to Bible study, but more casual) with a mom of teens. This mom pulled a fast one on me. I don't recall the topic, but whatever it was, it was *not* abortion or premarital sex. And that's what she chose to talk about. She was prepared. She had pictures and articles and materials and eyes full of thundering damnation, and I was . . . *gobsmacked.*

She lectured and accused these young girls and, Reader, I was *furious.* Shaking, sweating, stammering. Jesus flipping tables in the temple had nothing on me. All I could think was what if one of these girls had had an abortion? Or knew someone who'd had an abortion? Or, more likely, had had premarital sex? Or wanted to have premarital sex because that is a *normal desire* for a hormonal human being?

And what if they went home and cried after that and decided because of those things, because of those gory photos and damning articles written by nobody important, Jesus couldn't love them?

That night, I tried to patch the hole I saw growing in their hearts. I quoted the truth that "God is love" and the greatest commandment is love, and that no matter what you've done in your life, it doesn't matter, because God is grace and mercy and *he still wants you even if you're messy.*

I don't know if a single one heard my voice over the rushing accusations in their ears, but I pray they did.

I got into the car that night with my husband (who led the boys' group and was like, *You talked about what? We just prayed and listened to Relient K*) and cried. I was so angry, I cried. I felt helpless and hopeless and utterly defeated because like it or not, fear is a powerful motivator, and those girls were so afraid of themselves and their bodies and their decisions and that was . . . ugh. My stomach churns even now. *I'm crying even now.*

I think that's the night I stopped caring about hurting the church's feelings.

I went home and I looked at my piles and piles of Christian fiction scattered around our spare room, and I was angry. Yeah, sure, it's inspirational when a character in the 1870s can keep her faith and fight temptation because everything about her society and culture (of no one, because she's alone on the frontier) supports that.

But what about someone in 2008 (or 2021, for that

matter)? How does someone keep their faith when they are told that literally everything they do is an abomination to God? Cuss when you spill your soda while driving? Sin. Check out a guy when you're swimming? Sin. Check out a guy when you're a guy? Sin. Sip a beer at a party? Sin. And all those sins? Straight to hell. There's no middle ground. No grace. *No Jesus in that narrative.*

Who can live like that? Who wants that kind of belief system in their life?

I'm not a great public speaker, but I can write. And I decided I was going to write *alternative* Christian fiction. Of course, I'd never written a book before in my life, and writing books is hard, but I was determined to create an option C. Not quite secular but definitely not inspirational (at least in that way).

It took me a long time to finish something, and then I started querying my book to every Christian agency or publisher I could think of. I was met with immediate resistance. Granted, my early efforts were not great, but Christian agents would jump on my queries and almost immediately reject when they read the full, citing "not a good fit." I knew what they meant. They didn't care for my less-than-pious characters. (If you ever want to feel bad about yourself, pull up a Christian publisher and check out their submission guidelines. Mother Teresa would be rejected.)

I sat on it. Prayed about it. Cussed about it. Drank wine about it. I talked with my husband, who shrugged and said, "It's up to you, but you started writing because you wanted real characters out there, and I think you'll regret it if you take out the realness and it sells."

"But what if I leave it in and it never sells?"

"Then you write another one."

(By the way, that's the *last* thing an author ever wants to hear. "Just write another one.")

Well, I wrote another one. And another and another. I've been so, *so* lucky to have fallen in with my agent, Kate McKean, and my publisher, Wednesday Books, and my editor, Vicki Lame. Meg Hennessey started out as a side character in my second book, *More Than Maybe*. Over the course of writing that book, I spent some time getting to know Meg, and she bloomed in full color, faith struggle and all, in my heart. I knew she had her own story to tell, and to be honest, at first, I didn't want to pursue it. I've gotten a little flak in my previous books for hinting at faith, and I knew if I opened this can of worms, I couldn't go back. Meg's story would be polarizing, and I'm not super into confrontation.

And that was *before* I met Micah!

I figured, hey, I'll toss out this idea of Meg's faith search during her gap year to my editor, and *for sure* she'll say no. Who wants that? How would you even market that?

She did not say no. I tried other ideas! Safer ideas! "That's cool," she said. *"First Meg."*

I thought, maybe I could focus on the romance and go sort of light on the faith search. But then #MeToo happened, and a lead pastor at a church I grew up attending was in the news for using his position of power to sexually abuse women leaders in that church, and I was *devastated.* Sickened. All I could think about was the years and years I was told that as a female, I was responsible for not only my purity but the purity of the boys and men around me. How I was told that sex before marriage or outside marriage was a serious sin and would not only ruin me for my future husband but also curse our marriage. Tank tops and shorts and visible bra straps and V-necks and bathing suits and sitting with a boy on your bed . . . all these things were wrong and shameful. To this very day, if my husband tries to comment in a flirty way about my neckline, I have to fight the urge to change. It's ridiculous and I hate it and I'm so very certain this is not how God wants us to live.

Anyway. If you've made it to the end of this book, you know the rest. Meg and Micah have told you the rest. Clearly, there was no turning back for me after that. I had to write this story, and once I opened the floodgates and picked up my proverbial pen-as-sword, it was as though I'd purged something. I know not everyone who reads this will approve. I try not to care about that, but I do. Like Meg, I want approval. But in the end, it's not the approval of readers that I seek. I hope this story heals and helps. I suspect for some it will. It certainly has for me.

Friends, I've spent my life sinning. Like constantly. Little sins all day long; big sins, too, if you're into ranking. But I've also lived knowing that God's grace covers me, and his love is everything.

I don't give a shit if you sin. Or don't sin. What I care about, so deeply, is that you know that no matter what, no matter who you are, or aren't, God loves you. And so do I.

And Meg and Micah and every character I ever write would love you, too.

With love,
Erin Hahn

Acknowledgments

I feel like I've been writing this story in my heart for most of my life, but I never would have gotten it to the page if not for . . .

The encouragement and relentless enthusiasm from my editor, the Best Editor, Vicki Lame.

The calm and cool, levelheaded insight from my agent, the Best Agent, Kate McKean.

The backing and complete support of my publisher, the Best Imprint, Wednesday Books.

The ridiculous talent and patience of my publishing team at Wednesday Books, including, but never limited to, DJ DeSmyter, Kerri Resnick, Mary Moates, and Jennie Conway, and also the team over at Macmillan Audio who always do such a brilliant job bringing my stories to life.

The spot-on feedback from my earliest readers, Kelly Coon and Karen McManus.

The lovely and thoughtful blurbs (which made me feel like maybe I wasn't making a terrible error in judgment pouring my heart into a book like this) from Ashley

Schumacher (thank YOU for being my Vada and sending me a song when I needed it most), Erin Craig, Laura Taylor Namey, and Joy McCullough.

The twenty years of friendship, fellowship, prayer, and laughter that inspired Meg and her mom—my 915 Pine/Bible study girls: Kelly Laarman, Lindsay VonQualen, Katie Willett, Maria Gibson, Aimee Hougaboom, and Meg Markoya. I hope I've done it justice, friends.

My husband, Mike, who taught me about Jesus, who loved me as I was, whose discernment and patience inspired Micah Allen, and who has stood by my side and supported me even when I told him, "I think this book might get some people mad at me." I couldn't write a love interest better than the one God wrote for me.

My kids, the Best Kids: Jones and Al, I pray this book, if you read it one day, will give you peace in your hearts and the confidence to know you are so loved no matter what.

My mom, Deb Jenkins; sister, Cassie Canestrini; and best friends, Meg Turton and Cate Unruh, who all read this story before anyone else and told me that even though it hurt to write and hurt worse to read, it was important and necessary and would make a difference one day.

The Bandrowski family. I'm not even sure where you all are living these days, but there was a time many years ago when I was a poor college kid without a place to stay and you opened your home and your family to me. I've often thought about that month under your roof where I was shown firsthand a loving, Christian family. I don't know that I can fully express the impact that time had on me. I hope if I'm ever faced with the same situation one day, I will choose to be as generous as you were to me.

The ones who've done it right: the pastors, pastors' wives,

youth group leaders, camp counselors, worship leaders, church families, Bible study leaders, song writers, artists, authors, the ones who have loved with wild abandon and fierce determination—who looked at a face and saw only a soul worth their time and nothing else—to all of you, THANK YOU. Thank you from the bottom of my heart.

To Jesus. It feels flippant to thank you for helping me to write a book, so I won't do that, even if I feel gratitude deep in my bones. Instead, I'll thank you for never, ever letting go of me.